Gustav Meyrink

The GOLEM

With eight illustrations
by Hugo Steiner-Prag

Vitalis

© Vitalis, 2003
Translation: Isabel Cole
Cover: Karel Hruška
Layout: Leo Novotný
Typesetting: Cadis, Praha
Print: Finidr, Český Těšín
All rights reserved

ISBN 80-7253-071-2
www.vitalis-verlag.com

TABLE OF CONTENTS

SLEEP

The moonlight falls upon the foot of my bed and lies like a big, flat, pale stone.

When the full moon's form starts to shrink and its right side begins to wither – as one cheek of an aging face is first to wrinkle and waste away – at this hour a dull, tormenting unrest comes over me.

I sleep not and I wake not, and half in a dream my soul mingles things seen with things read and heard, like currents of different color and clarity flowing together.

I had read about the life of the Buddha Gotama before going to bed, and in a thousand variations, always starting over from the beginning, the words ran through my mind:

"A crow flew to a stone which resembled a piece of fat and thought: perhaps this is good to eat. Finding nothing good to eat, the crow flew away. Like the crow who came to the stone, so we – we, the tempters – abandon the ascetic Gotama when he no longer pleases us."

And the image of the stone which resembled a piece of fat waxes to monstrous proportions in my mind:

I walk along a dry riverbed and pick up smooth pebbles.

Grey-blue ones flecked with glittering dust, which I ponder and ponder and yet can make neither heads nor tails of – then black ones with sulfur-yellow dots like a child's petrified efforts to mold lumpish speckled salamanders.

And I want to hurl them far from me, these pebbles, but they slip from my hand every time, and I cannot ban them from my sight.

All the stones which ever played a role in my life crop up around me.

Some struggle cumbrously to work their way out of the sand toward the light – like big, slate-colored crabs when the tide comes in – as if making every effort to catch my eye and tell me things of infinite importance.

Others – exhausted – fall back feebly into their holes and abandon hope of ever being heard.

Sometimes I wake with a start from the twilight of these half-dreams, and again I see the moonlight lying on the bunched-up foot of my blanket like a big, flat, pale stone, before groping anew after my vanishing consciousness, restlessly seeking the stone which torments me – which must lie buried somewhere in the rubble of my memory and which resembles a piece of fat.

A drainpipe must once have emptied onto the ground next to it, I picture to myself – bent at an obtuse angle, its edges rust-eaten – and defiantly I try to summon up such an image in my mind's eye, to delude my panicked thoughts and lull them to sleep.

I cannot.

Again and again, with idiotic persistence, an obstinate inner voice insists – tireless as a shutter rhythmically banging against the wall in the wind: it wasn't like that at all, that wasn't the stone that resembles fat.

And the voice is impossible to escape.

If I object a hundred times over that all this is perfectly irrelevant, it falls silent for a little while, only to wake again unexpectedly and stubbornly begin anew: fine, fine, all very well, but it isn't the stone that resembles a piece of fat. –

Gradually an unbearable feeling of helplessness overcomes me.

What happens next, I do not know. Have I voluntarily abandoned all resistance, or have they overpowered and gagged me, my thoughts?

All I know is that my body lies in bed asleep, and my senses are severed and tied to it no longer. –

Who is now "I", I suddenly want to ask; but I remember that I no longer possess an organ for asking questions; then I am afraid the foolish voice will wake and begin the endless interrogation about the stone and the fat again.

And so I turn away.

DAY

There I stood all at once in a dark courtyard, looking through a reddish arch to the other side of the narrow, dirty street, where a Jewish junk dealer leaned outside a vault whose outside arch was hung with old metal gadgetry, broken tools, rusty stirrups and ice-skates and all sorts of other dead things.

This image was as tormentingly monotonous as all those impressions which cross the threshold of our consciousness day after day like peddlers, and it provoked neither my curiosity nor my surprise.

I realized that I had called these surroundings home for quite some time.

Though it contradicted what I had only just seen and how I had gotten here, this sensation made little impression on me either. – – –

As I climbed the worn-down stairs to my room and fleetingly noted the greasy appearance of the stone treads, it struck me that I must once have heard of a strange comparison between a stone and a piece of fat.

Then I heard footsteps climbing the stairs ahead of me, and as I reached my door I saw that it was the junk-dealer Aaron Wassertrum's fourteen-year-old, red-haired Rosina.

I had to squeeze past her, and she backed up against the banister and arched over it lewdly.

She grasped the iron bar in her filthy hands for support, and I saw her bare forearms gleam pale in the murky semi-darkness. I avoided her gaze.

Her insinuating smile and that waxy rocking-horse face revolted me.

I felt she must have spongy white flesh like the axolotl I had just seen in the salamander cage at the bird-seller's.

Redheads' eyelashes sicken me like a rabbit's.

And I unlocked the door and quickly shut it behind me. –

– – –

From my window I saw the junk-dealer Aaron Wassertrum standing outside his vault.

He lounged in the dark archway and picked at his nails with a pair of pincers.

Was red-haired Rosina his daughter or his niece? He did not resemble her at all.

Among the Jewish faces that appear before me on Hahnpassgasse day after day, I can clearly distinguish different tribes which are not blurred by the kinship of the individuals in question, any more than oil can mingle with water. You cannot say: those two there are brothers or father and son.

One belongs to this tribe and one to another, that is all you can read in their features.

Even if Rosina did resemble the junk-dealer, what would it prove!

These tribes nurse a secret mutual revulsion and abhorrence which bursts even the boundaries of kinship – but they hide it well from the outside world, as if guarding a dangerous secret.

Not one of them lets it show, and in this agreement they are like hate-filled blind men clinging to a filthy rope: one with both fists, another with one reluctant finger, all possessed by the superstitious fear that they will be doomed in a moment if they abandon the shared handhold and part from the others.

Rosina belongs to the tribe whose red-haired type is even more repellant than the others. Whose men are narrow-chested, with long chicken's necks and protruding Adam's apples.

Everything about them seems freckled, and all their life they suffer ruttish torments, these men – secretly waging a ceaseless, vain battle against their lusts, perpetually racked by a disgusting fear for their health.

I was not sure how I had ever come to think that Rosina was related to Wassertrum the junk-dealer.

I had never noticed her in the old man's vicinity nor seen them speak to each other.

And she was almost always in our courtyard, or skulking about the dark corners and corridors of our house.

Surely all my neighbors took her for the junk-dealer's close relative or at least his charge, yet I am convinced that not one would be able to offer a reason for these suppositions.

Hoping to take my mind off Rosina, I looked out the open window of my room and down at Hahnpassgasse.

As if sensing my gaze, Aaron Wassertrum suddenly lifted his face to me.

His hideous, rigid face with the bulging fish-eyes and the gaping hare-lip.

He struck me as a human spider, sensing the least disturbance to its web, however indifferent its demeanor.

And whatever does he live from? What does he think, and what are his designs?

I did not know.

In the opening of his vault the same dead, worthless things hang day after day, year in, year out.

I could have drawn them with my eyes shut: here the bent tin trumpet with no keys, the yellowed painting, on paper, of the so oddly assembled soldiers. Then a garland of rusty spurs on a moldy leather strap and other half-rotten junk.

And on the ground in the front, piled up so close together that no one can cross the threshold of the vault, a row of round iron stove lids. –

All these things increased rather than decreased in number, and whenever a passerby actually stopped and asked the price of something or other, the junk-dealer became violently agitated.

He would lift his hare-lip, ghastly to behold, and irritably blurt out something incomprehensible in a gurgling, stumbling bass until the customer lost all desire to inquire any further and went on his way, alarmed.

Quick as a flash Aaron Wassertrum's eyes had slid away from mine, now fixed with avid interest on the bare walls of the neighboring house which abut my window.

What on earth did he see there?

The house faces away from Hahnpassgasse, and its windows look out onto the courtyard! Only one faces the street.

By chance, at that very moment someone seemed to have entered the rooms on the same floor of the neighboring building – an oddly shaped studio, I believe – for through the walls I suddenly heard the voices of a man and a woman in conversation.

But the junk-dealer couldn't possibly have heard that from down there! – –

Someone moved outside my door, and I guessed: it's Rosina still, standing outside in the dark, in the greedy expectation that I might call her in to me after all.

And half a floor below pockmarked adolescent Loisa waits on the stairs with bated breath to see whether I will open the door, and his seething jealousy and the heat of his hatred seem to rise up to meet me.

He is afraid to come closer lest Rosina notice him. He knows he is at her mercy as a hungry wolf is at the mercy of its keeper, yet if he had his way he would leap up and blindly vent his rage! – – –

I sat at my workbench and hunted for my pincers and graver.

But I was good for nothing; my hand was not steady enough to restore the fine Japanese engravings.

The dark, sullen life which clings to this house refuses to leave me in peace, and old images keep looming up inside me.

Loisa and his twin brother Jaromir can hardly be a year older than Rosina.

I barely remember their father, who had been the host baker, and I believe an old woman takes care of them now.

But I did not know which one of the many old women who live hidden away in the house like toads in their holes.

She takes care of the two boys, that is to say: she gives them shelter; in return they must hand over whatever they happen to steal or beg. –

Does she feed them too? I supposed not, for the old woman does not come home until late at night. They say she lays out the dead.

I often saw Loisa, Jaromir and Rosina playing innocently in the courtyard together when they were children.

But that was a long time ago.

Now Loisa is after the red-haired Jew-girl all day long.

Sometimes he seeks and seeks her in vain, and when he can find her nowhere he sneaks to my door and waits, face contorted, for her to steal up.

As I sit at my work I picture him lurking outside in the crooked corridor, his head bent forward intently on his emaciated neck.

Sometimes the silence is broken by a frenzied clamor.

Jaromir, deaf and dumb, all his thoughts possessed by an incessant mad greed for Rosina, roams the house like a wild animal, and, half out of his mind with jealousy and suspicion, he utters harsh inarticulate howls enough to make the blood run cold.

13

He seeks the two, always imagining them together – hidden somewhere in one of the thousand filthy nooks – in blind rage, goaded on by the thought of sticking to his brother's heels so that nothing involving Rosina will happen without his knowledge.

And I sensed that the cripple's perpetual torment was the very stimulus which impelled Rosina to make free with the other again and again.

Whenever her inclination or willingness wanes, Loisa devises particularly beastly tricks to whet her voracity.

They let the deaf-mute catch them, or seem to catch them, and cunningly they lure the frantic boy after them into dark passageways where, with rusty barrel-hoops which whip up into the air when stepped on, and iron rakes with the points upward, they have set vicious traps into which he inevitably takes bloody falls.

From time to time Rosina thinks up something infernal on her own to increase the torment to the utmost.

All at once she alters her conduct toward Jaromir and pretends to have taken a sudden fancy to him.

With her ever-smiling demeanor she hastily tells the cripple things which send him into an almost demented state of excitement, concocting a mysterious, only half-intelligible sign language which inevitably ensnares the deaf-mute in an inextricable web of uncertainty and devouring hopes. –

Once I saw him standing in the courtyard in front of her, and she egged him on with such violent gesticulations and movements of her lips that I thought he would collapse any moment in frantic excitement.

Sweat poured down his face with the superhuman effort to grasp the sense of the purposely unclear, hasty communication.

And all the next day he hung about, feverish with excitement, on the stairs of another sagging house which lies in the continuation of the cramped, grimy Hahnpassgasse – until it was too late for him to beg a few kreuzers on the corner.

And when he came home late that night, half dead of hunger and excitement, his guardian had long since locked him out. – – –

– – –

A woman's cheerful laugh rang through the walls from the adjacent studio.

A laugh? – A cheerful laugh in these houses? There's not a soul in the ghetto capable of laughing cheerfully.

Then I remembered: several days ago the old marionette player Zwakh had confided in me that a distinguished young gentleman had rented the studio from him, and paid dearly for it – evidently in order to meet unobserved with the dear one of his heart.

The new tenant's valuable furniture had to be carried up secretly one piece at a time, little by little, night after night, so that no one in the house would notice.

The kindly old man had rubbed his hands in delight as he told me, childishly pleased at the cleverness with which he had pulled everything off: none of the other tenants could have the slightest suspicion of the romantic couple.

And the studio could be reached unnoticed from three different buildings. – There was even a trapdoor!

Yes, when the iron door of the attic floor was unlatched – and that was very easy to do from the other side – one could walk past my room to the stairs of our house and use them as an escape route...

Once again the cheerful laugh rings out and stirs the indistinct memory of a luxurious apartment and a noble family which often summoned me to perform minor restorations of precious antiquities. –

Suddenly I hear a piercing scream next door. I listen in horror.

15

The iron attic door crashes, and a moment later a lady bursts into my room.

Hair disheveled, white as the wall, a golden brocade thrown over her bare shoulders.

"Master Pernath, hide me – for God's sake, Christ's sake! – don't ask, hide me here!"

Before I could reply, my door was thrown open again and slammed shut immediately. –

For one second the face of the junk-dealer Aaron Wassertrum had grinned in at us like a hideous mask. – – –

A luminous round spot appears before me, and in the light of the moon I see the foot of my bed again.

Sleep still lies upon me like a heavy woolen cloak, and the name Pernath looms in my memory in golden letters.

Where on earth did I read this name? – Athanasius Pernath? –

I think, I think, a long, long time ago I took the wrong hat one day, and I was surprised at the time that it fit me so well, when my head is so unusually shaped.

And I looked inside the strange hat – back then and – – yes, yes, there it was, written in gold paper letters on the white lining:

ATHANASIUS PERNATH

The hat cowed and frightened me, though I did not know why.

Suddenly the voice which I had forgotten, which always demanded the whereabouts of the stone which resembled a piece of fat, shoots toward me like an arrow.

Hastily I conjure up the sharp, sickly-grinning profile of the red-haired Rosina, and thus manage to evade the arrow, which is immediately swallowed up by the darkness.

Yes, Rosina's face! That's stronger than the idiotic prattling voice after all; and now that I am about to be back safe in my room on Hahnpassgasse, I can set my mind at rest.

"I"

If I am not wrong in feeling that someone is climbing the stairs at a certain fixed distance behind me intending to pay me a visit, now he must almost have reached the last landing.

Now he turns the corner, where the archivist Shemajah Hillel lives, and passes from the worn flagstones to the corridor of the top story, which is paved with red bricks.

He gropes along the wall, and now, this very moment, laboriously spelling it out in the darkness, he must be reading my name on the door-plate.

And I stood upright in the middle of the room looking at the door.

The door opened, and he stepped inside.

He took only a few steps toward me, and did not remove his hat, nor say a word in greeting.

This is how he conducts himself when he is at home, I felt, and found it quite natural that he should act in this way and no other.

He reached into his pocket and took out a book.

Then he leafed through it for a long while.

The book's cover was made of metal, and the indentations in the shape of rosettes and signets were colored in and filled with small stones.

At last he had found the place he sought, and pointed to it.

The chapter was called "Ibbur", "the impregnation of the soul", I deciphered.

The big initial "I", executed in gold and red, took up almost half of the entire page, which I skimmed without thinking, and it was damaged at the edge.

I was to restore it.

The initial had not been glued onto the parchment, as I had seen in old books before, but rather seemed to consist of two thin sheets of gold soldered together in the middle, their ends clasping the edges of the parchment.

Then a hole must have been cut in the page where the letter stood?

In that case, the "I" ought to appear in reverse on the other side.

I turned the page and found my hypothesis confirmed.

Without thinking I read this page too, and the facing page. And I read on and on.

The book spoke to me as dreams speak, only much more clearly. And it touched my heart like a question.

Words poured from an invisible mouth, came to life and surged toward me. They turned and twirled before me like gaudily-dressed slave girls, then sank into the ground or vanished into the air like iridescent vapor, giving way to the next. Each hoped for a short while that I would choose her and forego the sight of those to come.

Some among them strutted like peacocks, in shimmering robes, and their steps were slow and measured.

Some like queens, yet aged and dissipated, their eyelids painted – with a trollop's turn to the mouth and their wrinkles plastered with ugly rouge.

I looked past them at the ones to come, and my eyes skimmed long processions of grey figures with faces so blank and common that it seemed impossible to stamp them on my memory.

Then they hauled up a woman stark naked and gigantic as a brazen colossus.

For a second the woman stood before me, and bowed down to me.

Her lashes were as long as my entire body, and she pointed mutely to the pulse of her left hand.

It throbbed like an earthquake, and I felt that the life of a whole world was in her.

From the distance a procession of Corybants came rushing up.

A man and a woman embraced. I saw them coming from afar, and the procession swept closer and closer.

Now I heard the resounding song of the celebrants close by, and my eyes sought the entwined couple.

But it had turned into a single form, ensconced, half-male, half-female – a hermaphrodite – on a throne of nacre.

And the crown of the hermaphrodite ended in a board of red wood wherein the worm of destruction had gnawed mysterious runes.

A herd of blind little sheep came trotting up hastily behind it in a cloud of dust: the feed animals which the gigantic androgyne kept in its retinue to sustain the host of Corybants.

Amidst the figures pouring from the invisible mouth were some risen from graves – their faces shrouded.

And when they stopped before me, they dropped their shrouds and stared hungrily at my heart with rapacious eyes, making icy terror shoot through my brain and my blood rise like a river when boulders fall from the sky – straight into its bed. –

A woman drifted past me. I did not see her face, for it was averted, and she wore a mantle of trickling tears. –

Carnival processions danced past, laughing and caring not for me.

Only a Pierrot looks back at me thoughtfully and returns. Plants himself in front of me and gazes into my face as though it were a mirror.

He twists his face into such strange grimaces, lifting and moving his arms, now hesitant, now lightning-fast, that I am overcome by the unearthly urge to imitate him, to wink my eyes as he does, to shrug my shoulders and twist the corners of my mouth.

Then impatient figures crowd up and push him aside, all wanting to enter my sight.

But none of the beings endure.

They are slipping beads, strung on a silken cord, nothing but single notes of a melody pouring from the invisible mouth.

What spoke to me was no longer a book. It was a voice. A voice demanding something from me that I did not understand, however hard I struggled. Tormenting me with burning, unintelligible questions.

But the voice which spoke these invisible words was extinct and without resonance.

Every sound made in the world of the present has many echoes, as every thing has one big shadow and many little shadows, but this voice had echoes no longer – long, long ago they had scattered and faded. – – –

And I had read the book to the very end and still held it in my hands, when suddenly it seemed to me that I had been leafing through my brain and not a book! – –

All that the voice had told me I had carried within me as long as I had lived, only it had been covered up and forgotten and had hidden from my thoughts to this day. –

– – –

I looked up.

Where was the man who had brought me the book?

Gone?

Will he fetch it when it is finished?

Or was I meant to bring it to him?

But I could not remember him saying where he lived.

I tried to recall his appearance, but failed.

How had he been dressed? Was he old, was he young? – And what color was his hair and his beard?

I could picture nothing, nothing more. – All the images I made of him dissolved without a trace even before I could piece them together in my mind.

I closed my eyes and pressed my hand to my eyelids, hoping to capture even the tiniest fragment of his image.

Nothing, nothing.

I went to the middle of the room and looked at the door, as I had done – just now, when he came, and pictured to myself: now he is turning the corner, now he is walking along the brick floor, now reading my door-plate "Athanasius Pernath" outside, and now he is stepping in.

In vain. Not the faintest memory of his appearance stirred within me.

I saw the book lying on the table and wished in spirit for the hand which had taken it out of the pocket and held it out to me.

I could not even remember whether it had been gloved or bare, young or wrinkled, adorned with rings or not.

Then I had a strange idea.

It was like an inspiration, something one cannot resist.

I put on my coat, donned my hat and went out into the corridor and down the stairs. Then I slowly returned to my room.

Slowly, very slowly, just as he had come. And as I opened the door I saw that my room was filled with twilight. Had it not been bright day when I went out just now?

How long I must have spent pondering, not to notice how late it is!

And I attempted to mimic the stranger in gait and gesture, but I could not remember them at all. –

How could I possibly mimic him, anyway, when I no longer had any idea how he could have looked?

But it turned out differently. Quite differently than I had thought.

My skin, my muscles, my body suddenly remembered without telling the brain. They made movements I neither wished nor intended.

As if my limbs no longer belonged to me!

When I took a few steps through the room my gait was suddenly strange and faltering.

That is the walk of a person who is constantly at the point of toppling forward, I said to myself.

Yes, yes, yes, he walked like this!

Vividly I knew: he was like this.

I wore a strange, beardless face with high cheekbones and gazed out through slanting eyes.

I felt it, though I could not see myself.

That is not my face, I nearly cried out in horror, and tried to feel it, but my hand, refusing to obey my will, descended into my pocket and took out a book.

Just as he had done. –

Suddenly I am sitting at the table again without a hat, without a coat and am myself. I, I.

Athanasius Pernath.

Dismay and terror shook me, my heart raced fit to burst, and I felt: ghostly fingers which groped through my brain just now have let me go.

In the back of my head I still felt the cold traces of their touch. –

Now I knew what the stranger was like, and I could have felt him within me once more – any moment – if only I had wanted to; but to call up his image so that I could *see* it before me eye to eye – that I still could not do, nor will I ever be able to.

He is like a negative, an invisible hollow-mould, I realized, whose contours I cannot grasp – I must slip into them myself if I am to become conscious of their form and their expression within my own "I". – –

In my desk drawer lay an iron coffer – I would lock the book inside it; not until this state of mental illness had abated would I take it out again and go about restoring the damaged initial "I".

I took the book from the table.

And I felt as if I had not touched it at all; I seized the coffer: the same feeling. As if the sensation of touch had to cover a long, long stretch of utter darkness before converging with my consciousness, as if all things were separated from me by a layer of years and belonged to a past which had long since passed me by!

– – –

The voice which circles in the darkness seeking to torment me with the fatty stone passed without seeing me. And I know it comes from the realm of sleep. But what I experienced was real life – that, I feel, is why it could not see me and why it seeks me in vain.

PRAGUE

Next to me stood the student Charousek, the collar of his thin, threadbare overcoat turned up, and I heard his teeth chattering in the cold.

He'll catch his death in this drafty, freezing archway, I said to myself, and I invited him to come across the way to my apartment.

But he refused.

"I thank you, Master Pernath", he murmured, shivering, "I'm afraid I don't have much time – I have urgent business in town. – And we'd be soaked to the skin if we went out onto the street now – the first few steps would do it! – – The downpour just won't let up!"

The torrents of water swept across the roofs and ran down the faces of the houses like a flood of tears.

Turning my head slightly, I could see my window over there on the fifth floor; streaming with rain, its panes seemed to have softened – grown lumpy and opaque like isinglass.

A yellow stream of filth gushed down the street, and the archways filled with passersby, all waiting for the storm to let up.

"There comes a bridal corsage", Charousek said suddenly, pointing to a bouquet of withered myrtle which came floating past in the filthy water.

Someone behind us laughed loudly at that.

Turning around, I saw that it had been an elegantly dressed old gentleman with white hair and a bloated, toad-like face.

Charousek also glanced behind him and muttered something to himself.

The old man had a disagreeable aura – I turned my attention away from him and studied the discolored houses which huddled together before me in the rain like listless old animals.

How abject and eerie they all looked!

Built slapdash, they stood there like weeds shooting up from the ground.

They had been propped against a low, yellow stone wall, the only surviving remnant of some earlier, elongated building – two or three centuries ago, haphazardly, with no consideration for the others. There half of a crooked house with a receding forehead – another beside it: protruding like a canine tooth.

Under the gloomy sky they seemed to lie in slumber, and one sensed none of the cunning, malignant life which they emanate at times, when the fog of the autumn evenings fills the alleys and helps conceal the faint, barely perceptible play of their features.

In the age I have now lived here the impression has lodged within me, and I cannot shake it off, that there are certain hours of the night and at the crack of dawn when they excitedly hold a silent, secret conference. And sometimes a faint inexplicable tremor runs through their walls, sounds skitter across their roofs and drop into the gutters – and we acknowledge them unmindfully with dulled senses, never seeking their cause.

Often I dreamed I eavesdropped on these houses' sinister doings and learned to my horror that they were the true secret masters of the street, able to cast off their life and feeling and gather it up once more – lending it by day to the people who dwell here only to demand it back that coming night with cutthroat interest.

And if I call before my mind's eye the strange people who live in them like phantoms, like beings – not born of woman – whose thoughts and deeds are pieced together at random, I am more than ever inclined to believe that such dreams hold dark truths which in my waking hours only glimmer on in my soul like the impressions of florid legends.

Then the legend of the unearthly golem wakes in me in secret, the artificial man whom a cabalistic rabbi here in the ghetto once formed from the elements, calling him to thoughtless, automatic being by thrusting a gematric word behind his teeth.

And as that golem turned to an image of clay the instant the secret syllable of life was taken from his mouth, so too, I thought, must all these *people* collapse unsouled in a moment if some trifling notion, an irrelevant aspiration, for one perhaps a pointless habit, for another nothing but the dull anticipation of something utterly amorphous, groundless – were extinguished in their brain.

What an everlasting anxious watchfulness is in these creatures!

You never see them work, these people, and yet they wake at the crack of dawn and wait with bated breath – as if for a victim who never comes.

And if ever someone does seem about to enter their territory, some defenseless person to feather their nests, a paralyzing fear suddenly overcomes them, chases them into their corner and makes them tremblingly desist from all designs.

It seems no one is so weak that their courage would suffice to overcome him.

"Degenerate, toothless beasts of prey, robbed of their strength and their weapons", Charousek said hesitantly, looking at me. –

How could he know what I was thinking? –

At times one's thoughts kindle so strongly that they can leap over to the mind of a bystander, I felt.

"– – – whatever do they live from?" I asked after a while.

"Live? What from? Some of them are millionaires!"

I looked at Charousek. What on earth could he mean by that?

But the student said nothing and looked up at the clouds.

For a moment the murmur of voices in the archway had fallen silent, and all that could be heard was the lashing of the rain.

What can he possibly mean by that: "Some of them are millionaires!"?

Once again Charousek seemed to read my mind.

He pointed to the junk shop next to us, where the water washed the rust from the iron gadgetry in trickling, brown-red puddles.

"Aaron Wassertrum! He's a millionaire, for one – almost a third of the Jewish Town is in his possession. Didn't you know that, Herr Pernath?!"

My breath caught in my mouth. "Aaron Wassertrum! The junk-dealer Aaron Wassertrum a millionaire!?"

"Oh, I know him quite well", Charousek went on doggedly, as if he had only been waiting for me to ask him. "And his son, Dr. Wassory. Haven't you heard of him? Of Dr. Wassory, the – prominent – ophthalmologist? – Only a year ago the whole city was enthusing about him – about the great – – scholar. At the time no one knew that he had changed his name and used to be called Wassertrum. – He like to play the un-worldly man of science, and whenever the conversation turned to his origins, he let it slip modestly and deeply moved, with half-words, that his father had come from the ghetto – had been forced to work his way up into the light from the basest begin-nings, with all kinds of trials and unspeakable tribulations.

"Yes! With trials and tribulations!

"But with whose trials and unspeakable tribulations, and by what means, that he did not say!

27

"But I know the story behind the ghetto!" Charousek seized my arm and shook it violently.

"Master Pernath, I'm so poor that I can hardly comprehend it myself; I must go about half-naked like a vagabond, look here, and yet I'm a student of medicine – I'm an educated man!"

He threw open his coat, and to my horror I saw that he had neither shirt nor jacket, wearing the coat on his bare skin.

"And that poor was I when I caused the downfall of that beast, that all-powerful, venerated Dr. Wassory – to this day no one suspects that I, I was the actual instigator.

"In the city it was said to have been a certain Dr. Savioli who brought his practices to light and then drove him to suicide. – Dr. Savioli was nothing but my tool, I tell you! I alone devised the plan and amassed the material, offered the proofs, quietly and imperceptibly loosening stone after stone in Dr. Wassory's edifice until no money in the world, no stratagem of the ghetto could have averted the collapse which was only an imperceptible nudge away.

"You know, just – just like a game of chess.

"Exactly like a game of chess.

"And no one knows that it was me!

"Likely the junk dealer Aaron Wassertrum can't sleep nights, with the terrible suspicion that someone he does not know, someone who is always close by, yet whom he cannot grasp – someone other than Dr. Savioli – must have been involved.

"Wassertrum may be the sort of person whose eyes can see through walls, but he cannot conceive that there are minds that gauge how to pierce those walls with long, invisible poisoned needles, past stone slabs, past gold and jewels, to strike the hidden vein of life."

And Charousek struck his forehead and laughed wildly.

"Aaron Wassertrum will soon find out; the very day he goes for Dr. Savioli's throat! That very day!

I have worked out this chess game as well, down to the very last move. – This time it will be a king's bishop gambit. To the bitter end, there is not a single move for which I lack a devastating rejoinder.

He who takes me up on this gambit will hang in the air, I tell you, like a helpless marionette on fine strings – on strings I pluck – hear me well, which *I* pluck, and his free will is no more."

The student spoke as if in a fever, and I stared him in the face, appalled.

"What have Wassertrum and his son done to you to make you hate them so?"

Charousek protested:

"Never mind that – ask instead what broke Dr. Wassory's neck! – Or would you rather discuss it some other time? – The rain has let up. Perhaps you want to go home?"

He lowered his voice as if suddenly turning quite calm. I shook my head.

"Have you ever heard how glaucoma is cured these days? – No? – Then I must explain that to you so that you will understand all the details, Master Pernath!

Listen: 'glaucoma' is a malignant disease of the inner eye which ends in blindness, and there is only one way to check the progress of the malady, namely the so-called iridectomy, in which a tiny wedge is plucked from the iris of the eye.

To be sure, the inevitable consequences are hideous episodes of dazzlement which remain life-long; in most cases, however, the loss of vision is halted.

But there is a peculiar twist to the diagnosis of glaucoma.

There are times, especially at the onset of the illness, when the most obvious symptoms seem to abate entirely,

29

and in such cases a doctor who finds no trace of any ailment can never say for certain that a previous doctor who was of a different opinion must necessarily have been in error.

But once the aforementioned iridectomy has taken place – and of course it can be performed on a healthy eye as well as on a sick one – it is impossible to determine whether glaucoma had been present or not.

And Dr. Wassory used these and other circumstances to devise a villainous plan.

Countless times – especially with women – he diagnosed glaucoma in cases of harmless vision impairments for the sole purpose of performing an operation which was extremely lucrative and required no effort on his part.

Now at last he'd gotten his hands on utterly defenseless people; now not an iota of courage was needed to plunder them!

You see, Master Pernath, the degenerate beast of prey had been transplanted into an environment where it could maul its victims even without strength or weapons.

With nothing at stake! – Do you understand? Without having to risk the least thing!

With a number of spurious publications in professional journals Dr. Wassory had managed to acquire the reputation of an outstanding specialist, hoodwinking even his colleagues, who were much too decent and guileless to see through him.

The natural result was a flood of patients all seeking his help.

When someone with minor vision impairments came to him for an examination, Dr. Wassory went to work with methodical cunning.

First he conducted the usual examination, but cleverly noted only the answers which pointed toward a diagnosis of glaucoma, so that he would be covered no matter what happened later. And he probed carefully to learn whether an earlier diagnosis had been made.

In the course of casual conversation he would mention that he had received an urgent summons from abroad on urgent scientific affairs and would be leaving town tomorrow. –

Then he would examine the patient's eyes with the ophthalmoscope, intentionally causing him as much pain as possible with the beams of electric light.

All with intent! All with intent!

When the examination was over and the patient had asked the usual fearful question as to whether there was cause for alarm, Wassory made his first move.

He took a seat across from the patient, let a minute pass, and then said in a measured, sonorous voice:

'Loss of sight in both eyes appears inevitable in the immediate future!'

– – –

The scene that naturally ensued was appalling. Often people would faint, weep and scream and throw themselves to the ground in a frenzy of despair.

To lose one's sight is to lose everything.

And when the equally inevitable moment came when the poor victim clutched at Dr. Wassory's knees and asked beseechingly whether there was no help on God's earth, the beast made his second move and transformed himself into the – God who offered aid!

Everything, everything in the world is like a chess game, Master Pernath! –

Operate immediately, Dr. Wassory would then muse, that alone could mean salvation, and, suddenly overcome by a frenzy of greedy vanity, he would wax eloquent in elaborate descriptions of this case and the other, all of which bore an uncommon resemblance to the one in question – how he

alone was responsible for saving the sight of countless patients, and more of the kind.

He reveled in the sensation of being taken for a kind of
superior being in whose hands lie the woe and well-being of
his fellow man.

But the helpless victim sat broken before him, heart filled
with burning questions, with clammy brow, not even daring to interrupt him, in fear: of angering him – the last remaining hope of succor.

And with the words that unfortunately he could proceed
to operate only several months from now, when he had returned from his journey, Dr. Wassory would bring his speech
to a close.

Hopefully – in such cases one should always hope for
the best– it would not be too late, he would say.

At that, of course, the patients would leap up in horror,
declare that under no circumstances would they wait even a
day longer, and implore him to advise them of another ophthalmologist in the city who could perform the operation.

Now the moment had come for Dr. Wassory to deal the
coup de grace.

He paced up and down, deep in thought, knit his brow
in deep concern and finally murmured, troubled, that if *another* doctor performed the operation it would unfortunately require a repeated examination of the eye with electric
light, and – the patient knew himself how painful it was –
the blinding rays could have a well-nigh catastrophic effect.

Thus – leaving aside the fact that many doctors lacked
the necessary practice in iridectomies – as the other doctor
would have to repeat the examination, he would not be able
to proceed with the surgical operation for some time, until
the optic nerves had recovered."

Charousek clenched his fists.

"In the language of chess we call that 'zugzwang', my
dear Master Pernath! – – What followed was zugzwang all
over again – one forced move after the other.

Now, half-mad with desperation, the patient would be-
seech Dr. Wassory to have mercy, to postpone his departure
for one day and perform the operation himself. – For it was
worse yet than a quick death, the horrible, tormenting fear
of going blind at any moment was the most terrible thing
imaginable.

And the more the monster resisted and moaned: a post-
ponement of his trip could cause him incalculable harm, the
higher were the sums the patient volunteered.

Once the sum struck Dr. Wassory as sufficient, he gave
in, and the very same day, before some chance could expose
his plan, he inflicted irremediable harm upon both this unfortunate person's healthy eyes, the constant feeling of dazzlement which inevitably made life a perpetual torment, yet
obliterated the evidence of the villainous trick forever.

With these operations on healthy eyes Dr. Wassory not
only enhanced his fame and his reputation as an incompa-
rable doctor who managed to check the imminent onset of
blindness every time – it also satisfied his boundless greed
and flattered his vanity when the unsuspected victims, physically and financially damaged, looked up to him as a helper and praised him as their savior.

Only a person with all the fibers of his being rooted in
the ghetto and its countless, covert but invincible resources,
one who had learned from childhood to lie in wait like a spider, knew every soul in the city and divined and penetrated
the finest details of their interconnections and financial circumstances – only such a – 'half-seer', one could almost say
– could practice such abominations year after year.

And if it had not been for me, he would still be practic-
ing his trade today, would have practiced it to a ripe old age,

finally enjoying his waning years as a venerable patriarch in the circle of his loved ones, decorated with high honors, a splendid model for future generations, until – until at last he bit the dust as well.

But I too grew up in the ghetto, my blood is saturated with the same atmosphere of infernal cunning, and thus I was able to cause his downfall – just as the invisible ones cause a man's downfall – like lightning striking from the blue.

Dr. Savioli, a young German doctor, took the credit for unmasking him – I used him as my front and heaped evidence upon evidence until the day the public prosecutor stretched out his hand toward Dr. Wassory.

Then the beast committed suicide! – Blessed be the hour!

As if my double had stood at his side and guided his hand, he took his life with the vial of amyl nitrite I had deliberately left in his examination room when I myself had him misdiagnose glaucoma in me – deliberately and with the ardent wish that this amyl nitrite should be his end.

In the city it was said he had died of a stroke.

Amyl nitrite, when inhaled, kills like a stroke. But the rumor could not persist for long."

– – –

Charousek suddenly stared off absently, as if lost in some profound problem; then he shrugged a shoulder in the direction of Aaron Wassertrum's junk shop.

"Now he's alone", he murmured, "all alone with his greed and – and – and the wax doll!"

– – –

My heart beat in my mouth.

I looked at Charousek in horror.

Was he mad? Feverish fantasies must have made him invent these things.

Of course, of course! He had invented it all, dreamed it up!

It can't be true, all the horrible things he said about the ophthalmologist. He's consumptive, the fevers of death reel in his brain.

And I was about to soothe him with a few joking words, divert his thoughts into cheerful channels.

Before I could find the words, Wassertrum's face with its harelip flashed through my memory like lightning, just like the time it had looked into my room through the flung-open door with round fish eyes.

Dr. Savioli! Dr. Savioli! – Yes, yes, that was the young man's name which the marionette player Zwakh had whispered to me, the genteel lodger who had rented the studio from him.

Dr. Savioli! – It rang out within me like a cry. A series of nebulous images darted through my mind, wheeling about with the fearful suppositions which closed in upon me.

I was about to ask Charousek, fearfully hasten to tell him what I had witnessed, when I saw that a violent attack of coughing had seized him and nearly knocked him off his feet. I watched him grope his way out into the rain, effortfully steadying himself against the wall with his hands.

Yes, yes, he was right, he was not raving, I felt – it is the impalpable ghost of crime which creeps through these streets day and night, seeking to take form.

It is in the air, and we do not see it. Suddenly it crystallizes in a human soul – we suspect nothing – there, there, and before we can come to grips with it, it has become formless, and all is over.

And nothing reaches us but the dark tidings of some appalling event.

All at once I grasped the innermost essence of the enigmatic creatures who lived all around me: they drift through existence without a will of their own, animated by an invisible magnetic current – – as the bridal corsage had floated past just now in the filthy rivulet.

The houses all seemed to stare over at me with cunning faces full of nameless malice – the archways: gaping black mouths, tongues rotted away – maws which might let out a piercing scream at any moment, so piercing and hate-filled that it would shock us to the core.

What was the last thing the student had said about the junk-dealer? I whispered his words to myself: – Now Aaron Wassertrum was alone with his greed and – – his wax doll.

What could he have meant by the wax doll?

It must have been a metaphor, I reassured myself – one of those morbid metaphors he likes to ambush people with, which one does not understand, and which, when they unexpectedly turn clear later on, can frighten one as deeply as unusually-shaped objects suddenly caught in a bright beam of light.

I took a deep breath, to calm myself and shake off the horrible impression which Charousek's story had made on me.

I look a closer look at the people waiting with me in the passage: now the fat old man was standing next to me. The one who had laughed so revoltingly just now.

He wore a black frock-coat and gloves and stared fixedly with bulging eyes at the archway of the house across the street.

His smooth-shaven face with the broad, vulgar features twitched excitedly.

I followed his eyes involuntarily and saw that they were glued as if spell-bound to red-haired Rosina, who stood on the other side of the street, that perpetual smile playing about her lips.

The old man was at pains to give her a sign, and I saw that she knew it, but pretended not to understand.

37

At last, unable to stand it any longer, the old man waded across on tip-toes, hopping over the puddles with ludicrous elasticity like a big black rubber ball.

They seemed to know him here, for I heard all sorts of gibes aimed at him. A rowdy behind me, with a red knitted scarf around his neck, a blue military cap and a Virginia cigar behind his ear, grinningly made insinuations I did not understand.

All I gathered was that in the Jewish Town the old man was known as the "Freemason", and that in their speech this was a nickname for those who were in the habit of violating adolescent girls, but protected from punishment by their intimate relations with the police. – – –

Then Rosina's face and the old man had vanished into the darkness of the vestibule.

PUNCH

We had opened the window to release the tobacco smoke from my room.

The cold night wind blew in and tugged at the shabby coats which hung on the door, making them sway softly to and fro.

"Prokop's worthy headdress is itching to fly off", said Zwakh, and pointed to the musician's big slouchhat, which moved its broad brim like black wings.

Josua Prokop twinkled merrily.

"Probably", he said, "probably it wants – – –"

"It wants to be off to 'Loisitschek' for the dance-music", Vrieslander took the words out of his mouth.

Prokop laughed, and with his hand he beat time to the strains the thin winter air carried over the roofs.

Then he took my old, broken guitar from the wall, pretended to pluck the broken strings, and sang a curious song in thieves' cant, in a screeching falsetto and with florid intonations:

> "An Bein-del von Ei-sen
> recht alt,
> An Stran-zen net gar
> a so kalt,
> Messinung, a'Räucherl
> und Rohn,
> Und immerrr nur putz-en – – –"

"How splendidly he commands the patter all of a sudden!" And Vrieslander laughed out loud and rumbled in accompaniment:

> "Und stok-en sich Aufzug

und Pfiff
Und schmallern an eisernes
G'süff.
Juch –
Und Handschuhkren, Harom net san – – –"[1]

"Every night at 'Loisitschek' the meschugge Nephtali Schaffranek with the green eye-shade drones out this queer little song, and a painted hussy plays the accordion and bawls the words to it", Zwakh explained to me. "You ought to come with us to this saloon some time, Master Pernath. Later on, perhaps, when we've finished the punch – what do you think? Because today is your birthday."

"Yes, yes, come along with us afterwards", said Prokop, shutting the window, "it's the kind of place you have to have seen."

Then we drank the hot punch and mulled over our private thoughts.

Vrieslander carved away at a marionette.

"You've virtually cut us off from the outside world, Josua", Zwakh broke the silence, "no one has said a word since you closed the window."

"I was just thinking, when the coats started flapping just now, how strange it is when the wind moves inanimate objects", Prokop replied quickly, as if to excuse his silence. "It looks so queer when things which usually lie there lifeless suddenly up and flutter about. Don't you think? – One time on a deserted square – without feeling a breath of wind, since I was standing in the shelter of a building – I saw big scraps of paper whirl about in a mad frenzy, chasing each other as if in mortal enmity. A moment later they seemed to have composed themselves, but suddenly a mad vehemence

---

[1] Couched in thieves' cant, the secret language of the underworld, this song is virtually indecipherable today and has thus been left in the original.

came over them again, and they raced about in senseless fury, crowding together in a corner only to scatter again as if possessed, finally vanishing around a corner.

One fat newspaper was unable to follow; it was left lying on the pavement, balefully flapping open and shut, as if it had lost its breath and was gasping for air.

A dark suspicion dawned upon me then: what if, in the end, we living creatures too are something like those scraps of paper? – Might an invisible, ungraspable wind chase us back and forth as well, determining our actions, while we in our innocence think ourselves governed by our own free will?

What if the life within us is nothing but a mysterious whirlwind? The wind of which the Bible says: Do you know whence it comes and whither it goes? – – – And do we not sometimes dream of reaching into deep water and catching silver fish, when all that has happened is that a cold draft has brushed our hands?"

"Prokop, you're speaking in words like Pernath's, whatever is the matter?" said Zwakh, looking at the musician suspiciously.

"The story of the Book of Ibbur just now – it's a pity you missed it by coming so late – that's what put him in such a pensive mood", said Vrieslander.

"A story about a book?"

"Actually about a strange-looking person who brought a book. – Pernath doesn't know his name, where he lives, what he wanted, and though his appearance is supposed to have been so striking, somehow it can't be described."

Zwakh pricked up his ears.

"How very odd", he said after a pause, "was the stranger beardless, perhaps, and did he have slanting eyes?"

"I believe so", I said, "that is, I – I'm positive of it. Do you know him?"

41

The marionette player shook his head: "He reminds me of the 'Golem', that's all."

The painter Vrieslander lowered his wood-carving knife:

"Golem? – I've heard so much talk of him. Do you know anything about the Golem, Zwakh?"

"Who can claim to *know* anything about the Golem?" Zwakh replied with a shrug. "He is banned to the realm of legend until one day on the streets some incident suddenly brings him to life again. And then for a time everyone speaks of him, and the rumors grow to monstrous proportions. Become so embellished and inflated that at last they're done in by their own implausibility. The story goes back to the seventeenth century, they say. Following lost instructions from the Cabala, a rabbi is said to have created an artificial man – the so-called Golem – to help and serve him, to ring the bells in the synagogue and perform all kinds of menial chores.

But it did not turn out as a real man, filled only with a dull, half-conscious, vegetable life. And even that, they say, was only during the day and thanks to a magical slip of paper stuck behind his teeth which tapped the free sidereal forces of the universe.

And one evening when the rabbi forgot to remove the seal from the Golem's mouth before the evening prayer, the Golem went into a frenzy, raging through the streets in the darkness and demolishing everything within reach.

Until the rabbi threw himself into his path and destroyed the slip of paper.

And then the creature collapsed lifeless. Nothing was left of him but the tiny clay figure which is still on display over in the Old-New Synagogue."

"The emperor is said to have summoned that same rabbi to the castle, where he invoked and revealed the shades of the dead", put in Prokop. "Modern scholars hold that he used a magic lantern."

"Yes indeed, no explanation is too preposterous to meet with approbation nowadays", Zwakh went on undeterred. – "A magic lantern! As if Emperor Rudolf, who went in for that sort of thing all his life, wouldn't have seen through such a clumsy hoax at first glance!

Admittedly, I have no idea what's at the bottom of the Golem legend, but it involves something which haunts this quarter and cannot die, of that I am certain. My ancestors have lived here for generation upon generation, and there is no one who can look back upon more first-hand and inherited memories of the Golem's periodic appearances than I!"

Zwakh suddenly broke off, and sympathetically we sensed how his thoughts strayed back into past times.

As he sat there at the table, propping his head on his hand, his red, youthful cheeks a strange contrast to his white hair in the lamplight, I could not help comparing his features with the mask-like faces of the marionettes he had so often showed me.

Strange, how the old man resembled them!

The same expression and the same cast to his features!

Some things in this world simply cannot break free of each other, I felt, and as I reflected upon Zwakh's simple fate, it suddenly struck me as ghastly and monstrous that a man such as he, who had enjoyed a better education than his forbears and was supposed to become an actor, could suddenly return to the shabby puppet theater to work the fairs once again with the same puppets which had earned his forefathers a miserable living, guiding them anew through their awkward obeisances and somnolent adventures.

He is unable to part from them, I realized; they draw their life from his, and when he was far from them they turned into thoughts, dwelled in his brain, and stole his peace of mind until he returned home once more. That is why he tends

43

them now so lovingly and clothes them proudly in tawdry finery.

"Zwakh, won't you tell us the rest of the story?" Prokop urged the old man, with a questioning look at Vrieslander and me to see whether we wished the same.

"I don't know where to start", the old man said hesitantly, "the story of the Golem is hard to put your finger on. As Pernath said just now: he knows exactly how the stranger looked, and yet he can't describe him. Every thirty-three years or so our streets are visited by a phenomenon which in itself is not so very exciting, yet which spreads a panic for which there is neither explanation nor justification:

"You see, again and again it comes to pass that a complete stranger, beardless, yellow of complexion and Mongoloid of feature, clothed in old-fashioned, faded garments, with a rhythmical and oddly stumbling gait, as if at the point of toppling forward, strides through the Jewish Town from the direction of the Altschulgasse and suddenly – is lost to sight.

Generally he turns into an alleyway and vanishes.

One time his path is said to have taken him in a circle, returning to his starting-point: an ancient house near the synagogue.

And then a few overwrought people claim to have seen him turn the corner toward them. Yet though he had quite clearly been approaching them, he grew smaller and smaller, just like someone dwindling into the distance, and – finally vanished entirely.

Sixty-six years ago he must have made an especially deep impression, for I remember – I was a very small boy at the time – that they searched the house on Altschulgasse from top to bottom.

And they discovered that in this house there really is a room with barred windows to which no door exists.

They found it out by hanging linens out all the windows to get a better view from the street.

As there was no other way to reach it, a man lowered himself from the roof on a rope to look inside. But as soon as he neared the window, the rope snapped, and the unfortunate man dashed his brains out on the pavement. And later, when the experiment was to be repeated, opinions as to the whereabouts of the window were so at odds that they let it be.

I myself encountered the 'Golem' for the first time in my life about thirty-three years ago.

He came toward me in a so-called passage house, and we nearly ran into each other.

To this day I fail to grasp what was in my mind back then. One doesn't go about day in, day out, expecting to meet the Golem, for heaven's sake.

But at that moment, distinctly – quite distinctly, even before I caught sight of him, something shrilled out within me: the Golem! And that very instant someone stumbled out of the darkness of the passage, and that stranger passed me. A second later a flood of pale, drawn faces surged toward me, assailing me with questions: had I seen him?

And as I replied I felt that my tongue was released from a paralysis of which I had felt nothing until that moment.

I was literally surprised that I could move, and vividly it dawned on me that, if only for the fraction of a heartbeat, I must have been in a kind of cataleptic trance.

I have pondered these things long and hard, and I think I come closest to the truth when I say: once a generation a psychic epidemic sweeps through the Jewish Town with lightning speed, gripping the souls of the living for some purpose which remains hidden to us, bringing forth like a mirage the silhouette of a characteristic being which may have lived here centuries ago and thirsts for form and features.

Perhaps it is among us, hour after hour, and we do not perceive it. Neither do we hear the note of a humming tuning-fork before it touches the wood and makes it vibrate in sympathy.

Perhaps it is only something like a psychic work of art, without innate consciousness – a work of art which arises as a crystal unfolds from formlessness in accordance with an immutable law.

Who can say?

As the electric tension builds past endurance on humid days and at last gives birth to lightning, might not the constant accumulation of the never-changing thoughts which poison the air here in the ghetto inevitably lead to a sudden, fitful discharge? – A psychic explosion which whips our dream-consciousness out into the daylight, creating – there nature's lightning– here a ghost whose countenance, gait and gestures would inevitably reveal the symbol of the collective soul to each and every one of us, if only we knew how to interpret the secret language of forms?

And just as various phenomena herald the lightning strike, here too certain fearful harbingers betray that phantom's imminent incursion into the realm of deeds. The flaking plaster of an old wall takes on the outlines of a striding figure; and in the frostwork on the window the features of staring faces emerge. The sand seems to sift differently from the roof, suggesting to the suspicious observer that an invisible intelligence, hidden, shunning the light, is tossing it down in furtive attempts to create all manner of strange shapes. – When our eyes rest on a monotonous weave or the irregularities of the skin, we are overcome by the thankless gift of seeing cautionary, significant forms everywhere. And through all these spectral attempts of the massed herd of thoughts to gnaw through the ramparts of banal reality, we are tormented by the certainty that our own innermost self is being sucked out deliberately and against our will, merely to let the phantom take on solid form.

When I heard Pernath confirm just now that he had encountered a beardless man with slanting eyes, the 'Golem' stood before me exactly as I saw him then.

He stood before me as if he had appeared out of thin air.

And for a moment I was overcome by a certain numb fear that once again something inexplicable was at hand, the same fear I had felt once in my childhood when the Golem's first uncanny manifestations began to cast their shadow.

Sixty-six years ago that must have been, and it started with the evening my sister's betrothed came to visit and the family was to decide the day of the wedding.

We told fortunes by pouring molten lead into a basin of water – as a joke – and I stood by gaping and not knowing what to make of it all – in my confused, childish mind I associated it with the Golem, of whom I had often heard my grandmother speak, and I imagined that any minute the door would open and the stranger would come in.

Then my sister emptied the spoonful of molten metal into the basin of water and laughed at me cheerfully as I watched agog.

With trembling, withered hands my grandfather fished out the gleaming lump of lead and held it up to the light. At once excitement broke out. They all began to talk at once; I tried to worm my way through, but was fended off.

Later, when I was older, my father told me that the molten metal had solidified in the shape of a tiny, very distinct head – smooth and round, as if cast in a mold, and so uncannily resembling the features of the 'Golem' that they had all taken fright.

I often spoke of it with the archivist Schemajah Hillel, who has the effects of the Old-New Synagogue in his safekeeping, including that certain clay figurine from Emperor

Rudolf's times. He has studied the Cabala, and believes that that lump of earth with human limbs may be nothing other than a one-time omen, as was the leaden head in my case. And the stranger who walks the streets must be the imaginative or mental image which that medieval rabbi first *thought to life* before he could clothe it in matter, and which now at regular intervals – under the same astronomical conjunctions under which it was created – returns, tormented by the thirst for material life.

Once Hillel's deceased wife stood face to face with the 'Golem', and felt as I had that one is in a cataleptic trance as long as the mysterious being is near. She said she was firmly convinced that it could only have been her own soul which – having departed her body – confronted her for a moment's time, staring her in the face with the features of an alien being.

Despite the terrible fear which came over her, not for a second did she lose the certainty that the other could only be part of her own inner being."

– – –

"Unbelievable", murmured Prokop, lost in thought.

The painter Vrieslander also seemed absorbed in contemplation.

There was a knock at the door, and the old woman who brought me water and other necessities in the evening came in, set the clay pitcher on the ground and left without a word.

We all looked up and gazed about the room as if awakening, but it was a long time before anyone spoke a word.

As if a new influence had slipped through the door along with the old woman, and needed getting used to.

"Yes! The red-haired Rosina, that's another one of those faces you can't get out of your mind, which you keep seeing pop up in every corner", Zwakh said out of the blue. "I've known that frozen grin all my life. First the grandmother,

48

then the mother! – And always the same face, not a feature altered! The same name, Rosina – one is always the resurrection of the other."

"Isn't Rosina the daughter of the junk-dealer Aaron Wassertrum?" I asked.

"So they say", replied Zwakh. – – "But Aaron Wassertrum has many a son and many a daughter we know nothing of. No one knew who the father of Rosina's mother was either – nor what became of her. – At fifteen she gave birth to a child and was never seen since. As far as I can remember, her disappearance was associated with a murder committed in this house because of her.

As her daughter does now, in her day it was *she* who possessed the thoughts of the adolescent boys. One of them is still alive – I see him quite often – but his name escapes me. The others soon died, and I believe it was she who drove them to their early graves. All I remember from that time are brief episodes which drift through my memory like faded pictures. There was a semi-imbecile who went from tavern to tavern at night cutting the guests silhouettes from black paper for a few kreuzers. And if you got him drunk he succumbed to an unspeakable sadness, and with tears and sobs he would keep cutting out the same sharp girl's profile until he had used up his whole supply of paper.

Judging from indications I have long since forgotten, when little more than a child he had loved a certain Rosina – probably the grandmother of today's – so deeply that he lost his mind.

When I count back the years, it can have been none other than the present Rosina's grandmother."

– – –

Zwakh fell silent and leaned back. – – –

In this house fate wanders in circles and keeps returning to the same place, the thought crossed my mind, and I

49

recalled an ugly scene I had once witnessed – a cat with an injury to one side of its brain, staggering about in a circle. – – –

"Now comes the head", I suddenly heard the painter Vrieslander say in a bright voice.

And he took a round piece of wood from his pocket and began to carve away at it.

Weariness pressed heavy on my eyes, and I moved my armchair out of the light and into the background.

The water for the punch seethed in the kettle, and Josua Prokop refilled the glasses. The sound of dance music came softly, very softly through the closed window – sometimes falling silent entirely, then picking up, as the wind lost it on its way or carried it up to us from the street.

Wasn't I going to join in the toast, the musician asked me after a while.

But I gave no reply – I had so utterly lost the will to move that it did not even occur to me to open my mouth.

I thought I was asleep, so stony was the inner calm which had seized me. And I had to peer over at Vrieslander's glittering knife, restlessly gnawing little shavings from the wood – to make certain that I was awake.

Zwakh's voice rumbled in the distance, continuing to tell all sorts of curious tales about marionettes and abstruse fairytales he had thought up for his puppet shows.

Dr. Savioli was mentioned too, and the genteel lady, wife of a nobleman, who paid secret visits to Savioli in the hidden studio.

And again I saw Aaron Wassertrum's taunting, triumphant face in my mind's eye. –

I wondered whether I should tell Zwakh what had happened that time – then thought it inconsequential and not worth the trouble. And I knew that my will would fail me if I tried to speak now.

Suddenly the three at the table looked over at me sharply, and Prokop said very loudly: "He's fallen asleep." – so loudly that it almost sounded like a question.

They went on in hushed voices, and I realized that they were talking about me.

Vrieslander's knife danced back and forth, catching the light which poured down from the lamp, and the reflected glare burned into my eyes.

A word like "madness" came up, and I listened intently to the talk of the little circle.

"Subjects like the 'Golem' ought to be avoided in Pernath's presence", Josua Prokop said reproachfully. "When he spoke of the Book of Ibbur just now, we held our tongues and asked no questions. I wager he merely dreamed it all."

Zwakh nodded: "You're absolutely right. It's like taking a candle into a dusty room, where the walls and ceiling are hung with tattered cloths and the dry tinder of the past lies foot-deep on the floor; the least touch, and the flames would shoot out from all sides."

"Was Pernath in the lunatic asylum for long? Too bad about him, he can't be much older than forty", Vrieslander said.

"I don't know, and I have no idea where he comes from or what his profession used to be. He looks like an old French nobleman with his slender figure and his goatee. Many, many years ago an old doctor of my acquaintance asked me to look after him and find him a little apartment here in these streets where no one will pry into his affairs and unsettle him with questions about days gone by." Again Zwakh looked over at me, moved. – "He has lived here ever since, making a modest living by restoring antiques and cutting cameos. Fortunately for him, he seems to have forgotten everything relating to his madness. But whatever you do, don't ask him about things which could stir his memories of the past – how often did the old doctor urge that upon me! You know, Zwakh, he always said, we have a certain method; we have walled up his illness with enormous effort, if I may – just as the scene of some tragedy is shut away because of the unhappy memory associated with it." – –

The words of the marionette player had ambushed me like a butcher a defenseless animal and wrung my heart with rough, cruel hands.

As long as I could remember, a dull torment had gnawed at me – the suspicion that something had been taken from me and that I had walked much of my life's path along an abyss like a somnambulist. And I had never been able to fathom the cause.

Now the solution to the riddle lay manifest before me, stinging unbearably like an opened wound.

My morbid reluctance to give rein to the memory of past events – then the strange, recurring dream that I was trapped in a house with a series of chambers I could not enter – the disturbing failure of my memory in things concerning my youth – all at once there was a terrible explanation: I had been insane, and hypnosis had been used to close off the "room" which led to those chambers of my brain, making me homeless amidst the life surrounding me.

And without hope of ever regaining the lost memory!

The motives of my thoughts and actions lie hidden in another, forgotten existence, I realized – never could I know them: a cut plant am I, a rice seedling that sprouts from a strange root. And if I managed to force my way into that locked "room", wouldn't I succumb once again to the ghosts which had been banned there?!

Zwakh's tale of the "Golem" an hour ago passed through my mind, and suddenly I saw an enormous, mysterious connection between the legendary chamber with no door where that stranger was said to live, and my portentous dream.

Yes! My rope, too, "would snap" if I tried to glimpse through the barred window of my inner life.

The strange connection grew ever clearer to me, taking on an indescribably terrifying quality.

I felt: things – inconceivable – are forged there and move side by side like blind horses, not knowing where the way leads.

In the ghetto too: a room, a space whose entry none can find – a shadowy being which dwells there, from time to time groping its way along the streets to spread fear and horror! – – –

Vrieslander was still carving away at the head, and the wood squeaked under the blade of the knife.

It almost pained me to listen, and I looked over to see when it would be over with.

As the head turned back and forth in the painter's hand, it seemed imbued with consciousness, peering from corner to corner. Then its eyes lingered upon me for a long time, glad to have found me at last.

And I could not look away either, staring fixedly at the wooden face.

For a while the painter's knife seemed hesitantly to seek something, then, resolute, it carved a line, and the features of the wooden head came to fearful life.

I recognized the yellow face of the stranger who had brought me the book.

Then I could make out nothing more, the vision had lasted only an instant, and I felt my heart leave off beating and flutter anxiously.

Yet – as then – I remained conscious of the face.

I myself was the face and lay on Vrieslander's lap, peering about.

My eyes roamed the room, and a strange hand moved my skull.

Then all at once I saw Zwakh's agitated face and heard his words: for God's sake, that's the Golem!

There was a scuffle; they tried to snatch the wood carving from Vrieslander by force, but he fended them off and cried laughingly:

"What do you want, it's completely botched." And he shook them off, opened the window and threw the head down onto the street.

I swooned, plunging into a profound darkness shot with shimmering strands of gold, and when I woke, after what seemed a long, long time, I heard the wood clatter on the pavement. – – –

"You were so sound asleep that you didn't feel us shake you", Josua Prokop said to me, "the punch is all gone, and you've missed everything."

The searing pain at what I had just heard overwhelmed me again, and I wanted to cry out that I had not been dreaming when I told them about the Book of Ibbur – I wanted to take it out of the casket and show it to them.

But I had no chance to voice these thoughts, and could not prevail against my guests' sudden restlessness.

Zwakh bundled me into my coat and cried:

"Just come along with us to 'Loisitschek', Master Pernath, that'll refresh the vital spirits."

NIGHT

Without a will of my own, I had let Zwakh lead me down the stairs.

The smell of the fog which seeped into the house from the street grew more and more distinct. Josua Prokop and Vrieslander had gone a few paces ahead, and could be heard talking to each other outside the archway.

"It must have fallen through the sewer grating. Devil of a business."

We came out onto the street, and I saw Prokop crouch to search for the marionette.

"I'm glad you can't find the stupid head", Vrieslander muttered. He leaned against the wall, and his face lit up luridly and flickered out at brief intervals as he sucked a match-flame into his short pipe with a hiss.

Prokop waved his arm vehemently in protest and bent over still further. He was almost kneeling on the pavement.

"Be quiet! Don't you hear?"

We came closer. He pointed mutely to the grating without a word and cupped his hand to his ear, listening. For a while we stood motionless and strained to hear down into the shaft.

Nothing.

"What was it?" the old marionette player whispered at last; but Prokop immediately seized him by the wrist.

For a moment – barely the space of a heartbeat – I had thought a hand was knocking against an iron plate down there – almost inaudibly. When I thought about it a second later, it was all over; only in my breast did it continue to reverberate like the echo of a memory, slowly giving way to an indeterminate feeling of horror.

Footsteps coming up the street banished the impression.

"Let's go; what are we standing around for!" Vrieslander reprimanded.

We walked down the block.

Prokop followed reluctantly.

"I'd bet my life that someone down there was screaming in mortal anguish."

None of us answered him, but I felt that our tongues were fettered by something like slowly dawning fear.

Soon we stood outside a red-curtained tavern window.

SALON LOISITSCHEK

"Today Big Konzert"

stood on a piece of pasteboard with faded pictures of women stuck to its edges.

Before Zwakh's hand could touch the knob, the door swung inward, and a strapping fellow with black, greased hair and no collar – a green silk cravat slung around his bare neck, his vest adorned with a cluster of pig's teeth – received us with bows and scrapes.

"Yeah, yeah, dat's vat I call guests. – – – Pane Schaffranek, quick, gimme a drum roll!" he hastily added over his shoulder into the crowded establishment.

The reply was a tinkling sound like a rat scampering across piano wires.

"Yeah, yeah, dat's vat I call guests, dat's vat I call guests. Just look at dat", the strapping fellow kept murmuring to himself as he helped us out of our coats.

"Yes, yes, I've got all de 'stinguished nobility of de country gaddered here today", he said triumphantly in reply to Vrieslander's astonished look as several distinguished-looking young men in evening attire came to view on a kind of platform in the back of the tavern, set off by two steps and a balustrade.

Clouds of pungent tobacco smoke hung over the tables, and behind them tatterdemalion figures crowded the long wooden benches against the walls: whores from the Bulwarks, unkempt, filthy, barefoot, their firm breasts barely veiled by discolored shawls; next to them pimps with blue military caps and cigarettes behind their ears; cattle-dealers with hairy fists and ponderous fingers, whose every movement spoke a mute language of baseness; roaming waiters with impudent eyes and pock-marked sales clerks in checkered trousers.

"I'll put up a screen around de table so you'll 'ave it nice an' private", the strapping man's fat voice wheezed, and a wheeled partition pasted over with little dancing Chinamen trundled in front of the corner table at which we had taken our seats.

The jangle of a harp silenced the babble of voices in the room.

For one second a rhythmic pause.

Deathly silence, as if everyone was holding their breath.

With appalling distinctness the iron gas jets could suddenly be heard blowing the flat, heart-shaped, hissing flames from their mouths – – – then the music pounced on the noise and devoured it.

As if they had only just taken form, two strange figures emerged from the tobacco smoke before my eyes.

With a long, flowing, white prophet's beard, a black silk skullcap – such as old Jewish patriarchs wear – on his bald head, his blind eyes milky blue and glassy – fixed on the ceiling – an old man sat moving his lips silently and plucking the strings of a harp with withered fingers like vulture's claws. Next to him, in a greasily-gleaming black taffeta dress, jet beads and cross on her neck and arms – the very image of sham bourgeois respectability – a spongy hussy with an accordion on her lap.

A wild throng of sounds stumbled from the instruments, then the melody petered out, exhausted, in mere accompaniment.

The old man snapped at the air a few times and opened his mouth wide enough to show the black stumps of his teeth. Slowly a wild bass struggled up from his chest, accompanied by strange guttural Hebraic sounds:

"Roo-n-te, blau-we Stern – – "

"Reeteeteet", the hussy shrilled, immediately snapping shut her yelpy lips as if she had said too much.

"Roonte, blaue Steern,
Hörndlach ess' i' ach geern."

"Reeteeteet."

"Rothboart, Grienboart,
allerlaj Stern – – "

"Reeteeteet, reeteeteet–"[2]

– – –

The couples began to dance.

"It's the song of 'chomezigen Borchu'", the marionette player explained to us with a smile, softly beating time with the pewter spoon which, curiously enough, was attached to the table with a chain. "A hundred years ago or even more two journeyman bakers, Rotbart and Grünbart, poisoned the bread – stars and crescents – on the eve of 'Schabbes Hagodel' to bring death aplenty to the Jewish Town; but the 'meschores' – the congregation attendant – discovered the plot in time with the help of divine illumination and was able to hand both criminals over to the police. To commemorate this miraculous deliverance from deadly peril the 'Lamdonim' and 'Bocherlech' composed the strange song which we are now hearing as a bordello quadrille."

"Reeteeteet – reeteeteet."

"Roote, blaue Steern – – – –" The old man's baying rang out ever more hollow and fanatical.

---

[2] Yiddish: "Red, blue star, I like to eat crescents too, Rotbart, Grünbart, all kinds of stars."

Suddenly the melody became muddled and gradually shifted into the rhythm of the Bohemian 'Schlapak', a gliding dance in which the couples ardently pressed sweaty cheek to sweaty cheek.

"Attaboy. Bravo! Hey there! Catch, hepp, hepp!" a slender bemonocled young cavalier in tails called to the harpist, reaching into his vest pocket and tossing a silver piece in his direction. It did not reach its destination: I saw it flash above the hurly-burly of the dancers; then it was gone. A rowdy – his face seemed so familiar; I believe it must have been the one who stood next to Charousek in the downpour the other day – took his hand out from behind his partner's neckerchief, where it had stubbornly rested all this time – a snatch in the air with monkey-like agility, not missing a single beat of the music, and the coin was palmed. Not a muscle twitched in the lad's face; only two or three nearby couples grinned faintly.

"Probably one of the boys from the 'Battalion', to judge by his skill", Zwakh said with a laugh.

"I believe Master Pernath hasn't heard about the 'Battalion' before", Vrieslander put in too quickly, and gave the marionette player a wink I was not supposed to see. – I understood well enough: as in my room just now, they thought I was sick. Wanted to cheer me up. And Zwakh was to tell a story. Any story.

When the good old man looked at me so pityingly, heat surged from my heart to my eyes. If only he knew how his pity hurt me!

I overheard the first words, the marionette player's introduction to his story – I know only that I felt I was bleeding to death. I grew ever colder and more rigid, as I had just now when I lay as a wooden face in Vrieslander's lap. Then all at once I was in the very midst of the story, which took me in its alien embrace – enveloping me like a lifeless piece from a school reader.

Zwakh began:

"The tale of the jurist Dr. Hulbert and his Battalion.

– – – Nu, what can I tell you: he had a face full of warts
and crooked legs like a dachshund. Even as a boy he knew
nothing but studying. Dry, enervating studying. The money
he earned from giving lessons went to support his sick
mother as well. How green meadows look, and hedges and
hills full of flowers and trees, that, I believe, he knew only
from books. And you know yourself how little sunshine
reaches Prague's black alleys.

He earned his doctorate with distinction; that went without saying.

Well, in time he became a famous jurist. So famous that
all the people – judges and old lawyers – came to ask him
questions when there was something they didn't know. Yet
he lived wretched as a beggar in a garret overlooking the
Tyn Yard.

Year after year passed this way, and Dr. Hulbert's reputation as a luminary in his field gradually became a byword
throughout the land. Surely none would have believed that a
man such as he could be susceptible to the heart's tender
sentiments, for his hair was already turning white and no
one could remember him ever having spoken of anything
but jurisprudence. But it is in such sealed hearts that passion
burns the hottest.

On the very day when Dr. Hulbert achieved the goal
which, ever since his student days, must have seemed the
loftiest: when, namely, His Majesty the Emperor gave
word from Vienna that he was to be appointed Rector
Magnificus at our university, word went around that he had
become engaged to a lovely young woman from a poor but
noble family.

And in truth, from then on fortune seemed to smile upon him. Though his marriage remained childless, he adored

61

his wife, and his greatest delight was to fulfill her every unspoken wish.

Yet in his good fortune he did not forget his suffering fellows, as many another has done. 'God has stilled my longing,' he said one time, 'he made a dreamlike vision come true, one which has hovered before me like a splendor since my childhood: he gave me for my own the loveliest being on earth. And so I wish that a glimmer of this happiness might reach others as well, as far as it is in my small power.'

– – –

And so it happened that when the occasion arose he took in a young student and treated him like a son of his own. Presumably reflecting how he himself would have profited from such a good deed in the days of his care-filled youth. But in this world many an act which seems good and noble has consequences like to a detestable one, no doubt because we cannot, after all, distinguish what contains virulent seed and what beneficial; so it happened that Dr. Hulbert reaped the bitterest suffering from his compassionate deed.

Soon the young wife was enflamed by a secret passion for the student, and as a merciless fate would have it, just when the rector came home unexpectedly to surprise her with a bouquet of roses for her birthday as a sign of his love, he found her in the arms of him upon whom he had heaped kindness after kindness.

The blue daisy is said to lose its color forever when struck by the livid, sulfurous gleam of the lightning which presages a hailstorm; it is certain, at any rate, that the old man's soul went blind forever the day his happiness was shattered. That very same evening he, who had never known the meaning of immoderation, sat here at 'Loisitschek' until dawn – almost senseless from cheap liquor. And 'Loisitschek' became his home for the rest of his ruined life. In the summer he slept somewhere amidst the rubble of a construction site, in winter here on the wooden benches.

He was tacitly allowed to retain the titles of Professor and Doctor. No one had the heart to reproach him with their grievance at his transformation.

Gradually the shady denizens of the Jewish Town came to gather about him, and that was the birth of the strange fellowship known to this day as 'the Battalion'.

Dr. Hulbert's exhaustive knowledge of the law became the bulwark for all those under police scrutiny. If some released convict was in danger of starving to death, Dr. Hulbert would send him stark naked to the Old Town Square – and the Office on the so-called "Fischbanka" would be compelled to provide him with a suit of clothes. If a homeless whore was expelled from the city, she would quickly marry a local hooligan and thus become a resident.

Dr. Hulbert knew a hundred such expedients, and his counsel rendered the police helpless. – Whatever these outcasts of human society 'earned', they deposited faithfully, down to the heller and kreuzer, in the common till which covered the necessities of life. Not one of them was ever guilty of the slightest dishonesty. Perhaps it was this iron discipline that gave rise to the name 'the Battalion.'

On the night of every December 1st, the anniversary of the old man's misfortune, a strange celebration was held in 'Loisitschek'. They crowded here shoulder to shoulder: beggars, vagabonds, pimps and whores, drunkards and rag-pickers, and it was silent as a church service. – And then, from the corner where the two musicians are now sitting, right under the coronation picture of His Majesty the Emperor, Dr. Hulbert told them his life story: how he had struggled his way to the top, acquired his doctorate and then become Rector Magnificus. Every time he reached the point when

he entered his young wife's room with the bunch of roses –
both to celebrate her birthday and in memory of the hour
when he had come to ask for her hand and she had become
his dear betrothed – his voice would fail, and he would collapse onto the table, weeping. Then, now and again, some
wanton female would drop a half-withered flower upon his
hand, bashfully and secretly so that none might see.

For a long time none of the listeners would move. These
people are too tough to weep, but they would look down at
their clothes and twist their fingers uncertainly.

One morning Dr. Hulbert was found dead on a bench
down on the Vltava. I believe he must have frozen to death.

Even now I see his funeral procession before me. The
'Battalion' members nearly tore themselves to pieces in the
effort to make everything as spectacular as possible.

The beadle of the university led the way in full regalia,
in his hands the purple cushion with the gold chain on it,
and behind the hearse, in endless ranks – the 'Battalion',
barefoot, filthy, ragged and tattered. One of them had sold
his last possessions and strode along: his body, legs and
arms wrapped and bound with layers of old newspaper.

Thus did they render him the last honors.

On his grave, out in the cemetery, stands a white stone
upon which three figures are carved: the Savior crucified
between two robbers. From an unknown donor. It is whispered that the monument was erected by Dr. Hulbert's wife.

– – – –

But the dead jurist's will provided a legacy stipulating
that every member of the 'Battalion' be treated to a free
midday soup at 'Loisitschek'; that is the reason for the
spoons hanging from the chains here at the table, and the
hollows in the tabletop are the plates. At twelve o'clock the
waitress comes and squirts the broth into them with a big
tin syringe, and if anyone fails to identify himself as a

member of the 'Batallion', she sucks the broth back up again.

Starting from this table, the custom traveled around the whole world in the form of a joke." – – –

– – –

A tumult in the tavern woke me from my lethargy. Zwakh's last words drifted past my consciousness. I saw him moving his hands to illustrate the pumping of a syringe piston; then the images which unreeled about us raced across my vision so quickly and mechanically and yet with such uncanny vividness that after a few moments I completely forgot myself and felt like a wheel in a living clock-work.

The room had turned into one great throng of people. Up on the platform: dozens of gentlemen in black dress-coats. White cuffs, glittering rings. A dragoon uniform with the aiguillettes of a cavalry captain. In the background a lady's hat with salmon-hued ostrich feathers.

Loisa's twisted face looked up through the posts of the balustrade. I saw: he could hardly stand upright. Jaromir was there too, staring up fixedly, his back pressed close to the side wall as if pushed against it by an invisible hand.

The dancing figures suddenly faltered: the tavern-keeper must have said something to frighten them. The music kept playing, but softly; it was unsure of itself now. It trembled; one felt that distinctly. And yet the tavern-keeper's face had an expression of gloating, savage joy.

– – – – Suddenly the Inspector of Police stands in the doorway in uniform. His arms are spread so that none can leave. Behind him a policeman.

"So there's dancing here after all. In spite of the ban? I'm closing the place. You're coming along, tavern-keeper! And everyone here, march, off with you to the station!"

That sounds like a command.

The strapping man gives no reply, but the gloating grin stays on his face.

It only grows more fixed.

The accordion, choked up, can only wheeze.

And the harp puts its tail between its legs.

Suddenly the faces all appear in profile: they gape expectantly up at the platform.

And then a genteel black figure comes coolly down the few steps and slowly approaches the Inspector.

The policeman's eyes are glued spellbound to the black patent leather shoes which come sauntering up.

The cavalier, having stopped a pace away from the police officer, runs his bored gaze over him from head to foot and back again.

The other young noblemen up on the platform lean over the railing and stifle their laughter with grey silk handkerchiefs.

The cavalry captain jams a gold piece into his eye socket and spits the butt of his cigarette into the hair of a girl lounging below him.

The Inspector of Police turns color and in his discomfiture stares fixedly at the pearl on the aristocrat's shirtfront.

He cannot endure the indifferent, lusterless gaze of this smooth-shaven, immobile face with its hooked nose.

It destroys his composure. Crushes him.

The deathly silence of the tavern grows more and more agonizing.

"That is how the statues of knights look, lying with folded hands on stone sarcophagi in Gothic churches", the painter Vrieslander whispers, glancing at the cavalier.

At last the aristocrat breaks the silence: "Eh – hm." – –
He copies the voice of the tavern-keeper: "Yeah, yeah, dat's vat I call guests. Just look at dat." A resounding howl explodes in the tavern, making the glasses jingle; the rowdies hold

their bellies with laughter. A bottle flies against the wall and shatters. The strapping tavern-keeper bleats at us in explanation and awe: "His Excellency Prince Ferri Athenstädt."

The prince has handed the officer a visiting card. The poor man takes it, salutes repeatedly and clicks his heels.

There is another hush, the crowd waits breathlessly to hear what will happen next.

The cavalier speaks again:

"The ladies and gentlemen you see gathered here – eh –, are my dear guests." His Excellency indicates the riff-raff with a negligent motion of his arm. "Might you, Herr Inspector – eh – care to be introduced?"

The Inspector demurs with a forced smile, awkwardly stammers something about "performing vexatious duties" and finally screws himself up to the words: "I can tell that this is a respectable affair."

That puts life into the cavalry captain: he hurries into the background to the lady's hat with the ostrich feather and a moment later, to the jubilation of the young noblemen – drags Rosina down into the hall by the arm.

She staggers with drunkenness and her eyes are closed. The big, expensive hat sits askew, and she has nothing on but long pink stockings and – a man's dress coat on her naked body.

A sign: the music breaks in frenetically – – – – – – – "reeteeteet – reeteeteet" – – – – – and washes away the gurgling cry uttered by deaf-mute Jaromir, over against the wall, upon seeing Rosina. – – –

We decide to go.

Zwakh calls the waitress.

His words are swallowed in the general ruckus.

The scenes before me turn fantastic like an opium dream.

The cavalry officer holds the half-naked Rosina in his arms and revolves slowly with her in time to the music.

The crowd has drawn back from them respectfully.

Then there is a murmur from the benches: "Loisitschek, Loisitschek." Necks are craned, and the dancing couple is joined by a second, still stranger one. An effeminate looking lad in pink underwear, with long blond hair down to his shoulders, his lips and cheeks painted like a whore and his eyes downcast in coquettish perplexity – clings languishing to Prince Athenstädt's breast.

The harp gushes a saccharine waltz.

A savage loathing of life rises in my gorge.

Anxiously my eyes seek the door: the Inspector stands there, turned away so as not to see a thing, whispering rapidly to the policeman, who slips something in his pocket. It sounds like handcuffs.

The two of them peer over at pock-marked Loisa, who makes as if to hide and then, paralyzed – his face white as chalk and twisted with fear – remains where he is.

An image flares up in my memory and fades: the image I saw an hour before, Prokop listening – bending over the grate – and a death-cry rings out from under the ground. – –
– I want to cry out and cannot. Cold fingers reach between my lips and bend my tongue down against my front teeth, so that it fills my mouth like a lump and I cannot utter a word.

I cannot see the fingers, I know they are invisible, and yet I feel them like physical things.

And it looms clear in my consciousness: they belong to the spectral hand which gave me the Book of Ibbur in my room on Hahnpassgasse.

"Water, water!" Zwakh cries out next to me. They hold my head and shine a candle into my pupils.

"Bring him to his apartment, fetch a doctor – the archivist Hillel understands this kind of thing – – take him there!" they consult in a murmur.

Then I lie stiff as a corpse on a stretcher, and Prokop and Vrieslander carry me out.

WOKE

Zwakh had gone up the stairs ahead of us; I heard the anxious questions of Mirijam, the daughter of the archivist Hillel, and his attempts to reassure her.

I made no effort to hear what they were saying, and I guessed, rather than understanding it in words, that Zwakh was explaining how I had had an accident and they had come to ask him to give me first aid and restore me to consciousness.

I was still unable to move a muscle, and the invisible fingers held my tongue; but my thoughts were steady and sure, and the sense of horror had released me. I knew exactly where I was and what was happening to me, and did not even find it odd to be carried up the stairs like a dead man, set down in Schemajah Hillel's room along with the stretcher and – left alone.

A calm, natural contentment filled me, as one feels upon returning home after a long walk. It was dark in the room, and the blurred outlines of the window frames loomed cruciform against the dull-lit haze which shimmered up from the street.

Everything seemed perfectly natural to me, and I wondered neither that Hillel entered the room with a seven-flamed Jewish menorah, nor that he calmly wished me "good evening" like someone whose arrival he had expected.

As he went back and forth, straightening several objects on the dresser and finally using the menorah to light another, also with seven candles, I was vividly struck by something I had never found unusual all the time I had lived in this house – though we had often met on the stairs three or four times a week –.

Namely: the harmony of his body and limbs and the narrow, delicate cast of his face with the nobly formed brow. As I now saw by the light of the candle, he could be no older than I: 45 years at most.

"You arrived a few minutes earlier than expected" – he began after a while – "otherwise I would have had the candles lit already." – He pointed to the two menorahs, came up to the stretcher and, it seemed, fixed his dark, deep-set eyes upon someone who stood or knelt at my head, but whom I could not see. At the same time he moved his lips in a silent utterance.

At once the invisible fingers released my tongue, and the paralysis left me. I sat up and looked behind me: aside from Schemajah Hillel and me, there was no one in the room. So his "you" and the remark that he had been waiting had been meant for me!?

Even stranger than these facts in themselves, I was incapable of feeling the slightest astonishment at them.

Hillel seemed to guess my thoughts, for he smiled kindly, helping me up from the stretcher and pointing to an armchair, and said:

"There is nothing marvelous about it. People are frightened only by the spectral things – the kischuph: life scratches and stings like a hair shirt, but the sunbeams of the spiritual world are mild and warming."

I was silent, unable to think of a reply. Neither did he seem to expect a response; he sat across from me and went on serenely: "Even a silver mirror, if it could feel, would suffer pain only when it is burnished. Once it is smooth and shining, it reflects all the images it captures without suffering and agitation. –

Happy is the man", he added softly, "who can say of himself: I am burnished." – For a moment he gave way to his musings, and I heard him murmur Hebrew words:

"*Lischuosècho Kiwisi Adoschem.*" Then once again his voice rang distinctly in my ear:

"You came to me in a deep sleep, and I woke you. In the Psalms of David it is said:

" '*Then I said within myself: now I begin: it is God's right hand that has wrought this change.*'

When people rise from their beds they believe they have cast off sleep, not knowing that they have fallen victim to their senses, prey to a new, much deeper sleep than the one they have just escaped. There is only one true waking, and that is the one you are now approaching. Speak of it to other people, and they will say you are sick, for they cannot understand you. And thus it is useless and cruel to tell them of it.

> They pass like a river –
> And are as a sleep,
> As grass which soon withers –
> Which is reaped in the evening and dries."

Who was the stranger who visited me in my room and gave me the Book of Ibbur? Did I see him awake or in a dream?" I wanted to ask, but Hillel answered me before I could put words to the thought:

"Suppose that the man who came to you and whom you call the Golem signifies the waking of the dead through the innermost spiritual life. Everything on earth is naught but an eternal symbol, clothed in dust!

How do you think with your eyes? Every form you see, you think with your eyes. Everything which has taken form was once a ghost."

Concepts which had once been anchored in my brain tore loose and drifted out upon a boundless sea like ships without rudders.

Tranquilly Hillel went on:

"He who has been woken can die no more; sleep and death are one."

"– – can die no more?" – A dull pain seized me.

"Two paths run side by side: the path of life and the path of death. You took the Book of Ibbur and read in it. The spirit of life has impregnated your soul", I heard him say.

"Hillel, Hillel, let me take the path all men take: the path of death!" my every fiber cried out wildly.

Schemajah Hillel's face went rigid with gravity.

"Men take no path at all, neither that of life nor that of death. They drift along like chaff in a storm. The Talmud says: 'Before God created the world, he held a mirror up to his creatures; there they saw the spiritual torments of existence and the delights to follow. Some took on these torments. But the others refused, and these God struck from the book of the living.' But you *take* a path and have set out upon it of your own free will – even if you no longer know it: you have summoned yourself. Do not despair: gradually, when knowledge comes, memory will come as well. *Knowledge and memory are the same.*"

The friendly, almost affectionate tone in which Hillel's speech ended restored my composure, and I felt sheltered like a sick child who knows his father is at his side.

I looked up and saw that many figures had suddenly filled the room, encircling us: some in white shrouds, such as the old rabbis wore, others with three-cornered hats and silver buckles on their shoes – but Hillel passed his hand over my eyes, and the room was empty once again.

Then he accompanied me out to the stairs and gave me a burning candle to light my way back to my room. – – –

I went to bed and tried to sleep, but slumber did not come, and I passed instead into a strange state which was neither dreaming nor waking nor sleeping.

I had snuffed the light, yet everything in the room was so clear that I could distinguish each separate form. At the same time I felt quite at ease and free of that unrest which usually torments one in such a state.

72

Never in my life had I been capable of thinking so sharply and precisely. The rhythm of health surged through my nerves and marshaled my thoughts in rank and file like an army waiting only for my command.

I needed only to give the summons, and they would step up to me and fulfill my wishes.

I remembered an aventurine cameo I had been trying to cut the past few weeks – without success, for the many scattered spangles in the mineral refused to correspond to the features of the face I pictured – and at once I saw the solution before me and knew exactly how I must wield the cutter to do justice to the structure of the material.

Once slave to a horde of fantastic impressions and dream visions, often doubtful whether they were ideas or feelings, I suddenly saw myself as lord and ruler of my own realm.

Arithmetical problems which once I could only have solved on paper, groaning with exertion, suddenly yielded their results in my mind like child's play. All with the help of a newborn ability to see and grasp just what I needed: numbers, forms, objects or colors. And when the questions could not be solved with tools of that kind – philosophical problems and the like – hearing took the place of this inner vision, and the voice of Schemajah Hillel assumed the role of the speaker.

Thus was I granted perceptions of the strangest kind.

Things I had heedlessly let slip past my ear a thousand times, as mere words, loomed before me imbued with value in their innermost fiber; all at once I "grasped" what I had learned "by heart" as my "proper"ty. The unguessed-at secrets of word formation lay bare before me.

The "lofty" ideals of mankind, which had hitherto looked down on me with the bland faces of Councilors of Commerce, their swelled chests daubed with medals – humbly now they raised the masks from their ugly faces and begged pardon: they themselves were only beggars, yet crutches for – a still more outrageous fraud.

Was I dreaming after all? Could it be that I had not spoken to Hillel at all?

I reached for the armchair next to my bed.

Right: there lay the candle Schemajah had given me, and, happy as a little boy on Christmas Eve who has assured himself that the miraculous jumping jack is really and truly there, I burrowed back into the pillows.

And like a bloodhound I plunged on into the thicket of psychic riddles which surrounded me.

First I tried to go back to the point in my life to which my memory extended. Only from there – I believed – could I set eyes upon that part of my existence which, by some strange twist of fate, darkness hid from me.

But however I tried, the most I could do was to picture how I had stood in the dark courtyard of our house that time, making out the figure of Aaron Wassertrum in the junk shop through the archway – as if I had lived in this house for a century, working the trade of lapidary, always the same age and never once a child!

I was about to abandon hope of delving deeper in the shafts of the past when suddenly I grasped with brilliant clarity that though the broad road of events ended at that certain archway in my memory, a number of narrow little footpaths did not; they must have accompanied the main road all along without my noticing. "Where", the cry resounded in my ears, "did you acquire the skills with which you now eke out your livelihood? Who taught you cameo-carving – and engraving and all the rest? Reading, writing, speaking – and eating – and walking, breathing, thinking and feeling?"

At once I acted upon this inner voice. Systematically I traced back my life.

I forced myself to think, in reverse but without interruption: What happened just now, what was its starting point, what came before that, and so forth?

Once again I had reached that certain archway – – now! Now! One little leap into the void, and the abyss which separated me from memory would be vaulted – suddenly an image I had overlooked while retracing my thoughts rose before me: Schemajah Hillel passed his hand over my eyes – as he had done just now in his room.

And everything was erased. Even the desire to seek on.

Only one thing stood firm as a lasting good – the realization that life's sequence of events is a dead end, however broad and navigable it may seem. It is the narrow, hidden paths which take us back to our lost homeland: the fine, barely visible writing graven on our body, not the hideous scar left by the rasp of outward life – holds the solution to the ultimate secrets.

Thus, just as I could find my way back to the days of my youth if I learned the primer's alphabet in reverse order, from Z to A, arriving where I had begun to learn in school – thus, I realized, I should also be able to make my way into the other distant homeland which lies beyond all thought.

A world of work descended upon my shoulders. Hercules, too, bore the vault of heaven above him for a time, I recalled, and the legend's hidden meaning glimmered out at me. And just as Hercules regained his freedom through a ruse, by begging the giant Atlas: "Just let me wrap a bundle of rope around my head, so that the terrible burden does not crush my brain", there might– it dawned on me – be some dark way around this obstacle.

Suddenly I was deeply suspicious of putting blind faith in the leadership of my thoughts. I stretched out and covered my eyes and ears with my fingers so as not to be distracted by the senses. To kill every thought.

But my will foundered upon the iron law: I could drive out one thought only with another, and when one died, the next had already come to gorge upon its flesh. I fled into the roaring torrent of my blood, but the thoughts followed at my heels; I hid in the forge of my heart: a little while only, and they had discovered me.

Once again Hillel's friendly voice came to my aid, saying: "Keep to your path and waver not! The key to the art of forgetting belongs to our brothers who walk the path of death; but you have been quickened by the spirit of – life."

The Book of Ibbur appeared before me, and two letters flared up within it: the one which signified the brazen woman, with the pulse as mighty as an earthquake – the other at an immeasurable distance: *the hermaphrodite on the nacreous throne, on its head a red wood crown.*

Then for the third time Schemajah Hillel passed his hand over my eyes, and I fell asleep. – –

Snow

"My dear, revered Master Pernath!

I write you this letter in great haste and the utmost fear. Please, destroy it immediately after reading it – or better yet, bring it to me along with its envelope. – Otherwise it will not leave me in peace.

Do not tell a soul that I have written you. Or where you will go today!

Your honest, good face inspired such trust in me – 'the other day' – (This little allusion to an incident you witnessed will permit you to guess who is writing you this letter, for I am afraid to sign my name) – and the fact that your dear, deceased father gave me lessons as a child – all this gives me the courage to turn to you, perhaps the only person left who can help me.

I beg you, come today, at 5 in the evening, to the Cathedral Church on the Hradschin.

A lady known to you."

– – –

I sat there for what must have been a quarter of an hour holding the letter in my hand. The strange, solemn mood which had still enveloped me from the night before fled in a trice – blown away by the fresh breeze of a new earthly day. A young fate came toward me, smiling and full of promise – a child of spring. A human heart sought help from me. – From me! How different my room suddenly looked! The worm-eaten carved cabinet had such a contented mien, and the four armchairs struck me as old people who sit around the table playing tarok with cozy chuckles.

My hours were filled, filled with wealth and splendor.

Was the withered tree to bear fruit after all?

I felt a vital force seep through me, a force which till now had slept within me – hidden in the depths of my soul, buried in the rubble heaped up by daily life, as a spring breaks free of ice when winter gives way.

And as I held the letter in my hand I *knew* with such certitude that I would be able to help, whatever the matter was. The jubilation in my heart gave me this assurance.

Over and over I read the words: "– and the fact that your dear, deceased father gave me lessons as a child – – – –"; – my breath caught. Didn't that sound like a promise: "Even today you will be with me in paradise"? The hand which reached out to me, seeking help, extended a gift: *the memory I thirsted for* – it would reveal the secret to me, help lift the curtain which had closed over my past.

"Your dear, deceased father – –", how strange the words sounded when I said them to myself! – Father! – For a moment I saw the weary face of an old man with white hair appear in the armchair next to my trunk – a stranger, a perfect stranger, and yet so terribly familiar; then my eyes came to themselves, and the hammer strokes of my heart struck the tangible hour of the present.

I jumped up in alarm: had I dreamed away the time? I looked at the clock: God be praised, only four-thirty.

I went next door into my bedroom, fetched my hat and coat and went down the stairs. What did I care today for the dark corners' whispering, the spiteful, fretful objections which always rose up from them: "We won't let you – you're ours – we don't want you to be happy – that would be a fine thing, happiness here in the house!"

The fine, poisoned dust of all these corners and corridors which ordinarily settled around me with choking hands – today it fled before the living breath of my lips. For a moment I paused at Hillel's door.

Should I go in?

A furtive awe kept me from knocking. I felt so utterly different today – as if I were *forbidden* to go in there to him. And already the hand of life propelled me forward, down the stairs. – –

The street lay white in the snow.

I believe many people greeted me; I do not remember whether I returned the favor. Over and over I put my hand to my bosom to feel whether I still had the letter:

The place radiated warmth. – – –

– – –

I wandered through the arches of the stone arcades on the Old Town Square and past the bronze fountain whose Baroque grille was hung with icicles, over the stone bridge with its statues of saints and the figure of John of Nepomuk.

Below the river foamed spitefully against the piles.

Half in a dream, my gaze fell upon the hollowed-out sandstone of Saint Luitgard with the "Torments of the Damned" inside: the snow lay thick upon the eyelids of the penitents and the shackles on the hands they had raised in prayer.

Archways gathered me up and released me, palaces marched slowly past with haughty carved portals on which lions' heads bit bronze rings.

Here too, snow, snow everywhere. Soft, white as the fur of an enormous polar bear.

High, proud windows, the sills be-glittered and iced, gazed up indifferently at the clouds.

It astonished me to see the sky so full of birds on the wing.

As I climbed the countless granite steps to the Hradschin, each as broad as four human bodies are long, the city with its roofs and gables receded step by step from my senses. – – – Dusk was already creeping along the facades when I stepped out onto the lonely square from whose center the cathedral rears up to the angels' throne.

Footsteps – the edges crusted with ice – led to the side door.

From some distant apartment the soft, forlorn sounds of a harmonium drifted out into the evening stillness. They fell into this desolation like teardrops of melancholy.

Behind me I heard the sigh of the leather cushion as the church door admitted me; then I stood in the darkness, and the golden altar gazed over at me in rigid tranquility through the green and blue shimmer of dying light which fell through the stained-glass windows and onto the pews. Sparks flew from red glass hanging lamps.

A faded smell of wax and incense.

I lean back in a pew. My blood grows strangely still in this realm of immobility.

A life without pulse fills the room – a secret, patient waiting.

There! – From a great, great distance the sound of horses' hooves reached my ear, muffled and barely audible, strove closer and fell silent.

A dull thump like a carriage-door closing. – – –

The rustling of a silk dress had approached, and a lady's thin, delicate hand touched my arm.

"Please, please, let us go over there by the pillars; I hate to speak of the things I must tell you here in the pews."

The solemn pictures all around took form in sober clarity. The day had suddenly laid hands on me.

"I hardly know how to thank you, Master Pernath, for coming all this way in such awful weather for my sake."

I stammered a few banal words.

"– – But I could think of no other place where I would be safer from scrutiny and harm. I'm sure no one has followed us here, into the cathedral."

I took out the letter and handed it to the lady.

She was almost entirely swathed in costly furs, but by the mere sound of her voice I had recognized her as the woman who had fled terrified into my room on Hahnpassgasse with Wassertrum at her heels. And this did not surprise me, for I had expected none other.

I could not take my eyes away from her face; in the twilit niche it must have seemed even paler than it really was. Her beauty took my breath away, and I stood spellbound. I felt like falling down before her and kissing her feet for being the one I was to help, for choosing me to do so. – – –

"I ask you with all my heart, please forget – at least as long as we are here – the situation in which you saw me that time", she went on in a choked voice, "and I have no idea what you think of that sort of thing – – "

"I've lived to a ripe old age, but never in my life was I so presumptuous as to think myself the judge of my fellow man", was all I could utter.

"I thank you, Master Pernath", she said warmly and simply. "And now listen to me patiently and tell me whether you can help me or at least give me advice in my distress." – I felt terror seize her, and heard her voice tremble. – "That time – – in the studio – – – that time I was seized by the terrible certainty that the hideous ogre had gone after me with intent. – For months it had struck me that wherever I went – alone or with my husband or with – – – with – with Dr. Savioli – the horrible, criminal face of that junk dealer would always crop up nearby. Asleep and awake his squinting eyes hounded me. As yet there has been no sign of his intentions; but the fear that chokes me at night is all the more tormenting: when will he fling the noose around my neck!

At first Dr. Savioli sought to reassure me: what could a wretched junk dealer like this Aaron Wassertrum possibly be capable of – at worst it could only be trivial blackmail or the like – but his lips turned white every time the name Wassertrum was mentioned. I fear: to reassure me, Dr.

Savioli is hiding something from me– something terrible which could cost him or me our life.

And then I learned what he had painstakingly concealed from me: that *the junk dealer had paid him several visits in his apartment at night!* I *know* it, I sense it in every fiber of my body: something is brewing, closing about us slowly like the coils of a serpent. – What business does this cut-throat have there? Why can't Dr. Savioli shake him off? No, no, I won't stand by and watch any longer; I must do something. Anything, before it drives me mad."

I wanted to say a few comforting words in reply, but she cut me off.

"And in the past few days the nightmare which threatens to strangle me has taken on increasingly concrete forms. Dr. Savioli suddenly fell ill – I can no longer communicate with him – dare not visit him for fear that my love of him be discovered at any moment; he lies in delirium, and all I could learn is that in his fever he fancies himself persecuted by a monster with a harelip: Aaron Wassertrum!

I know how brave Dr. Savioli is; it is all the more terrible for me – can you see that? – to see him paralyzed now in the face of a menace which I myself sense only as the dark presence of a terrible destroying angel.

You will say I am a coward, and ask why I do not acknowledge Dr. Savioli openly, cast everything from me, if I love him so: everything, wealth, honor, reputation and so on, but –" she cried so that it resounded from the choir galleries, "I *cannot*! – there's my child, my dear, blond little girl! I *can't* give up my child! – Do you suppose my husband would let me have her!? There, there, take this, Master Pernath" – in a frenzy she tore open a little purse stuffed full of pearl necklaces and jewels –, "and bring it to the criminal; I know he's greedy – he can take all I possess, but he must leave me my child. – He'll keep silent, won't he? –

Speak, for Christ's sake, say but a word, say that you will help me!"

With a supreme effort I managed to soothe the raving woman until she sank down on a pew.

I said whatever came into my head. Confused, incoherent words.

All the while thoughts raced through my mind, so that I hardly understood myself what left my lips – fantastical ideas which collapsed as soon as they were born.

Absently I gazed at the painted statue of a monk in the niche. I talked and talked. Gradually the features of the statue altered, the habit became a threadbare overcoat with the collar turned up, and a youthful face with wasted cheeks and hectic spots loomed up above of it.

Before I had a chance to understand the vision, the monk had reappeared. My heart beat far too loudly.

The unhappy woman bent over my hand, weeping softly.

I gave her the strength which had filled me in the hour when I read the letter, and which now filled me overwhelmingly once again, and I saw it slowly restore her.

"I want to tell you why I have turned to you, Master Pernath", she began again softly after a long pause. "It was a few words you once said to me – words I have been unable to forget all these many years –"

Many years? My blood ran cold.

"– – you were saying goodbye to me – I don't remember why, I was only a child – and you said so kindly and yet so sadly:

'The time may never come, but if ever you are at your wit's end, remember me. Perhaps the Lord God will grant that *I* may be the one to help you.' – I turned away and quickly dropped my ball into the well so that you wouldn't see my tears. And then I wanted to give you the red coral heart I wore around my neck on a silken band, but I was ashamed to, it would have been too silly." – – –

Memory!

– The fingers of paralysis reached for my throat. Something glimmered before me as if from a forgotten, distant land of longing – sudden and fearful: a little girl in a white dress and all around the dark meadow of a manor garden, bordered by old elms. I saw it vividly before me once more. – – –

I must have turned color; I saw that from the haste with which she went on: "I know that your words back then were only meant in the spirit of parting, but they were often a comfort to me, and – and I thank you for them."

With all my strength I clenched my teeth and chased back into my breast the howling pain which lacerated me.

I understood: a merciful hand had slid the bolt before my memory. A brief glimmer from days gone by, and it stood clearly engraved in my consciousness: a love too strong for my heart to bear had gnawed at my thoughts for years, and my wounded spirit had sought succor in the pall of madness.

Gradually the calm of extinction came over me and cooled the tears beneath my lids. The pealing of bells passed through the cathedral, solemn and proud, and I was able to look with a joyful smile into the eyes of her who had come to seek help from me.

– – –

Once again I heard the dull slam of the carriage door and the clatter of hooves.

– – –

Through night-blue glittering snow I went down into the city.

The lanterns goggled at me with twinkling eyes, and from the tiered mountains of pine trees came a whisper of tinsel and silver nuts and Christmas drawing near.

At the Mary Column on Old Town Square the old beggar women with the grey head-shawls murmured their rosaries to the Holy Virgin by candlelight.

The booths of the Christmas market squatted outside the dark entrance to the Jewish Town. In their midst, draped with red cloth, the open stage of a marionette theater shone luridly in the light of smoldering torches.

Zwakh's Punchinello in purple and violet, in his hand a whip which ended in a skull, rode clattering across the stage on a wooden dapple-grey.

Crowded together in rows, the small children – fur caps pulled down over their ears – stared up open-mouthed, listening spellbound to the verses of the Prague poet Oskar Wiener which my friend Zwakh recited from inside the booth:

> "Foremost marched a jumping-jack
> Skinny as a versifier,
> Motley rags upon his back,
> Staggering and making faces." – – –

I turned onto the alley which opened up black and crooked onto the square. A silent crowd stood there shoulder to shoulder in the darkness in front of a notice:

A man had lit a match, and I managed to read fragments of several lines. With dulled senses my mind took in a few words:

Missing!
1000 fl. Reward
Elderly gentleman .... dressed in black ....
.... personal description:
.... fleshy, smooth-shaven face ....
.... hair: white ....
.... Police Headquarters ..... Room No. ....

Uncaring, listless, a living corpse, I walked slowly on into the unlit rows of houses.

A handful of tiny stars glittered on the narrow, dark celestial path over the gables.

My thoughts drifted peacefully back to the cathedral, and the tranquility of my soul grew deeper and still more beatific, when from the square, piercingly distinct – as if in my very ear – the voice of the marionette player came through the winter air:

> "Where is the heart of red, red stone?
> It hung upon a silken band
> And in the glow of dawn it shone." – – –

HAUNT

Long into the night I had paced up and down my room and racked my brains for a way to help "her".

Often I was at the point of going down to Schemajah Hillel to tell him of the trust that had been placed in me and ask his advice. But each time I thought better of it.

In spirit he loomed before me so gigantic in stature that it seemed sacrilegious to trouble him with matters of outward existence; then again, sometimes I had excruciating doubts as to whether I had really experienced all the things which had happened such a short time ago, yet seemed so strangely faded in comparison with the keenly vital events of the past day.

Had I been dreaming after all? Could I – a man with the unheard-of misfortune to lose his memory – for a single second take as a certainty something to which only my memory testified?

My gaze fell upon Hillel's candle, which still lay on the armchair. Thank God, at least one thing was certain: I had been in personal contact with him!

Shouldn't I hurry down to him without a second thought, throw my arms about his knees and lament to him as one man to another that an unspeakable pain was devouring my heart?

As soon as I put my hand on the doorknob, I let it fall again; I already saw what would come of it: Hillel would pass a gentle hand over my eyes and – – no, no, anything but that! I had no right to demand relief. "She" counted upon me and my help, and even if the danger she thought herself in seemed small and trifling to me at times – *she* surely felt it to be immense!

There would be time enough to ask Hillel for advice tomorrow – I forced myself to think coolly and soberly; to disturb him now – in the middle of the night? – It wouldn't do. Only a madman would act that way.

I was about to light the lamp, but let it be: the reflection of the moonlight on the roofs across the way fell into my room and gave me more light than I needed. And I feared that if I lit the lamp the night would pass even more slowly.

The thought of lighting the lamp only to wait for day was so desolate – a faint fear told me this would make the morning recede past knowing.

I went to the window: up above, the ranks of ornate gables rose like a ghostly cemetery floating in the air – gravestones with years erased by wind and rain, towering above the dark moldering vaults, these "dwelling places" in which the throngs of the living gnawed out lairs and passages.

I stood there for a long time, gazing up, until I began to wonder faintly, very faintly, why I was not alarmed at the distinct sound of furtive steps coming through the wall beside me.

I pricked up my ears: no doubt about it, someone was there again. The little creaks of the floorboards gave away the hesitant sidling feet.

At once I was in complete possession of myself. I virtually shrank as everything in me squeezed together under the pressure of the will to hear. All sense of time froze to the present.

One quick rustle which took fright at itself and broke off hastily. Then a deathly silence. The horrible, watchful silence which is its own traitor and makes minutes grow to monstrous proportions.

Motionless, I stood with my ear pressed to the wall, in my throat the menacing feeling that someone was standing there on the other side, just like me, and doing the same thing.

I listened and listened.

Nothing.

The studio next door seemed deserted.

Silently – on tip-toes – I stole to the armchair next to my bed, took Hillel's candle and lit it.

Then I thought it over: the iron attic door out in the corridor which led to Savioli's studio could only be unlocked from the other side.

At random I picked up a hook-shaped piece of wire which lay amidst my engraving instruments on the table: that kind of lock opens easily. At the slightest pressure on the bolt-spring!

And what would happen then?

Only Aaron Wassertrum could be spying next door – perhaps rummaging through drawers to find new weapons and proofs, I speculated.

Would it do much good for me to intervene?

I spent little time deliberating: act, don't think! Anything to shatter this terrible waiting for the morning!

And already I stood outside the iron attic door, pushed against it, cautiously slid the hook into the lock and listened. Right: a scraping noise inside the studio, as if someone were opening a drawer.

The very next moment the bolt shot aside.

I took in the room at a glance, and though it was almost completely dark and my candle only blinded me, I saw a man in a long black cloak jump up from a desk in fright – uncertain for a moment where to turn – make a move as if to rush at me, and then tear his hat from his head and hastily cover his face with it.

"What are you after?" I was about to cry, but the man was quicker:

"Pernath! Is that you? For God's sake! Put out the light!" The voice seemed familiar, but was definitely not that of the junk dealer Wassertrum.

Automatically I blew out the candle.

The room was filled with gloom – lit only faintly by the shimmering haze which shone in from the window recess – and I had to strain my eyes to the utmost to recognize the features of the student Charousek in the wasted, hectic face which suddenly appeared above the cloak.

"The monk!" sprang to my lips, and all at once I understood my vision in the Cathedral yesterday! *Charousek!* That was the man I must turn to! – And once again I heard the words he had said that day in the rain under the archway: "Aaron Wassertrum will learn that these walls can be pierced with long, invisible poisoned needles. The very day he flies at Dr. Savioli's throat!"

Could Charousek be an ally? Did he also know what had happened? His presence here at such an unusual hour suggested as much, but I was reluctant to ask him directly.

Having hurried to the window, he peered down at the street from behind the curtain.

I guessed: he was afraid Wassertrum could have seen the light of my candle.

"Surely you think me a thief, Master Pernath, rummaging through a strange apartment here at night", he began in an uncertain voice after a long silence, "but I swear to you – –"

At once I cut him off, reassuring him.

To show that I harbored no suspicions of him, but rather saw him as an ally, I told him, with some minor omissions I felt necessary, the story behind the studio, and that I feared a woman close to me was in danger of somehow falling victim to the junk dealer's extortionate desires.

From the courteous manner in which he listened without interrupting to ask questions, I gathered that he knew most of this already, if not down to the last details.

"It's true", he mused when I was finished. "So I wasn't mistaken after all! The fellow wants to go for Savioli's throat, but it seems he hasn't gathered enough material yet. Why else is he always lurking here! The other day, you see, I 'happened', shall we say, to come down Hahn-passgasse", he explained, noting my questioning look, "and saw how Wassertrum first strolled up and down outside the gateway down there – with a show of nonchalance – and then, when he thought no one was watching, quickly slipped into the house. I lost no time in following him, and pretended I had come to visit you; that is, I knocked at your door, and I surprised him fiddling around at the iron attic door with a key. Of course he gave it up the moment I came, and knocked at your door too, as a pretext. You must not have been at home, for no one answered.

After some discreet inquiries in the Jewish Town, I learned that someone who, to go by the descriptions, could only be Dr. Savioli, had secretly taken lodgings here. As Dr. Savioli is seriously ill, I figured out the rest for myself.

You see: and I've cleaned these out of the drawers to forestall Wassertrum just in case", Charousek finished, pointing to a bundle of letters on the desk; "those are all the papers I could find. Hopefully there's nothing more. At least I rummaged through all the chests and closets as well as I could in the dark."

As he spoke my eyes explored the room, focusing involuntarily on a trapdoor in the floor, and I recalled dimly that Zwakh had once told me of a secret passageway which led to the studio from below.

It was a rectangular slab with a ring for a handle.

"Where should we keep the letters?" Charousek resumed. "You, Herr Pernath, and I are probably the only people in the whole ghetto Wassertrum thinks harmless – why *me*, there – are – very – special – reasons – for – that" (I saw his feature twist in savage hatred as he virtually bit the last sentence to pieces) – "and he thinks you're – – " Charousek stifled the word "mad" with a hasty, forced cough, but I guessed what he had been about to say. It did not pain me; the feeling of being able to help "her" made me so happy that all my sensitivity was extinguished.

At last, agreeing that I should hide the bundle, we went back to my room. – – – Charousek was long gone, but still I could not bring myself to go to bed. A kind of inner discontent gnawed at me and held me back. I felt there was something else I had to do, but what? What?

Make the student a plan of what to do next?

That alone could not be it. Charousek would not let the junk dealer out of his sight anyway, there was no doubt about that. I shuddered at the thought of the hatred his words had breathed.

What could Wassertrum possibly have done to him?

The strange unrest within me grew, almost driving me to despair. Something invisible, something from beyond was calling me, and I did not understand.

I felt like a horse being trained, feeling the tug at the reins and not knowing which trick he is supposed to perform, not grasping his master's will.

Go down to Schemajah Hillel?

My every fiber gainsaid it.

Yesterday's vision of the monk in the cathedral church, upon whose shoulders Charousek's head had appeared in answer to a mute plea for counsel, was indication enough that from now on I must not despise vague feelings out of hand. For some time now secret powers had been budding within me, that was certain: I felt it too overwhelmingly to make any attempt at denial.

To *sense* letters, not merely read them in books with my eyes – to post an interpreter within me to translate what the instincts whisper without words, that must hold the key, I grasped, to communicate with one's own inner self in plain language.

"They have eyes and see not; they have ears and hear not", a passage from the Bible came to mind as if in explanation.

"Key, key, key", I suddenly realized that as my mind conjured up those strange notions, my lips had mechanically been repeating these words.

"Key, key – –?" My eyes fell on the crooked wire in my hand which I had used just now to open the attic door, and a searing curiosity goaded me to find out where the rectangular trapdoor in the studio might lead.

And without thinking twice I went back to Savioli's studio and tugged at the ring of the trapdoor until I finally managed to lift the slab.

Nothing but darkness at first.

Then I saw: narrow, steep stairs led down into profound gloom.

I climbed down.

For a time I groped along the walls with my hands, but there was no end to it: niches, damp with mold and mildew – twists, nooks and corners – passageways straight on, to the left and to the right, the remains of an old wooden door, forks and then stairs, stairs, stairs again, up and down.

Everywhere the stagnant smell of dirt and rot.

And still not a glimmer of light. –

If only I had taken along Hillel's candle!

At last flat, even ground.

From the crunching underfoot I gathered that I was walking on dry sand.

It had to be one of those countless passages which, seemingly without purpose and destination, run beneath the ghetto to the river.

I was not surprised: since time out of mind half the city rested upon such subterranean passageways, and the inhabitants of Prague had always had good reason to shun the light of day.

The utter absence of noise above me told me that though I had already been wandering for an eternity, I must still be in the area of the Jewish Town, which seems completely deserted at night. Busier streets or squares above me would have betrayed themselves with the distant rattle of carriages.

For an instant fear choked me: what if I was walking in circles!? What if I fell into a hole, hurt myself, broke a leg and couldn't go on!?

Then what would happen to *her* letters in my room? They would fall into Wassertrum's hands for certain.

The thought of Schemajah Hillel, whom I vaguely saw as a helper and guide, automatically calmed me.

But to be on the safe side I proceeded more slowly, feeling my way, and raised my arms so as not to bump my head if the ceiling of the passageway dropped unexpectedly.

From time to time, then more and more frequently, my hand struck the ceiling, and at last the stone sank so low that I had to bend over in order to fit through.

Suddenly my raised arm reached into empty space.

I stopped in my tracks and stared up.

At length I seemed to see a faint, barely perceptible shimmer of light coming from the ceiling.

Perhaps a shaft from some cellar ended here?

I straightened up and groped around me with both hands at eye level: the opening was perfectly rectangular and lined with masonry.

Gradually I made out the shadowy silhouette of a horizontal cross at the top, and at last I managed to grasp its bars, pull myself up and squeeze through.

Now I *stood* on the cross, taking my bearings.

This seemed to be one end of a ruined iron spiral staircase, if my fingers did not deceive me. I groped for a long, unspeakably long time before I finding the second step; then I heaved myself up.

There were eight steps in all. Each one almost a man's height above the last.

Strange: at the top the stairs ended at a kind of horizontal panel, its regular, intersecting lines admitting the glimmer of light which I had seen all the way down in the passageway!

I bent down as far as I could, hoping that from a somewhat greater distance I could make out the pattern of the lines, and saw to my surprise that they formed the exact shape of a hexagram such as one sees on the synagogues.

What could that be?

Suddenly I had it: it was a trap door letting light through at the corners! A wooden trapdoor in the shape of a star.

I planted my shoulders against the slab, pushed it up, and stood a moment later in a chamber filled with the glare of moonlight.

It was quite small, completely empty but for a pile of rubbish in the corner, and had only one stoutly barred window.

I could find no door or any other entryway but the one I had just used, though I searched the walls over and over again.

The bars of the window were too close together for me to put my head through them, but I saw this much:

The room was about at the level of the fourth floor, for the houses across the way had only two floors and were significantly lower.

I could just barely see the far shore of the street below, but the dazzling moonlight shone me full in the face and plunged it into a deep shadow which made it impossible for me to distinguish details.

The street had to be in the Jewish Quarter, for the windows across the way were all walled up, or merely hinted at by sills in the wall, and only in the ghetto do the houses turn their backs on each other so strangely.

In vain did I rack my brains to ferret out the identity of the strange building in which I found myself.

Could it be an abandoned side tower of the Greek Orthodox Church? Or was it somehow a part of the Old-New Synagogue?

The neighborhood was wrong.

I looked about the room again: not the slightest clue. – The walls and ceiling were bare, plaster and whitewash long since shed, and neither nail holes nor nails indicated that the room had ever been inhabited.

The floor was covered foot-high with dust, as if no living creature had set foot there in decades.

The thought of rummaging through the junk in the corner revolted me. It lay in utter darkness, and I could not tell what it was.

To all appearances it consisted of rags balled up in a heap.

Or were they several old, black suitcases?

I prodded the junk with my foot, and with my heel I managed to drag part of it near the beam of moonlight that lay across the room. It seemed a broad, dark band, slowly unrolling there.

A glint like an eye!

Perhaps a metal button?

At last it dawned on me: a sleeve of a strange, old-fashioned cut dangled from the bundle.

97

And a little white box or something of the kind lay under it, giving way under my foot and falling apart into many spotty layers.

I nudged it: a leaf flew into the light.

A picture?

I bent over: a pagat?

What had seemed a white box was a deck of tarok cards.

I picked it up.

What could be more absurd: a deck of cards in this unearthly place!

Oddly, I had to force myself to smile. A vague feeling of dread crept over me.

I sought a banal explanation of how the cards could have gotten here; meanwhile I counted the deck mechanically. It was complete: 78 cards. But even as I counted something struck me: the cards seemed made of ice.

They gave off a crippling chill, and when I held the pack in my closed hand I could hardly let it go again, so stiff were my fingers. Again I cast about for a matter-of-fact explanation:

My thin clothing, the long expedition through the underground passageways without coat and hat, the cruel winter night, the stone walls, the terrible chill which poured through the window along with the moonlight – it was odd enough that I was only just starting to feel cold. The excitement I had been in the entire time must have prevented me from noticing it. –

Shudder after shudder chased across my skin. They penetrated my body layer by layer, deeper and deeper.

I felt my skeleton turn to ice, conscious of each separate bone like cold metal bars to which my flesh froze fast.

No amount of walking helped, no stamping my feet nor beating my arms. I clenched my teeth so that I would not hear them chatter.

This is death, I told myself, laying its cold hands on your head.

And I fought frantically against the stupefying sleep of exposure which closed over me like a cloak, snug and suffocating.

The letters in my room – *her letters*, the cry rang out within me: they'll be found if I die here. And she has set her hopes on me! Laid her salvation in my hands! – Help! – Help! – Help!

And I shouted down into the deserted street through the bars of the window: Help, help, help!

Threw myself to the ground and got up again. I could not die, could not! For her sake, for her sake only! Even if I had to strike sparks from my own bones to warm myself.

The rags in the corner caught my eye, and I rushed over and pulled them on over my clothes with shaking hands.

A tattered suit of thick, dark cloth in a strange archaic cut.

It gave off a smell of rot.

Then I cowered in the opposite corner and felt my skin slowly, slowly grow warmer. Only the hideous sense of my own, iron skeleton within me refused to abate. I sat motionless and let my eyes roam: the card I had seen first – the pagat – still lay in the middle of the room in the beam of light.

I could not take my eyes away from it.

As far as I could tell at this distance, it seemed a child's clumsy watercolor, showing the Hebrew letter aleph in the form of a man in old Franconian garb, with a close-cropped grey goatee, his left arm raised, while the other pointed downward.

Didn't the man's face bear a strange resemblance to mine? a suspicion dawned upon me. – The beard – it was completely wrong for a pagat. – – I crawled up to the card and tossed it toward the rest of the junk in the corner, to be rid of the tormenting sight.

There it lay now, shimmering across at me – a vague, grey-white fleck – in the darkness.

I forced myself to think what I must do to get back to my apartment:

Wait for morning! Shout out the window to the passers-by that they should fetch a ladder and bring me up candles or a lantern! – Without light I would never manage to find my way back along the endless, eternally intersecting passageways, of this I was uneasily certain. – Or, if the window was too high, could someone climb up to the roof and use a rope to – –? God in heaven, it shot through me like a bolt of lightning: now I knew where I was: *A room without a door* – with nothing but a barred window – the ancient house on Altschulgasse, shunned by all! – Once before, many years ago, a person had let himself down on a rope from the roof to look through the window, and – Yes: *I was in the house into which the unearthly Golem had always disappeared!*

All further thought was crippled by a profound terror which I resisted in vain, which not even the memory of the letter could fight down, and my heart began to convulse.

Hastily I told myself, numb-lipped, that it was only the window blowing so icily from the corner, repeated it to myself, faster and faster, with whistling breath – it was too late: the whitish fleck over there – the card – it swelled to a blistered bulk, groped its way to the edge of the moonbeam and crept back into the dark once more. – Dripping sounds woke – half thought, guessed-at, half-real – in the room and yet outside it, around me and yet elsewhere – deep in my own heart and then again in the middle of the room: sounds like a compass falling, its point stabbing the wood!

Over and over: the whitish fleck – – the whitish fleck – –! It's a card, a wretched, stupid, silly playing card, I screamed into my own mind – – – in vain – – now – all the same – he has seized form – the pagat – and squats in the corner staring over at me with *my own face.*

– – –

For hours upon end I cowered there – motionless – in my corner, a skeleton frozen stiff in strange, decaying clothes! – And the man yonder: I myself.

Mute and motionless.

Thus we stared into each other's eyes – one the ghastly mirror image of the other. – – – – –

Does he also see how the moonbeams suck their way across the floor with snail-like languor, creeping up the endless expanse of the wall like hands moved by an invisible clockwork, growing dimmer and dimmer? –

I held him with my gaze, it was no use his trying to dissolve into the glimmer of dawn which came through the window to his aid.

I held him.

Step by step I struggled with him for my life – for the life that is mine because it no longer belongs to me. –

He grew smaller and smaller and when, at dawn, he crept back into his card again, I stood up, went over to him, and slipped him into my pocket – the pagat.

– – –

The street below was still deserted, not a soul to be seen.

I rummaged through the corner of the room, now filled with the dull morning light: broken crockery, a rusty pan, rotten rags, a bottleneck. Dead things, yet so strangely familiar.

And the walls too – as the cracks and crevices came to light – where had I seen them?

I picked up the pack of cards – it dawned on me: hadn't I painted them myself? As a child? A long, long time ago?

It was an ancient tarok deck. With Hebrew letters. – Number twelve must be the "Hanged Man", it came to me like a half-memory. – Head downward. His arms behind his back. – I leafed through: There! There he was.

Again, half dream, half certainty, an image loomed before me: *a soot-black schoolhouse*, hunchbacked, crooked, a sullen witch house, its left shoulder drawn up, the other grown together with the next house. – – – There are several of us adolescent boys – somewhere there is an abandoned cellar.

– – –

Then I looked down at my body, to my renewed confusion: the old-fashioned suit was completely unfamiliar to me. – – –

The noise of a jolting cart startled me, but when I looked down: not a soul. Only a butcher's dog stood lost in thought by a kerb-stone.

There! At last! Voices! Human voices!

Two old women came trotting slowly down the street, and I pushed my head halfway through the bars and called out to them.

They gaped up and consulted. But when they saw me they let out piercing cries and ran away.

They took me for the Golem, I realized.

And I thought that a crowd would gather, people to whom I could make myself understood, but a good hour passed, and only now and then did a pale face peer up cautiously at me, immediately recoiling in mortal fear.

Should I wait until the police came, perhaps hours later or not until tomorrow – the state scoundrels, as Zwakh called them?

No, I'd be better off going a short distance down the subterranean passages to see where they led.

Perhaps in the daytime some gleam of light would fall through crevices in the stone?

I climbed down the ladder and continued on the path I had taken yesterday, over whole heaps of broken bricks and through submerged cellars, climbed a ruined staircase and suddenly stood – – in the vestibule of the *black schoolhouse* I had seen just now as if in a dream.

At once memories flooded in upon me: desks spattered with ink from top to bottom, sum-books, shrill song, a boy who releases ladybugs in class, readers with squashed sandwiches inside, and the smell of orange peels. Now I knew with certainty: I had been here once as a boy. – But I hurried home without giving myself time to reflect.

The first person I encountered, on Salnitergasse, was a crippled old Jew with white sidelocks. As soon as he saw me he covered his face with his hands and loudly wailed Hebrew prayers.

People must have rushed out of their lairs at the noise, for an indescribable clamor broke out behind me. I turned around and saw a throng of faces surging after me, deathly pale and contorted in fear.

Astonished, I looked down at myself and understood – over my clothes I was still wearing that night's strange medieval clothing, and the people thought they were looking at the "Golem".

I dashed around the corner and behind the door of a house and tore the rotten rags from my body.

A moment later the crowd rushed past me screaming with swung sticks and slavering mouths.

– – –

LIGHT

I had knocked at Hillel's door several times that day– I would find no peace until I could speak to him and ask the meaning of all these strange events; but every time I was told that he was not yet home.

When he returned from the Jewish Town Hall, his daughter would let me know at once. –

And what a strange girl this Mirjam was!

A type such as I had never seen before.

A beauty so alien that at first one cannot grasp it – a beauty the sight of which strikes one mute, and which arouses an inexplicable feeling within one, something like a faintness of heart.

This face must have been shaped to laws of proportion lost for millennia, I reflected when I saw it in my mind's eye.

And I wondered which precious stone I would have to choose to render it in a cameo while remaining true to artistic expression: the outward appearance alone defied it, the blue-black gloss of the hair and the eyes which surpassed all I could imagine. – How could the unearthly delicacy of the face be captured in a cameo, true to sense and vision, without bogging down in the mindless likeness-making of canonical "art"!

A mosaic could be the only solution, I realized vividly, but what material would do? It would take a lifetime to assemble. – – –

What had become of Hillel!

I longed for him as if for a dear old friend.

Strange, how dear he had grown to me these past few days – and, strictly speaking, I had spoken to him only once in my life.

105

Yes, right: I ought to hide the letters – *her* letters. To ease my mind in case I should ever have to leave home for any length of time again.

I took them out of the chest – they would be safer in the casket.

A photograph slipped out from between the letters. I did not mean to look, but it was too late.

She gazed into my eyes, the brocade thrown over her bare shoulders – just as I had seen "her" the first time, when she fled into my room from Savioli's studio.

A frenzied anguish bored its way into me. I read the dedication under the picture without grasping the words, and the name:

Your Angelina.

– – –

Angelina!!!

I spoke the name, and the curtain hiding my youth from me tore from top to bottom.

I thought I would collapse with grief. I clawed at the air and whimpered – bit myself in the hand – – to be blind once more, God in heaven – better to go on living in a trance as I had done until now, I begged.

The pain rose in my gorge. – Welled. – Tasted strangely sweet – like blood. – –

Angelina!!

The name whirled in my veins and became – an unbearable, unearthly caress.

With a mighty effort I pulled myself together and forced myself – gritting my teeth – to stare at the picture until slowly I became its master!

Its master!

As of the playing card last night.

– – –

At last: Footsteps! A man's tread.

He was coming!

Jubilantly I ran to the door and flung it open.

Schemajah Hillel stood outside, and behind him – I reproached myself slightly for sensing it as a disappointment – with red cheeks and round child's eyes: old Zwakh.

"I see to my pleasure that you are well again, Master Pernath" Hillel began.

A cold "Master Pernath"?

Frost. Biting, numbing frost filled the room.

Stunned, I listened with half an ear as Zwakh chattered away at me, breathless with excitement.

"Do you know that the Golem is at large again? We were just speaking of it, remember, Pernath? The whole Jewish Town is up and about. Vrieslander saw it himself, the Golem. And once again, as always, it started with a murder." –

I pricked up my ears in surprise: a murder?

Zwakh shook me: "Yes, haven't you heard, Pernath? There's a high and mighty police notice hanging on every corner: fat Zottmann, the 'Mason' – oh, I mean the life insurance director Zottmann – is said to have been murdered. Loisa – from this very house – has already been arrested. And red-haired Rosina: vanished without a trace. – The Golem – the Golem – it's simply appalling."

I gave no reply and searched Hillel's eyes: why was he staring at me so fixedly?

Suddenly a restrained smile twitched at the corners of his mouth.

I understood. It was meant for me.

I could have fallen on his neck with exultation.

Beside myself with delight, I wandered around the room distractedly. What should I bring first? Glasses? A bottle of burgundy? (I had only one.) Cigars? –

At last I found words: "But why don't you sit down!?" – Quickly I pulled up armchairs for both my friends.

– – –

Zwakh began to grow irritated: "Why do you keep smiling like that, Hillel? Don't you believe the Golem is on the loose? It seems to me you don't believe in the Golem at all."

"I wouldn't believe in him even if I saw him in the room before me", Hillel answered coolly, looking at me. – I understood the double entendre.

Zwakh stopped drinking, surprised: "The testimony of hundreds means nothing to you, Hillel? – But just wait, Hillel, mark my words: now the Jewish Town will see murder after murder! Well do I know. The Golem brings a sinister entourage."

"There is nothing marvelous in the succession of similar events", returned Hillel. As he spoke he went up to the window and looked down through the panes at the junk shop. – "When the wind of thaw blows, the roots stir. The sweet and the poisonous alike."

Zwakh winked at me merrily and nodded in Hillel's direction.

"If the Rabbi had a mind to talk, he could tell us things to make your hair stand on end", he put in under his breath.

Schemajah turned around.

"I am no 'Rabbi', even if I am allowed to use the title. I am only a humble archivist in the Jewish Town Hall, keeping the register – of the living and the dead."

I felt there was a hidden meaning in his words. Even the marionette player seemed to sense it subconsciously – he fell silent, and for a while none of us spoke a word.

"Listen, Rabbi – pardon me: I meant 'Herr Hillel'", Zwakh began again after a while, and his voice was conspicuously earnest, "I've wanted to ask you something for a long time. You don't need to answer if you don't want to, or may not – – –"

Schemajah went to the table and played with his wineglass – he drank nothing; perhaps the Jewish ritual forbade it him.

"Ask at your pleasure, Herr Zwakh."

"– – Do you know anything about the Jewish esoteric teachings, the Cabala, Hillel?"

"Only a little."

"I have heard there is a document from which one can learn the Cabala: the 'Sohar' – –"

"Yes, the Sohar – the Book of Splendor."

"You see, there you have it", Zwakh swore. "Isn't it a shameful injustice that writings said to contain the key to the understanding of the Bible and happiness itself –"

Hillel interrupted him: "– only some of the keys."

"Very well, some at any rate! – Well, that these writings, due to their great value and their rarity, are available only to the rich? In one single copy, buried in a London museum at that, or so I'm told! And on top of everything written in Chaldean, Aramaic, Hebrew – or who knows what! – Have *I*, for example, ever in my life had the opportunity to learn any of these languages or go to London?"

"Have you bent all your desires so ardently toward this goal?" Hillel asked with a touch of mockery.

"To be perfectly honest – no", Zwakh admitted, some-what abashed.

"Then you should not complain", Hillel said dryly. "He who does not cry for the spirit with all the atoms of his body – like a choking man for air – will never behold the secrets of God."

"All the same, there is said to be a book containing all the keys to the riddles of the other world, not just some of them", the thought flashed through my mind, and my hand toyed automatically with the pagat, which I still carried in my pocket; but before I could clad the question in words, Zwakh had already uttered it.

Hillel smiled sphinx-like: *"Every question which a man can ask is answered the very moment he asks it in spirit."*

"Do *you* understand what he means by that?" Zwakh turned to me.

I gave no reply, holding my breath so as not to miss a word of Hillel's speech.

Schemajah went on:

"All of life is *nothing* but questions taken form, carrying the germ of the answer within them – and answers pregnant with questions. Only a fool sees anything else in it."

Zwakh pounded his fist on the table:

"Yes indeed: Questions which are different every time, and answers which each person understands differently."

"That is exactly the point", Hillel said amiably. "To cure everyone with the same spoon is the sole privilege of the doctors. The questioner receives the answer he needs: otherwise creatures would not take the path of their longing. Do you think it is by chance that our Jewish scriptures are written only in consonants? – Each must find for *himself* the secret vowels revealing the meaning which is meant for him alone – the living word must not ossify to dead dogma."

The marionette player protested passionately.

"Those are *words*, Rabbi, *words*! Call me Pagat ultimo if I can make heads or tails of it."

Pagat – The word struck me like lightning. I almost fell from my chair in horror.

Hillel avoided my eyes.

"Pagat ultimo? Who knows if that isn't your real name, Herr Zwakh!" Hillel's words reached my ear as if from far away. "One should never be all too sure of oneself. – By the way, speaking of cards: Herr Zwakh, do you play tarok?"

"Tarok? Of course. Ever since childhood."

"Then it astonishes me how you can ask about a book containing the entire Cabala when you yourself have held it in your hands a thousand times."

"I? Held it in my hands? I?" – Zwakh's hands went to his head.

"Yes, *you*! Has it never struck you that the tarok deck has twenty-two trumps – as many as the Hebrew alphabet has letters? And as if that weren't enough, don't our Bohemian cards display pictures which are clearly symbols: the Fool, Death, the Devil, the Last Judgement? – How loudly, my dear friend, do you ask life to shout the answers in your ears? – – What you do not need to know, however, is that 'tarok' or 'Tarot' means as much as the Jewish 'Tora' = the law, or the ancient Egyptian 'Tarut' = the questioned one, and in the ancient Zend tongue the word 'tarisk' = 'I demand the answer'. – But the scholars ought to know that before putting forth the assertion that tarok originated in the days of Karl the Sixth. – And thus, just as the pagat is the first card in the game, the human being is the first figure in his own picture book, his own double: – – the Hebrew letter aleph, which, designed in the shape of a man, points one hand to the heavens and one hand downward: that is to say: 'As it is above, so is it below; as it is below, so is it above.' – That is why I said just now: Who knows whether your name is really Zwakh and not: 'Pagat' – Don't tempt fate." – All the while Hillel looked at me fixedly, and I felt an abyss of ever-new meanings yawning beneath his words – "don't tempt fate, Herr Zwakh! *One can lose one's way in dark passages* from which none ever found his way back unless – *he carried a talisman with him.* Tradition tells that three men once descended into this realm of darkness; one went mad, the other blind, and only the third, Rabbi ben Akiba, came home unscathed, saying that he had met himself. Many a man, you will say, has met himself, Goethe for example, usually on a bridge or other crossing from one bank of a river to another – has looked himself in the eye and has *not* gone mad. But then it was only a reflection of his own consciousness and not the true double: not what is called 'the breath of the bones', the 'Habal Garmin', of which it is said: *As he went into the grave, incorruptible in his bones, so he will rise again on the day of the last judgment.*" Hillel's eyes bored deeper and deeper into mine. – "Our grandmothers say of him: '*He lives high above the earth in a room without a door, with one window only,* from which it is impossible to communicate with men. He who learns how to bind and to – – refine him, will be his own true friend.' – – – Finally, as far as tarok is concerned, you know as well as I: the cards lie differently for each player, but he who plays the trumps well, wins the game – – –. But come now, Herr Zwakh! Let us go; otherwise you'll drink up all of Master Pernath's wine, and there will be none left for him."

NEED

A snowflake battle raged outside my window. Regiment upon regiment the snow-stars – miniature soldiers in shaggy white coats – raced past the panes – for minutes at a time – always in the same direction, as if fleeing en masse from an especially fearsome enemy. Then, suddenly sick of running away, possessed by a mysterious fit of rage, they rushed back again, until from above and below new hostile armies took them in the flank and scattered everything in a whirl of confusion.

The strange things I had just experienced seemed to lie months in the past, and had it not been for the ever-new, bizarre rumors about the Golem which found their way up to me several times a day, making everything come to life afresh, I believe that in moments of doubt I could have suspected myself of having fallen victim to mental confusion.

Amidst the colorful arabesques these events had woven about me, what Zwakh had told me about the still-unsolved murder of the so-called "Freemason" stood out in screaming colors.

I failed to see quite what pockmarked Loisa could have to do with it, though I could not shake off a certain dark suspicion – that night, when Prokop thought he heard an unearthly noise from the grating, we had seen the boy at "Loisitschek" almost immediately afterwards. However, there was no reason to interpret the noise under the ground as a person's cry for help, and, moreover, it could just as well have been a hallucination. – – –

The snow whirling before my eyes blinded me, and I began to see everything in dancing lines. I turned my attention back to the cameo before me. The wax model I had made of

Mirjam's face ought to translate perfectly to the moonstone with its bluish luminosity. – I was delighted: it was a stroke of luck that I had found something so fitting in my store of minerals. The deep black matrix of hornblende lent the stone just the right light, and the contours fit as flawlessly as if nature had created it solely to make a lasting likeness of Mirjam's exquisite profile.

My original intent had been to make it into a cameo depicting the Egyptian god Osiris, and the vision of the hermaphrodite from the Book of Ibbur, which I could call to memory with striking vividness at all times, was a powerful artistic stimulus, but after the first few strokes I gradually discovered such a resemblance to the daughter of Schemajah Hillel that I changed my plan. – – –

– The Book of Ibbur! –

Shaken, I set down the graving needle. It was beyond comprehension, what had entered my life in this brief period of time!

Like one abruptly transported to the midst of a boundless sandy desert, all at once I grasped the vast, profound loneliness which separated me from the people around me.

Could I ever speak to a friend – aside from Hillel – of what I had experienced?

In the quiet hours of the past nights I had remembered that throughout the years of my youth – from earliest childhood – I had been tormented to the point of mortal anguish by an unspeakable thirst for the miraculous, but the fulfillment of my longing had come like a storm, its violence stifling my soul's joyful cry.

I trembled to think of the moment when I would come to myself and grasp what had happened as *the present*, in its full, marrow-searing vitality.

But let it not come now! First let me savor the pleasure: of watching unspeakable splendor approach!

It was in my power! I needed only to go over to my bedroom and throw open the casket where the Book of Ibbur lay, the gift of the Invisible Ones!

How long ago my hand had brushed it as I locked away Angelina's letters!

– – –

Dull thumps outside from time to time as the wind tossed the accumulated masses of snow from the roofs, followed by intervals of profound silence when the flakes blanketing the pavement absorbed every sound.

I turned back to my work – then, suddenly, steel-sharp hoof-beats down the street almost made one see the sparks fly.

It was impossible to open the window and look out: muscles of ice fused its edges to the masonry, and white drifted halfway up the panes. All I saw was Charousek standing next to the junk dealer Wassertrum, apparently quite amicably – they must have been conversing – saw the astonishment on both their faces grow as they seemed to stare at the carriage which was hidden to me.

It's Angelina's husband, flashed through my mind. – It couldn't be she herself! To drive up in her carriage to see me – on Hahnpassgasse – with her carriage, in front of everyone! It would have been sheer madness. – But what should I tell her husband if it was he and he asked me to my face?

Deny, of course, deny everything.

Hastily I ran through the possibilities: it can only be her husband. He received an anonymous letter – from Wassertrum – that she came here for a rendezvous, and she used an alibi: probably that she ordered a cameo from me, or something of the sort. – – –There! A furious knocking at my door and – Angelina stood before me.

She was unable to utter a word, but the expression on her face told me everything: she no longer needed to hide. The game was up.

Yet something within me rebelled against this assumption. I simply could not believe that I had been deceived in feeing that I could help her.

I led her to my armchair. Stroked her hair mutely; and she nestled her head against my chest, weary as a child.

We heard the crackling of the burning logs in the stove and saw the red glow dart across the floorboards, flame up and fade – flame and fade – flame and fade – – –

"Where is the heart of red, red stone – – –" the words chimed out within me. I started: where am I? How long has she been sitting here?

And I questioned her – cautiously, gently, very gently, so that she would not wake up and my probe would not touch the aching wound.

Piece by piece I learned what I needed to know, and fitted it together like a mosaic:

"Your husband knows– –?"

"No, not yet; he's away."

So Dr. Savioli's life was at stake – Charousek had been right. And she was here because Savioli's life was at stake, not hers. She no longer thinks of hiding, I realized.

Wassertrum had been to Dr. Savioli again. Had made his way to the sickbed with threats and force.

And then! Then! What did he want from him?

What did he want? She had half-guessed, half-learned: he wanted – – he – he wanted Dr. Savioli – – to do himself harm.

And now she knew the reason for Wassertrum's wild, insensate hatred: "Dr. Savioli hounded his son to death, the ophthalmologist Wassory."

A thought struck me like lightning: run down, tell the junk dealer everything: that *Charousek* had dealt the blow, from behind the scenes – not Savioli, who was only the tool – – –.

"Treachery! Treachery!" came the howl in my mind. "So you'd sacrifice poor, consumptive Charousek, who wanted

to help *you* and *her*, to the vengeance of this scoundrel?" –
And I was torn in bleeding halves. – Then one thought
voiced the solution, calm and icy cold: "Fool! It lies in your
hands! You need only take that file from the table, hurry
down and ram it through the junk dealer's throat until the
point comes out at his nape."

My heart exulted in a cry of thanks to God. – – –

I probed deeper: "And Dr. Savioli?"

No doubt about it, he would lay hands upon himself if
she did not come to his rescue. The nurses watched him like
hawks, had drugged him with morphine, but perhaps he
would wake suddenly – perhaps even as we spoke – and –
and – no, no, she had to go, could not waste a moment's
time – she would write to her husband, confess everything –
let him take away her child, but Savioli would be saved, for
she would have struck from Wassertrum's hands the only
weapon he had to threaten with.

She would reveal the secret herself before he could betray it.

"That you will *not*, Angelina!" I cried, thinking of the
file, and my voice failed me in exultation at my own power.

Angelina tried to tear away: I held her fast.

"One thing: think carefully, will your husband believe
the junk dealer out of hand?"

"But Wassertrum has proof, my letters, it seems, maybe
a picture of me – all the things that were hidden in the desk
next door in the studio."

Letters? Picture? Desk? – I knew not what I did: I clutched Angelina to my breast and kissed her. On the mouth, on
the brow, on the eyes.

Her blond hair fell before my face like a golden veil.

Then I held her slender hands and told her in hasty words
that Wassertrum's mortal enemy – a poor Bohemian student

– had secured the letters and everything else and that they were safe in my possession:

And she fell on my neck and laughed and wept in the same breath. Kissed me. Ran to the door. Turned around and kissed me again.

Then she was gone.

I stood as though stunned, still feeling the breath of her lips on my face.

I heard the carriage wheels thundering over the cobblestones, and the hooves' frantic gallop. A moment later all was still. As a grave.

In me, too.

– – –

Suddenly the door creaked softly behind me, and Charousek stood in the room:

"Pardon me, Herr Pernath, I knocked for a long time, but you didn't seem to hear."

I only nodded mutely.

"I hope you don't think I've been reconciled with Wassertrum because you saw me speaking to him just now?" – Charousek's mocking smile told me that he was only making a grim joke. – "For you must know: fortune smiles upon me; the scoundrel down there is growing fond of me, Master Pernath. – – It's a strange thing, the voice of the blood", he added softly – half to himself.

I had no idea what he meant by that, and assumed I had heard wrong. The excitement I had gone through still trembled too violently within me.

"He wanted to give me a coat", Charousek went on aloud. "Of course I gracefully declined. I'm already enough ill at ease in my own skin. – And then he forced money on me."

"You accepted it?!" it almost escaped me, but quickly I curbed my tongue.

Round red patches appeared on the student's cheeks.

"Of course, I accepted the money."

My head spun!

"Ac – cepted?" I stammered.

"I never imagined that one could feel so pure a joy in this world!" – Charousek paused for a moment and grimaced. "– Is it not an elevating feeling to see the invisible hand of 'Mother Providence' holding sway throughout Nature's household in wisdom and prudence!?" – He spoke like a pastor and jingled the money in his pocket. – "Truly, I see it as my sacred duty one day to use heller and pfennig of the treasure entrusted to me by a charitable hand for the noblest of all goals."

Was he drunk? Or mad?

Suddenly Charousek changed his tone:

"There is a satanic humor in Wassertrum's paying for his own – medicine. Don't you think?"

The hidden meaning of Charousek's words began to dawn on me, and his feverish eyes filled me with horror.

"But let's leave that aside for now, Master Pernath. First let's take care of unfinished business. The lady just now, that was *'she'*, wasn't it? What possessed her to drive up here in front of everyone?"

I told Charousek what had happened.

"Surely Wassertrum has no evidence in his hands", he interrupted me cheerfully, "otherwise he wouldn't have searched the studio again this morning.– Strange, you didn't hear him!? He spent a whole hour over there."

I was astonished that he knew everything in such detail, and told him so.

"May I?" – to demonstrate he took a cigarette from the table, lit it and explained: "You see, if you open the door now, the draft coming in from the stairwell makes the to-bacco smoke change direction. That is probably the only law of nature Herr Wassertrum knows in and out, and for all eventualities – the house belongs to him, as you know – he had a small, hidden, open niche built into the outside wall of the studio: a kind of air shaft, and in it a little red flag. Whenever someone enters or leaves the room, that is: opens the door which causes the draft, Wassertrum can tell from below by the lively fluttering of the flag. Of course, *I* know it too", Charousek added dryly, "when I make it my business to know, and I can observe it quite well from the air-hole of the cellar vis-à-vis wherein a benevolent fate graciously permits me to dwell. – The prank with the ventilation is a patent of the venerable patriarch, but for years I've been familiar with it as well."

"What a superhuman hatred you must feel for him to watch his every step that way. And for years at that, as you say!" I interjected.

"Hatred?" Charousek forced a smile. "Hatred? – Hatred is not the right expression. The word for my feelings toward him has not yet been invented. – Strictly speaking, I don't hate *him* at all. I hate his blood. Do you understand that? Like a wild animal, I can smell a single drop of his blood flowing in a person's veins – and" – he clenched his teeth – "here in the ghetto that is 'known to happen'." Too agitated to go on speaking, he went to the window and stared out. – I heard him suppress his panting. For a while both of us were silent.

"Hallo, what's that?" he said suddenly, jumping up and, waving me over urgently: "Quick, quick! Don't you have opera glasses or something like that?"

We peered out cautiously from behind the curtains:

Deaf-mute Jaromir stood at the entrance to the junk shop and, as far as we could tell from his sign language, was offering to sell Wassertrum a glittering object half-hidden in his hand. Wassertrum swooped down on it like a vulture and retreated into his lair with it.

A moment later he rushed out again – deathly pale – and seized Jaromir by the shirtfront: a violent struggle ensued. – All at once Wassertrum let go and seemed to reconsider. Gnawed furiously at his harelip. Glanced up at us broodingly and then amicably took Jaromir by the arm and drew him into his store.

We must have waited a quarter of an hour: they seemed unable to reach a bargain.

At last the deaf-mute reemerged with a satisfied expression and went his way.

"What do you think of that?" I asked. "It doesn't seem to be anything important, does it? The poor boy must have cashed in on something he begged."

The student gave no reply, and silently returned to his seat.

Evidently he did not ascribe any importance to the incident either, for after a pause he continued where he had left off:

"Yes. As I said, I hate his blood. – Stop me, Master Pernath, if I get excited again. I want to remain cold. I cannot afford to squander my best feelings like that. Otherwise it's as if I suddenly sober up afterwards. A person with a sense of decency ought to speak in cool words, not with pathos like a prostitute or – or a poet. – Since the dawn of time it never would have occurred to anyone to 'wring their hands with grief' if the actors hadn't concocted this gesture as particularly 'vivid'."

I realized that he was intentionally chattering away blindly in order to recover his inward composure.

It was beyond his power. He paced up and down the room nervously, picked up all sorts of objects and put them back again absently.

Then all at once he had returned to the heart of the matter.

"A person's tiniest involuntary movements betray this blood to me. I know children who resemble 'him' and are *thought to be* his, yet they are not of the same tribe – nothing fools me. It was years before I learned that Dr. Wassory is his son, but – I might say – I smelled it.

Even as a little boy, when I could not guess at Wassertrum's relationship to me" – for a moment his eyes rested upon me searchingly – "I had this gift. I had been kicked, beaten – there is probably no spot on my body that does not know the meaning of searing pain – was made to hunger and thirst until I went half mad and ate moldy dirt, but never could I hate the people who tortured me. I simply *could* not. I had no room left for hatred. – Do you understand? And yet my whole being was saturated with it.

Wassertrum had never done the least thing to me – I meant that he never beat me or threw anything at me or even cursed me in any way when I loafed about down there, a street urchin: I know that perfectly well – and yet all the rage and thirst for revenge which seethed within me was aimed at him. At him alone!

Even so, strangely enough, I never played tricks on him as a child. When the others did, I beat an immediate retreat. But I could stand in the archway for hours, hiding behind the front door and staring at his face through the crack at the hinges until everything went black before me with this inexplicable feeling of hatred.

It was then, I believe, that I laid the foundation for the clairvoyance which stirs within me as soon as I encounter beings, even things connected to him. Back then I must have unconsciously learned his every movement *by heart*: the way he wears his coat, how he touches things, coughs and drinks and all those thousands of details, until they ate their way into my soul, and I recognized their traces at first glance, infallibly, as his heirlooms.

Later this almost became a mania with me: I cast away harmless objects, tormented by the mere thought that his hand could have touched them – while others I grew fond of; I loved them like friends who wished him ill."

Charousek fell silent for a moment. I watched him gaze absently into space. His fingers mechanically stroked the file on the table.

"Later, when a few sympathetic teachers had collected money for me and I studied philosophy and medicine – and, in passing, learned how to think for myself – I began to realize what hatred is:

To hate something as deeply as I do, it must be a part of oneself.

And later on, when I found out – learned everything bit by bit: what my mother was and – and still must be, if – if she is still alive – and that my own body –" he turned away so that I would not see his face – "is filled with *his* loathsome blood – well, Pernath, why shouldn't you know it: *he is my father!* – then I realized where the root lay. – – – Now and then I even see a mysterious significance in the fact that I am consumptive and spit blood: my body resists all that is 'his' and thrusts it away with revulsion.

Often this hatred has followed me into my dreams, attempting to comfort me with visions of all the conceivable tortures I might inflict upon 'him', but I always shrugged them off, for they left me with the stale taste of – dissatisfaction.

When I think about myself and marvel at the fact that there is no one and nothing in the world I could hate – or even feel antipathy toward – but him and his tribe, the awful feeling often creeps over me: I could be what they call a 'good person'. But fortunately I am not. – As I said: there is no room left in me.

And you mustn't suppose that my sad fate embittered me (besides, I only found out years later what he had done to my mother) – I experienced *one* joyous day which far eclipsed the ordinary mortal lot. I do not know whether you know the meaning of inward, genuine, ardent piety – I had not known it before either – but the day when Wassory exterminated himself, when I stood below the shop down there and saw how 'he' took the news – 'indifferently', as an amateur ignorant of life's true stage would have thought – standing there impassively for what must have been an hour, his blood-red harelip drawn up only a tiny bit more than usual over his teeth, and his gaze turned inward so surely – – so – so – so strangely – – – then I felt the scent of frankincense from the archangel's pinions. – – Do you know the miraculous image of the Black Madonna in the Teyn Church? I prostrated myself before it, and the darkness of paradise enveloped my soul."

– – –

– – – – Watching Charousek stand there like that, his big, dreamy eyes filled with tears, I recalled Hillel's words about the enigma of the dark path taken by the brothers of death.

Charousek went on:

"The external circumstances which 'justify' my hatred or might make it seem understandable in the minds of the stipendiary judges may not interest you at all. – Facts look like milestones and are nothing but empty eggshells. They are the officious popping of champagne corks at the tables of the upstarts, which only the weak of mind take for the substance of the feast. – With all the infernal means customary among his kind, he made my mother submit to his will – if not something even worse. And then – – well – and then he sold her to – a disorderly house – – – that's not hard to do when your business friends are police counsels – but not because he had grown weary of her, oh no! I know the sneak-holes of his heart: he sold her *the very* day he realized in terror how ardently he really loved her. A man like him may seem to act senselessly, but always consistently. The pack rat in him squeals aloud as soon as someone comes to buy something from his junk shop, no matter how good the money: all he feels is the compulsion to 'cough it up'. He'd like to gobble up the very concept of 'having', and if he were could conceive of an ideal, it would be to dissolve at last into the abstract concept of 'property'. – –

And back then it swelled in him gigantically to a mountain of fear: of 'no longer being sure of himself' – not: *wanting* to surrender something to love, but *having* to surrender: sensing the presence of something invisible within him which secretly shackled his will, or what he wanted to be his will. – That was the beginning. What followed, came automatically. As the pike must bite automatically – like it or not – when a glittering object floats past at the right moment.

For Wassertrum the natural consequence was to barter away my mother. It satisfied the rest of the traits slumbering within him: the greed for money and the perverse delight in self-torment. – – – Forgive me, Master Pernath" – – Charousek's voice took on such a hard and emotionless tone that I took alarm – "forgive me for all this horribly clever talk, but at the university one gets one's hands on a lot of foolish books; one involuntarily adopts an asinine mode of expression." –

For his sake, I forced myself to smile; inwardly I understood quite well that he was fighting tears.

I must help him somehow, I thought, try at least to alleviate his bitterest need as far as it is within my power. I had one hundred gulden note; I removed it surreptitiously from the dresser drawer and slipped it into my pocket.

"One day, when you move on into a better environment and practice your profession as a doctor, you will find peace of mind, Herr Charousek", I said to give the conversation a more conciliatory turn; "will you soon take your degree?"

"Shortly. I owe it to my benefactors. There is no use in it, for my days are numbered."

I was about to make the stock objection that he saw things too darkly, but he headed me off with a smile:

"It's all for the best. Besides, surely it's no pleasure to playact the healer and end up boasting a noble title as well-poisoner with a diploma. – – On the other hand" – he added with his caustic humor – "unfortunately it shall put an end to my good works here in the ghetto of this world." He reached for his hat. "But I shall disturb you no longer. Or is there anything more to discuss regarding the Savioli affair? I think not. At any rate, let me know if you learn anything new. The best thing would be for you to hang a mirror here in your window as a sign for me to visit you. By no means should you come to me in the cellar: Wassertrum would immediately suspect that we are in league. – Incidentally, I'm quite curious to see what he will do now that he has seen the lady call on you. Just say she brought you a piece of jewelry to repair, and if he badgers you, play the madman."

I had found no suitable opportunity to press the bill upon Charousek, so I picked the modeling wax back up from the windowsill and said: "Come, I'll walk you part of the way down the stairs. – Hillel is expecting me", I lied.

He gave a start: "You're friends with him?"

"Acquainted. Do you know him? – – Or do you", – I smiled involuntarily – "mistrust him too?"

"God forbid!"

"Why so serious?"

Charousek hesitated, thinking:

"I don't know myself. It must be unconscious: whenever I meet him on the street, I'd like to step down from the sidewalk and fall to my knees as if before a priest carrying the host. – You see, Master Pernath, there you have a person who is the opposite of Wassertrum in every atom. For example, the Christians in the quarter, misinformed as usual, hold him to be a miser and a secret millionaire, and yet he is unspeakably poor."

I jumped up, horrified: "Poor?"

"Yes, maybe even poorer than I. I believe he knows the word 'take' only from books; and when he leaves the 'Town Hall' on the first day of the month, all the Jewish beggars run away from him, knowing that he would thrust his whole meager salary into the hands of the first one he met, and starve to death himself a few days later – along with his daughter. – If there is truth to what an ancient Talmudic legend claims: that of the twelve Tribes of Israel ten are accursed and two are holy, then he embodies the two holy ones and Wassertrum all the other ten together. – Have you never noticed how Wassertrum turns all the colors of the rainbow when Hillel walks past him? Interesting, I tell you! You see, *such* blood *cannot* mix; the children would be stillborn. If the mothers didn't die of horror first. – Incidentally, Hillel is the only person Wassertrum dares not molest – he shuns him like fire. No doubt because he sees Hillel as the inscrutable, the utterly indecipherable. Perhaps he also senses the cabalist in him."

We were already going down the stairs.

"Do you believe that there are still cabalists nowadays – that there could be anything to the Cabala?" I asked, curious what he would reply, but he did not seem to be listening.

I repeated my question.

Hastily he deflected it and pointed to a door off the stairwell which was nailed together out of crate lids.

"You have new neighbors there, a poor though Jewish family: the meschugge musician Naphtali Schaffranek with his daughter, son-in-law and grandchildren. When it grows dark and he's alone with the little girls, the madness comes over him: then he ties them together by the thumbs so that

127

they can't run away, drives them into an old chicken coop and gives them 'singing lessons', as he calls it, so that they can earn their own living later on – that is, he teaches them the craziest songs there are, German words, fragments which he picked up somewhere and which his fogged mind takes for – Prussian battle songs or something of the sort."

And sure enough, strange music drifted faintly out into the corridor. The bow of a fiddle scratched out the outlines of a street-ballad, hideously high and on one and the same perpetual note, and two children's voices, thin as threads, sang:

> "Frau Pick
> Frau Hock,
> Frau Kle-pe-tarsch,
> Se stehen beirenond
> Und schmusen allerhond – – "[3]
> – – –

It was madness and comedy at once, and against my will I had to laugh out loud.

"The Schaffranek son-in-law – his wife sells schoolchildren pickle brine by the glass at the Egg Market – spends the whole day going from office to office", Charousek went on grimly, "begging for old stamps. Then he sorts them, and if he happens to finds some that were cancelled only on the edge, he lays them on top of each other and cuts them up. He sticks together the uncanceled halves and sells them as new. At first the business thrived, sometimes yielding almost a – gulden a day, but in the end Prague's big Jewish industrialists got wise to it – and now they do it themselves. They skim off the cream."

---

[3] Yiddish: "They stand there together, chatting (or: 'schmoozing') about all kinds of things."

"Charousek, would you alleviate need, if you had money to spare?" I asked quickly. – We were standing outside Hillel's door, and I knocked.

"Do you think me so despicable that I would not?" he asked back, baffled.

Mirjam's steps drew nearer, and I waited for her to press down the door handle; then I slipped the bill into his pocket: "No, Herr Charousek, I do not, but you would *have to* think me despicable if I failed to do so."

Before he could reply, I shook his hand and shut the door behind me. As Mirjam greeted me, I listened to hear what he would do.

He stood where he was for a while, then gave a quiet sob and went down the stairs slowly, with groping steps. Like someone who must cling to the banister for support. – – –

It was the first time I had entered Hillel's room.

It was as austere as a prison. The floor scrupulously clean and strewn with white sand. No furniture but two chairs, a table and a dresser. A wooden ledge along the walls to the left and to the right.

Mirjam sat across from me at the window, and I modeled my wax.

"Must one have a face *before* one to capture the resemblance?" she asked timidly, only to break the silence.

Shyly we avoided each other's eyes. She did not know which way to look in shame and torment at the wretchedness of the room, and my cheeks burned with inner reproach for having so long ignored the conditions in which she and her father lived.

But I had to say something!

"Not so much to capture the resemblance as to judge the rightness of one's inward vision."

Even as I spoke I felt the profound falsity of everything I said.

For years I had unthinkingly parroted and followed the painters' erroneous axiom that one must study outward nature in order to create art; only since Hillel had woken me that night had my inner vision emerged: the true sight behind closed lids which is extinguished as soon as one opens one's eyes – the gift which all believe they have, and not one in a million actually possesses.

How could I even speak of the *possibility* of measuring the infallible plumb-line of spiritual vision against the eyes' crude resources!

Mirjam seemed to be thinking along similar lines, to judge by the surprise in her expression.

"You mustn't take it so literally", I excused myself.

Attentively she watched me carve out the form with the stylus.

"It must be infinitely difficult to transfer all the details to stone afterwards."

"That's nothing but mechanical work. More or less, anyway."

Pause.

"May I see the cameo when it's finished?" she asked.

"Why, it's meant for you, Mirjam."

"No, no; that's impossible – – that – that – – " I saw her hands grow nervous.

"You won't accept even this trifle from me?" I quickly interrupted her. "I wish I could do more for you."

Hastily she averted her face.

What had I said! I must have wounded her to the quick. It had sounded as if I were alluding to her poverty.

Could I put a good face on it? Wouldn't that only make it far worse? I took a stab:

"Listen to me calmly, Mirjam! I implore you. – I owe your father so very much – You can't possibly comprehend – – "

She looked at me uncertainly; appeared not to understand.

"– Yes, yes: so very much. More than my life."

"Because he helped you when you fainted? But that went without saying."

I sensed: she did not know the nature of the bond between me and her father. Cautiously I probed how far I could go without betraying what he kept from her.

"I believe inward aid must be rated much higher than outward aid. – I mean the aid which a person's spiritual influence radiates toward others. – Do you understand what I mean by that, Mirjam? – One can heal a person spiritually, not only physically, Mirjam."

"And that is – – ?"

"Yes, that is what your father did for me!" – I seized her hand. – "Don't you understand that it must be my heart's desire to do some favor, if not for him, at least for someone who is as close to him as you are?,– Have a little faith in me! – Is there no wish that I could fulfill for you?"

She shook her head: "You think I feel unhappy here?"

"Certainly not. But perhaps now and then you have cares of which I could relieve you? You are obliged – do you hear! – obliged to share them with me! Why do the two of you live here in this dark, sad street if you don't need to? You are so young still, Mirjam, and – – "

"You live here yourself, Herr Pernath", she interrupted me with a smile, "what ties you to this house?"

I was taken aback. – Yes. Yes, that was right. Why did I live here? I could not explain it. What ties you to this house, I repeated to myself absently. I was unable to find an explanation, and for a moment I completely forgot where I was. – Then, suddenly transported, I stood somewhere far above – in a garden – smelled the magical scent of blossoming elderflower clusters – gazed down at the city – – –

131

"Did I touch a wound? Did I hurt you?" Mirjam's voice reached me from far, far away.

She leaned over me and looked into my face with anxious scrutiny.

I must have sat there motionless for a long time, to make her worry like that.

For a while something wavered back and forth within me, then suddenly burst forth, flooding me, and I poured out my heart to Mirjam.

As if she were a dear old friend I had known all my life, from whom I had no secrets, I told her how things stood with me and how I had learned from Zwakh's story that I had been mad in earlier years and robbed of the memory of my past – how images had recently begun to stir within me, images whose roots must reach back to those days, and that I trembled to think of the moment when everything would be revealed to me, tearing me apart all over again.

I left out only those things which touched upon her father: my adventures in the underground passageways and all the rest.

Drawing close to me, she listened with a deep, breathless sympathy which did me a world of good.

At last I had found a person to whom I could spill my heart when my isolation of spirit weighed heavy on me. – Certainly: there was also Hillel, but for me he was like a being beyond the clouds, coming and going like a light which I could not approach when I longed for it.

I told her that, and she understood. Though he was her father, she saw him that way too.

He was devoted to her in unending love, and she to him – "and yet a glass wall seems to separate me from him", she confided in me, "and I cannot break through it. It has been like that as long as I can remember. – When I was a child and dreamed I saw him standing at my bedside, he always wore

the robes of the high priest: the golden tablets of Moses with
the twelve stones on his breast, and blue rays shone from his
temples. – I believe his love is of the kind that reaches beyond the grave, and is too great for us to grasp. – My mother
always said that too, when we spoke of him in secret." – – –
All at once she shuddered, trembling all over. I was about to
leap up, but she held me back: "Don't worry, it's nothing.
Only a memory. When my mother died – only I know how
he loved her, I was only a little girl at the time – I thought
pain would suffocate me, and I ran to him and clung to his
coat and wanted to cry out and couldn't, because everything
in me was paralyzed – and – and then – – – – the shivers run
down my spine again at the thought – – he looked at me with
a smile, kissed me on the brow and passed his hand over my
eyes. – – – – And from then on, to this very day, all the pain
at losing my mother was extinguished in me. I did not shed
a single tear when she was buried; I saw the sun in the sky,
God's radiant hand, and wondered why the people were cry-
ing. My father walked next to me, behind the coffin, and
every time I looked up he smiled faintly, and I felt horror rip-
ple through the crowd as they saw it."

"And are you happy, Mirjam? Completely happy? At the
same time, isn't there something fearful for you in the
thought of having as a father a being who has outgrown all
humanity?" I asked softly.

Mirjam shook her head joyfully.

"I live my life as if in a blissful sleep. – Just now, Herr
Pernath, when you asked me whether I have cares and why
we live here, I almost had to laugh. Is Nature beautiful?
Well, yes, the trees are green and the sky is blue, but with
my eyes closed I can picture all that much more beautifully.
Must I sit in the middle of a meadow in order to see it? –
And the little bit of need and – and – and hunger? That is a
thousand times outweighed by the hope and the waiting."

"The waiting?" I asked in astonishment.

"The waiting for a miracle. Don't you know that? No? You poor, poor person. – To think that so few people know it?! You see, that too is the reason why I never go out or associate with anyone. I used to have a few friends – Jewish girls, of course, like me – but we always talked at cross-purposes; they didn't understand me, and I didn't understand them. When I spoke of miracles, they thought I was joking at first, and when they realized how seriously I meant it and that for me miracles were not what the bespectacled Germans call them: the growth of the grass in accordance with nature's laws and so forth, but exactly the opposite – they would have thought I was crazy, but then my mind is fairly agile, I have learned Hebrew and Aramaic, can read the Targumim and Midrashim and other irrelevancies of the sort. At last they hit upon a word meaning absolutely nothing: they called me 'overwrought'.

When I attempted to explain to them that what is significant – essential – for me in the Bible and other holy scriptures is the *miracles* and only the miracles, and not precepts on morals and ethics, which can only be roundabout ways to arrive at miracles – they could respond only with platitudes, reluctant to admit openly that all they believed in the religious scriptures were the things which could just as well be set down in the Civil Code. The mere mention of the word 'miracle' made them uncomfortable. They said they were losing the ground beneath their feet.

As if there could be anything more magnificent than to lose the ground beneath one's feet!

The world is there for us to think it to pieces, I once heard my father say – then, only then does life begin. – I don't know what he meant by 'life', but sometimes I feel that one day I will 'awaken', so to speak. Even if I cannot imagine into what state. And before then miracles must happen, I always think.

'Have you ever seen any, that you're constantly waiting for one?' my friends often asked me, and when I replied in the negative, they were suddenly gleeful and sure of their triumph. Tell me, Herr Pernath, can you understand hearts like those? That I *have* experienced miracles, if only small – tiny ones –" – Mirjam's eyes gleamed – "I didn't want to tell them – –"

Tears of joy almost choked her voice.

"– But *you* will understand me: often, for weeks, even months" – Mirjam's voice grew very quiet – "we lived from miracles alone. When there was no bread left in the house, not a single bite, then I knew: the time has come! – And then I sat here and waited and waited, until I could hardly breathe what with the pounding of my heart. And – and then, when I suddenly felt the tug, I ran downstairs and up and down the streets, as quickly as I could, to be home before my father returned. And – and each time I found money. One time more, one time less, but always enough for me to buy the bare necessities. Often a gulden lay in the middle of the street; from far away I saw it glittering, and the people stepped on it, tripped over it, but no one noticed it. – Sometimes that made me so presumptuous that I didn't even go out, only searched the floor of the kitchen to see whether money or bread had dropped from Heaven."

– A thought flashed through my mind, making me smile with pleasure. –

She saw it.

"Don't laugh, Herr Pernath", she begged. "Believe me, I know that these miracles will grow and that one day they –"

I reassured her: "But I'm not laughing, not at all, Mirjam! Whatever are you thinking! I'm infinitely glad that you're not like the others who seek the usual cause behind every effect and balk when – in such cases *we* cry: Thank God! – it happens differently for once."

She reached her hand out to me:

"And you'll never say again, Herr Pernath, will you, that you want to help me – or us? Now that you know you'd rob me of the opportunity to experience a miracle if you did so?"

I promised. But in my heart I made one reservation.

Then the door opened, and Hillel came in.

Mirjam embraced him, and he greeted me. Warmly and full of friendship, but once again with the cool "Master Pernath".

And something seemed to weigh upon him like slight weariness or uncertainty. – Or was I mistaken?

Perhaps it was only the gloom of the chamber.

"You must have come here to ask my advice", he began after Mirjam had left us alone, "in the matter regarding the strange lady – –?"

In my astonishment I was about to interrupt him, but he cut me off:

"I heard it from the student Charousek. I spoke to him in the street because he struck me as oddly changed. He told me everything. In the fullness of his heart. Even that – you gave him money." He gave me a penetrating look, laying a most peculiar emphasis on each of his words, but I did not understand his meaning.

"Certainly, that made a few more drops of happiness rain down from Heaven – and – and in this – case it may not have done any harm, but –" – he thought for a while – "but sometimes that only causes suffering for oneself and others. It is not as easy to help as you think it is, my dear friend! Otherwise it would be very, very easy to save the world. – Don't you think?"

"Don't *you* give to the poor? Often enough all that you possess, Hillel?" I asked.

He shook his head, smiling: "You seem to have become a Talmudist overnight, answering a question with another question. Of course, that makes it hard to argue."

He paused, as if expecting me to reply to that, but again I failed to understand what in fact he was waiting for.

"Incidentally, to return to the subject", he went on in an altered tone, "I don't believe that your protégé – I mean the lady – is in any danger at the moment. Let things come to you. It is said: 'the wise man takes precautions', but the wiser man, it seems to me, waits and is prepared for everything. Perhaps the opportunity will arise for me to meet with Aaron Wassertrum, but he must make the first move – I won't take a single step, *he* must come over. Whether to you or to me, it makes no difference – and then I will speak with him. It will be for *him* to decide whether or not he follows my advice. I wash my hands of it."

Anxiously I tried to read his face. Never before had he spoken so coldly and with such strange menace. But an abyss slumbered behind these dark, deep-set eyes.

"A glass wall seems to separate him and us", I recalled Mirjam's words.

I could only press his hand silently and – go.

He accompanied me out the door, and when I turned around once more on the stairs, I saw that he had remained where he was, waving to me affectionately, but like someone who wants to say something more and cannot.

FEAR

I meant to take my coat and walking-stick and go eat in the little tavern "Zum alten Ungelt", where Zwakh, Vrieslander and Prokop always sat until late at night telling outlandish stories; but as soon as I entered the room the intention dropped from me – as if hands had torn away a cloth or something else I carried on my person.

The air was filled with a tension for which I could not account, present nonetheless like a tangible thing, within a few seconds infecting me so acutely that for sheer anxiety I hardly knew what to do first: light a candle, lock the door behind me, sit down, or pace the room.

Had someone crept in and hidden here in my absence? Was it a person's fear of discovery that infected me? Could Wassertrum be here?

I reached behind the curtains, opened the closet, glanced into the next room: no one.

The casket, too, stood in its place untouched.

Wouldn't it be best to bite the bullet and burn the letters, and be freed from worrying about them once and for all?

I groped for the key in my vest pocket – but would it have to be taken care of now? I had time enough until tomorrow morning.

First light the candle!

I could not find the matches.

I began to accuse myself of cowardice – the thought failed. In mid-sentence.

An insane notion seized me: quick, quick, climb onto the table, grab a chair and lift it up and, from on high, smash in the skull of "what" was crawling around there on the floor – – if – if it came close.

"There's no one here", I said out loud, angrily, "have you ever been afraid before in your life?"

It did not help. The air I breathed turned thin and piercing like aether.

If I had *seen anything*: the most hideous thing imaginable – the fear would have left me in an instant.

Nothing came.

I bored into all the corners with my eyes:

Nothing.

Nothing but familiar things all around: furniture, chests, the lamp, the painting, the wall clock – lifeless, old, faithful friends.

I hoped to see them shift before my eyes and give me reason to believe a hallucination was the cause of the choking fear within me.

That was not it either. – They remained rigidly true to their forms. Much more rigid than natural in the semidarkness.

"They are under the same constraint as you", I felt. "They don't dare make the slightest move."

Why didn't the wall clock tick?

The lurking on all sides drank up every sound.

I shook the table and was surprised to hear the noise.

If only the wind would at least whistle around the house! – Not even that! Or if the wood in the stove would crackle: the fire had died out.

And all the while the same terrible lurking in the air – ceaseless, unbroken as the trickling of water.

This vain standing-at-the-ready of all my senses! I thought I would never survive it. – The room was full of eyes I could not see – full of aimlessly wandering hands I could not grasp.

"It is the horror which gives birth to itself, the paralyzing terror of the ungraspable no-thing which has no form and gnaws away the bounds of our thought", I realized dimly.

I stood there stiffly and waited.

Waited for what must have been a quarter of an hour: maybe "it" could be tricked into creeping up on me from behind – and I could catch it in the act?!

I whirled around: again, nothing.

The same marrow-devouring "nothing" which *was not* and yet filled the room with its ghastly life.

And if I left the room? What was stopping me?

"It would go with me", I knew at once with incontrovertible certainty. And I realized that it would do no good to light the candle – all the same I groped for the lighter until I found it.

But the wick was reluctant to burn, and for a long time did no more than glow: the little flame could neither live nor die, and when at last it managed to cling to a consumptive existence, it remained lusterless like dirty yellow metal. No, darkness was better.

I snuffed it out and flung myself on my bed, fully dressed. Counted the beats of my heart: one, two, three, four – to a thousand and over again – hours, days, weeks it seemed to me, until my lips were dry and my hair stood on end: not a second of relief.

Not a single one.

I began to say words to myself, whatever sprang to my lips: "prince", "tree", "child", "book" – repeating them compulsively until suddenly they stood before me naked, senseless, terrible sounds from a barbarian age, and I had to think with all my might to find my way back into their meaning: p-r-i-n-c-e? – b-o-o-k?

Wasn't I mad already? Or dead? – I clutched at myself.

Get up!

Sit in the armchair!

I dropped onto the chair.

If only death would come at last!

Anything to stop feeling this bloodless, awful lurking!
"I – refuse – I – refuse –" I screamed. "Don't you hear me?"

I fell back, drained.

Could not believe I was still alive.

Incapable of thinking or doing a thing, I stared straight ahead of me.

– – –

"Why is he holding the seeds out so insistently?" a thought ebbed toward me, retreated and returned. Retreated. Returned.

At last I realized that a strange being stood in front of me – might have been standing by the whole time I had sat here – holding out its hand:

A grey, broad-shouldered creature, the size of a thick-set man, leaning on a spiral-twisted thorn-stick of white wood.

Where the head ought to have been, I could make out only a ball of pale vapor.

The apparition gave off a cloying smell of sandalwood and wet slate.

A feeling of utter defenselessness nearly robbed me of my senses. The nerve-gnawing torments I had gone through all this time now condensed to mortal fear, taking solid form in this being.

My instinct of self-preservation told me that I would go mad with horror and fear if I saw the face of the phantom – warned me of it, shouted it in my ears – and yet it drew me like a magnet, so that I could not take my eyes from the pale ball of mist and searched it for eyes, nose and mouth.

But however hard I tried: the vapor did not move. I managed to place all manner of heads on the torso, but each time I knew they were only figments of my imagination.

And they always dissolved – the very same second I created them.

The shape of an Egyptian ibis head held the longest.

The silhouette of the phantom blurred ghost-like in the darkness, contracting almost imperceptibly and expanding again as if with slow breaths which suffused the entire figure, the only movement to be seen. Instead of feet, bony stumps touched the ground, the flesh – grey and bloodless – drawn up a hand's breadth to form swollen rims.

The creature held its hand out to me unmoving.

It held little seeds. The size of a bean, red and edged with black dots.

What was I supposed to do with them?!

Dimly I felt: an immense responsibility would weigh upon me – a responsibility reaching far beyond all that was earthly – if I did the wrong thing now.

I sensed: two scales, each burdened with the weight of half the cosmos, hang somewhere in the realm of causes – if I cast a grain of dust on one of the two, it would sink to the ground.

That was the terrible lurking all around, I realized. "Don't move a finger", my reason advised. "Even if for all eternity death should refuse to come and redeem me from this torment." –

But then you would have made your choice: you would have *refused* the seeds, came the whisper within me. There is no turning back.

Helplessly I looked around, seeking a sign that might tell me what to do.

Nothing.

And *within* me no counsel, no inspiration – all was dead, extinct.

The lives of myriads of human beings weigh light as a feather in this terrible moment, I realized – –.

143

It must have been late at night already, for I could no longer make out the walls of my room.

Feet stomped in the room next door; I heard someone moving cabinets, tearing open drawers and throwing them to the ground with a crash, thought I recognized Wassertrum's voice letting out savage curses in his gurgling bass; I paid little heed. It was as insignificant as the scrabbling of a mouse. – I closed my eyes:

Human faces drifted past me in long rows. Their eyelids shut – rigid death masks: my own kin, my own ancestors.

Always with the same shape to the skull, no matter how the type might seem to change, they rose from their graves – with smooth, parted hair, curly and short-cropped, with full-bottomed wigs and ringlets – on through the centuries, until the features grew more and more familiar to me and converged in one last face: the face of the Golem, ending the procession of my forebears.

Then the darkness of my room dissolved into an infinite empty space, at whose center, I knew, I sat in my armchair, the grey shadow with the outstretched arm before me once again.

And when I opened my eyes, strange beings stood around us in two overlapping circles which formed a figure eight:

Those of the one circle draped in robes with a violet shimmer, those of the other in reddish black. People of an alien race, of tall, unnaturally slender build, their faces hidden by shining cloths.

The pounding of my heart in my breast told me that the moment of decision had come. My fingers jerked toward the seeds – and I saw a tremor run through the forms in the reddish circle. –

Should I refuse the seeds? The tremor seized the bluish circle – I looked sharply at the man with no head; there he stood – in the same pose: motionless as before.

144

Even his breathing had ceased.

I raised my arm, still undecided, and – struck the phantom's outstretched hands, making the seeds roll across the floor.

For a moment, sudden as an electric shock, I lost consciousness, thought I was plunging into endless depths – then I stood firmly on my feet.

The grey creature had vanished. As had the beings of the reddish circle.

But the bluish figures had formed a ring around me; they bore inscriptions in golden hieroglyphs on their breasts and mutely – it looked like an oath – held up between thumb and forefinger the red seeds which I had struck from the hand of the headless phantom.

I heard showers of hail rage against the window outside, and roaring thunder rent the air:

A winter thunderstorm swept across the city in all its senseless fury. From the river the dull canon shots announcing the breaking of the ice on the Vltava resounded through the howling of the storm at rhythmic intervals. The room blazed in the uninterrupted succession of lightning flashes. Suddenly I felt so weak that my knees trembled and I had to sit down.

"Be at ease", a voice said clearly beside me, "be quite at ease, today is the Lelschimurim, the Night of Protection." – – –

Gradually the storm subsided, and the deafening noise gave way to the monotonous drumming of the hail-stones on the roofs.

The weariness in my limbs grew so intense that I took in the events around me with dulled senses, half in a dream:

Someone in the circle said the words:

"He whom you seek is not here."

The others replied in a strange language. At this the first quietly said another sentence containing the name

"Henoch",

but I did not understand the rest: the groaning of the ice floes from the river carried too loudly on the wind.

– – –

Then one of them left the circle, stepped up to me, pointed to the hieroglyphs on his breast – they were the same letters as the others' – and asked me whether I could read them.

And when I replied in the negative – stammering with weariness – he stretched his palm out to me, and the writing appeared radiant on *my* breast in letters which were Roman at first:

CHABRAT ZEREH AUR BOCHER

and gradually changed into those I knew not. – – –

And I succumbed to a deep, dreamless sleep such as I had not known since the night Hillel loosed my tongue.

URGE

The hours of the last few days had passed as if in flight. I scarcely allowed myself time for meals.

An irresistible thirst for external activity kept me tied to my workbench from morning to evening.

The cameo was finished, and Mirjam had rejoiced in it like a child.

The letter "I" in the Book of Ibbur was mended as well.

I leaned back and calmly let all the little events of that day pass before me.

How the old charwoman burst into my room the morning after the storm with the news that the Stone Bridge had caved in that night. –

Strange: caved in! Perhaps in the very hour when I struck – – – no, no, don't think about that; all that had happened then might take on a prosaic veneer, and I had vowed to leave it buried in my breast until it woke again of its own accord – hands off!

How long ago had I crossed the bridge, seen the stone statues – and now it lay in ruins, the bridge that had stood for centuries.

It almost made me melancholy to think that I would never set foot on it again. Even if it were rebuilt, it would no longer be the old, mysterious stone bridge.

I thought about it for hours, as I carved the cameo, and as naturally as if I had never forgotten them, things came to life within me: how often, as a child and in later years, I had gazed up at the effigy of St. Luitgard and all the others who now lay buried beneath the raging water.

In my mind's eye I saw all the little things I called my own in my youth – and my father and my mother and the throng of school friends. Only I could no longer remember the house where I had lived.

I knew that suddenly, one day when I least expected it, it would stand before me again; and I looked forward to that.

The sense that all at once everything was developing within me naturally and simply was so comforting.

The day before last, when I took the Book of Ibbur out of the casket – there was nothing astonishing about the fact that it looked, well, the way an old vellum tome decorated with precious initials looks – I took it quite for granted.

I could not understand why it had ever made a sinister impression on me!

It was written in the Hebrew tongue, completely unintelligible to me.

When would the stranger return for it?

The joy in life which had secretly taken possession of me while I worked revived in all its invigorating freshness and chased away the night-thoughts which sought to waylay me again.

Quickly I seized Angelina's portrait – I had cut away the dedication written below – and kissed it.

All of it was so foolish and absurd, but why not dream for once of – happiness, holding on to the glittering present and rejoicing in it like a soap bubble?

For could not the vision which my heart's longing conjured up before me come true after all? Was it so utterly impossible that I might become a famous man overnight? Her equal, if not by birth? At least Dr. Savioli's equal? I considered the cameo of Mirjam: if I brought off more like this one – no doubt about it, the foremost artists of all times had done nothing better.

And assuming a mere accident: if Angelina's husband should suddenly die?

I went hot and cold: the slightest accident – and my hope, the most audacious hope, would take form. The fortune ready to fall into my lap was suspended on a fine thread which could snap at any moment.

Had I not already experienced miracles a thousand-fold? Things whose existence humanity did not even suspect?

Was it *no* miracle that in the space of a few weeks I had felt the stirrings of artistic abilities which already elevated me far above the average?

And I was only at the *start* of the path!

Had I no right to happiness?

Is mysticism tantamount to the lack of all desires?

I drowned out the "Yes" within me: just one more hour of dreaming – a minute – a brief existence!

And I dreamed with open eyes:

The gems on the table grew and grew and surrounded me on all sides with waterfalls of color. Opal trees stood in groves and scattered the light-waves of the sky, iridescent blue like the wings of a gigantic tropical butterfly, in a rain of sparks over boundless meadows filled with the hot fragrance of summer.

I thirsted, and cooled my limbs in the icy foam of the brooks which plunged over boulders of shimmering mother-of-pearl.

Sultry breezes wafted across slopes covered with blooms and blossoms, intoxicating me with the scent of jasmine, hyacinth, narcissus, daphne. – – –

Unbearable! Unbearable! I extinguished the picture. – I thirsted.

Those were the torments of paradise.

I tore open the window and let the wind of thaw caress my brow.

It smelled of spring's approach. – – –

Mirjam!

I thought of Mirjam. In her excitement she'd had to cling to the wall to stay on her feet when she came to tell me that a miracle had happened, a real miracle: she had found a gold piece in the loaf of bread the baker reached through the bars of their kitchen window from the corridor.

– – –

I reached for my wallet. – Hopefully it was not yet too late today, and I would be in time to *conjure up another ducat for her!*

She had visited me every day to keep me company, as she called it, but hardly spoke a word, so full was she of the "miracle". The experience had stirred her down to her innermost depths, and when I pictured how she sometimes turned deathly pale to the lips without any evident reason – merely under the influence of memory – I felt dizzy at the thought that in my blindness I could have done things whose import knew no bounds.

And when I recalled Hillel's final, dark words in connection with that, I went ice-cold.

The purity of my motive was no excuse – the end does *not* sanctify the means, I saw that now.

And what if, moreover, the motive: "wanting to help" only *seemed* "pure"? Did it not, perhaps, conceal a secret lie? The smug, unconscious desire to revel in the role of the helper?

I began to doubt myself.

I had judged Mirjam much too superficially, that was clear.

As Hillel's daughter alone she had to be different than other girls.

How could I have presumed to interfere so foolishly in her inner life, which might well be elevated sky-high above my own!

I should have been warned by the very cast of her face, a hundred times better suited to the sixth Egyptian dynasty – and much too ethereal even for that – than to ours with its rationalists.

"Only the true fool mistrusts external appearances", I had once read. – How true! How true!

By now Mirjam and I were good friends; should I admit to her that it was I who had slipped the ducats into the bread day after day?

The blow would come too suddenly. Would stun her.

I could not risk that, must proceed more cautiously.

Moderate the "miracle" somehow? Instead of slipping the money into the bread, lay it on the step so that she would find it when she opened the door, and so on, and so forth? Something new, less abrupt could be devised, I reassured myself, a new path which would gradually lead her away from the realm of the miraculous and back to daily life.

Yes! That was the right solution.

Or sever the knot? Let her father in on the secret and ask his advice? A flush of shame rose to my face. There would be time enough to take that step if all else failed.

Now to work, no time to lose!

I had a good idea: I must convince Mirjam to do something quite out of the ordinary, tear her from her usual surroundings for a few hours to provide her with new impressions.

We would take a carriage and go on an outing. Who would recognize us, if we avoided the Jewish Quarter?

Perhaps she would like to look at the caved-in bridge?

Or old Zwakh or one of her former friends should go driving with her if she should find my presence intolerable.

I was determined not to take no for an answer. – – –

I nearly bowled a man over on the threshold.

Wassertrum!

He must have been spying through the keyhole, for he was bending over when I ran into him.

"Are you looking for me?" I asked brusquely.

He stammered a few words of apology in his intolerable dialect; then he assented.

I asked him to come in and sit down, but he stopped at the table, twisting the brim of his hat spasmodically. His face and all his movements radiated a profound hostility which he vainly attempted to hide.

I had never seen the man at such close quarters. It was not his hideous ugliness which was so repellant (rather, it made me pity him: he looked like a creature whom nature itself had kicked in the face at birth, filled with rage and revulsion) – the fault lay in something different, inscrutable, which emanated from him.

The "blood", as Charousek had aptly called it.

Instinctively I wiped off the hand I had offered him when he entered.

As discreetly as I did so, he seemed to have noticed it after all, for suddenly he fought down a flare of hatred in his features.

"Nice place you got here", he began at last, falteringly, when he saw that I would not do him the favor of beginning the conversation.

In contradiction to his words, he shut his eyes as he spoke, perhaps to avoid meeting my gaze. Or did he think it would give a more harmless look to his face?

One distinctly heard the effort he made to speak proper German. I did not feel obliged to respond and waited to see what he would say next.

At a loss, he reached for the *file*, which – God knows why – had lain on the table ever since Charousek's visit, but immediately recoiled as if snake-bitten. I marveled inwardly at his subconscious psychic sensitivity.

"Natch, it comes with the job, the cushy pad", he said, pulling himself together, "when you – get classy visitors like that." He opened his eyes to see the effect the words had on me, but, evidently judging it premature, quickly shut them again.

I decided to corner him: "You mean the lady who drove up here the other day? Why don't you come out with it!"

He hesitated for a moment, then seized me hard by the wrist and tugged me to the window.

The strange, gratuitous way he did it reminded me how he had dragged the deaf-mute Jaromir down into his lair a few days before.

With crooked fingers he held a glittering object out to me:

"Whaddaya think, Herr Pernath, can anything be done?"

It was a golden watch with a case so deeply dented that it looked as if someone had warped it intentionally.

I took up a magnifying glass: the hinges were half torn-off, and inside – wasn't something engraved there? Barely legible and marred with a number of fresh abrasions besides. Slowly I deciphered:

K-rl Zott-mann..

Zottmann? Zottmann? – Where had I read that name? I could not remember.

Wassertrum nearly struck the magnifier out of my hand:

"There ain't nothing with the works, I had a look myself. But the case, that stinks."

"It just needs to be hammered into shape – a little soldering at most. Any old jeweler could do that for you, Herr Wassertrum."

"But I want it to be a respectable piece a work. You know like they say: artistic", he interrupted me hastily. Almost anxiously.

"Very well, if means that much to you –"

"Means that much!" His voice broke with zeal. "I'm going to wear it myself, this watch. And when I show somebody, I want to say: look here, *that's* the way Herr von Pernath woiks."

The man sickened me; he virtually spat his revolting flatteries into my face.

"Come back in an hour, and everything will be ready."

Wassertrum writhed: "Forget about it. Nothing doing. Three day. Four day. Next week is plenty of time. I'd be kicking myself my whole life if I rushed you."

What on earth did he want, that made him go so wild? – I stepped into the next room and locked the watch away in the casket. Angelina's photograph lay on top. I closed the lid again quickly – in case Wassertrum was looking my way.

When I came back I saw that he had turned color.

I looked at him sharply, but abandoned my suspicion again immediately: impossible! He *couldn't* have seen anything.

"Well then, next week perhaps", I said to put an end to his visit.

Suddenly he no longer seemed to be in a hurry; he took a chair and sat down.

Unlike before, now he kept his fisheyes wide open as he talked and stared fixedly at the top button of my vest. – –

Pause.

"Of course the duksel told you not to let on a thing if it comes out. What?" he suddenly burst out at me without any transition whatsoever, pounding his fist on the table.

There was something peculiarly alarming in the abruptness with which he shifted from one manner of speech to another – suddenly leaping from flattering tones to brutality – and I thought it quite probable that most people, especially women, would be in his power in the wink of an eye if he had the least little weapon against them.

I wanted to leap up, seize him by the throat and throw him out the door, that was my first thought; then I reflected that it might be wiser to sound him out thoroughly first.

"I really don't understand your meaning, Herr Wassertrum." I made an effort to put on as foolish a face as possible. "Duksel? What's that: duksel?"

"Should I maybe teach you Joiman?" he snapped at me rudely. "You'll have to lift up your hand in court when push comes to shove. Do you get me?! I'm telling you!" – He began to yell: "You won't lie to my face and tell me 'she' didn't come running outta there into your room" – he pointed his thumb toward the studio "– with a rug on and – nothing else!" Rage rose and filled my eyes; I seized the scoundrel by the shirtfront and shook him:

"If you say another word in that tone of voice, I'll break every bone in your body! Understood?"

He sank onto the chair, ashen, and stuttered: "Whatsa matter? Whatsa matter? Whaddaya want? I'm just saying."

I paced up and down the room a few times to calm myself. Not listening to all the things he slavered out in apology.

Then I sat right in front of him, determined to clear up the matter with him once and for all, as far as Angelina was concerned, and if this could not be done peacefully, force him to open hostilities and spend his few weak arrows prematurely.

Without paying the slightest attention to his interruptions, I told him to his face that extortion of whatever kind – I emphasized the word – was doomed to failure, that he could not provide evidence for a single accusation and that I would *certainly* be able to avoid testifying (assuming this were even within the realm of possibility). Angelina was so dear to me that I could not fail to rescue her in her hour of need, cost what it may, *even perjury!*

155

Every muscle in his face twitched, his harelip parted all the way up to the nose, he bared his teeth and kept interrupting me, gobbling like a turkey: "Do I want anything from the duksel? Listen to me, will you!" – He was beside himself with impatience, seeing that I would not be deterred. "It's about Savioli, the goddamned dog – the – the –" he suddenly bellowed out.

He gasped for breath. Immediately I stopped: at last I had him where I wanted him, but already he had seized hold of himself and fixed his eyes on my vest again.

"Listen, Pernath", he forced himself to imitate the cool, considered tone of a tradesman, "you keep going on about the duk – – about the dame. Fine! She's married. Fine: she got involved with the – with the young rascal. What's it to me?" He moved his hands back and forth in front of my face, fingertips pressed together as if he were holding a pinch of salt. – "Let her settle that herself, the duksel. – I'm a man of the woild, and you're a man of the woild. We know the ropes. Nuuu? All I'm after is my money. Get my meaning, Pernath?"

I listened in astonishment:

"What money? Does Dr. Savioli owe you something?"

Wassertrum evaded the question:

"I have scores to settle with him. It comes down to the same thing."

"You want to murder him!" I cried.

He jumped up. Reeled. Hemmed and hawed a few times.

"Yes indeed! Murder! How much longer will you insist on playing this farce!" I pointed to the door. "Get out of here."

Slowly he reached for his hat, put it on, and turned to go. Then he stopped once more and said with a calm of which I never would have dreamed him capable:

"All right. I wanted to let you off. Fine. No is no. Merciful barbers make stinking wounds. My tsarbichel is full. If

youda been clever: Savioli's just in your way, no!? – *Now –
all – three of you*" – he made it clear what he meant with a
gesture of strangulation – "*get presscolleh.*"

His face expressed such a satanic cruelty, and he seemed
so sure of himself, that my blood ran cold. He must have
possessed a weapon which I had not suspected, nor Charousek guessed at. I felt the ground give way beneath me.

"*The file! The file!*" I heard the whisper in my brain. I
gauged the distance: one step to the table – two steps to
Wassertrum – – I was about to spring – – – when Hillel appeared on the threshold out of nowhere.

The room swam before my eyes.

All I saw – as if through a mist – was that Hillel stood
motionless and Wassertrum retreated to the wall, step by
step.

Then I heard Hillel say:

"You know the saying, Aaron: *All Jews are each other's
bondsmen?* Don't make it too difficult." – He added a few
words in Hebrew which I did not understand.

"Whaddaya need to go snooping around the door for?"
the junk dealer spat out with trembling lips.

"It is none of your concern whether I was eavesdropping
or not!" – again Hillel ended with a Hebrew phrase, this
time sounding like a threat. I thought a quarrel was brewing,
but Wassertrum said not a syllable in reply; he thought for a
moment and left the room sullenly.

A minute must have passed before the junk dealer's
dragging footsteps came back up the stairs. Without a word,
Hillel went out and made room for him.

Wassertrum waited until he was out of earshot, and then
growled at me savagely:

"Gimme my watch back."

– – –

SHE

Where was Charousek?

Almost twenty-four hours had passed, and still he had not made his appearance.

Could he have forgotten the sign we had agreed upon? Or didn't he see it?

I went to the window and adjusted the mirror so that the ray of sun which shone upon it fell straight onto the barred spy-hole of his basement dwelling.

Hillel's intervention – yesterday – had reassured me quite a bit. Surely he would have warned me if danger were at hand.

Besides: Wassertrum could not have done anything else of significance; right after leaving me he had returned to his shop – I glanced down; sure enough, there he slouched motionless behind his stove lids, just as I had seen him early this morning. – – –

Unbearable, the endless waiting!

The mild spring air streaming in through the open window in the next room made me sick with longing.

That melting trickle from the roofs! And how the filaments of water gleamed in the sunlight!

I felt drawn outside on invisible threads. Impatiently I paced up and down the room. Dropped into an armchair. Stood up again.

The greedy budding of an amorphous infatuation in my breast – it refused to relent.

It had tormented me all night. Once it was Angelina who nestled against me, then again I seemed to be talking quite innocently with Mirjam, and hardly had I rent that

image, when Angelina came again and kissed me; I smelled
the scent of her hair, and her soft sable tickled my neck,
slipped from her bared shoulders – and she turned into
Rosina, dancing with drunken, half-closed eyes – in a
dress-coat – naked – – – and all of it in a half-sleep which
was exactly like waking. Like sweet, consuming, twilit
waking.

Toward morning my double stood at my bedside, the
shadowy Habal Garmin, "the breath of the bones" Hillel had
alluded to – and I saw it in his eyes: he was in my power:
had to answer every question I asked him about things of
this world or the other, and was only *waiting* for it, but the
thirst for mystery made no headway against the heat of my
blood and seeped away in the parched ground of my reason.
– I sent away the phantom away to become Angelina's mirror image, and it shrank to the letter "aleph", grew tall
again, stood there stark naked as the colossal woman I had
once seen in the Book of Ibbur, with a pulse like an earthquake, and bent over me, and I breathed in the dazing scent
of her hot flesh.

– – –

Would Charousek never come? – The bells sang out
from the steeples.

I would wait another quarter of an hour – and then it was
time to go out! Stroll down bustling streets filled with people in festive dress, mingle with the cheerful tumult in the
wealthy neighborhoods, see beautiful women with coquettish faces and slender hands and feet. Perhaps I would run
into Charousek, I told myself in excuse.

I took the ancient tarok game from the bookshelf to pass
the time. –

Perhaps the pictures would inspire me to a cameo?

I searched for the pagat.

Nowhere to be found. Where could he have gotten to?

I leafed through the cards again and soon lost myself in re-
flections on their hidden significance. Especially the "Hanged Man" – whatever could he mean?

A man hangs from a rope between heaven and earth,
head down, arms tied behind his back, his right shin crossed
over his left leg, giving the appearance of a cross superim-
posed on an upside-down triangle.

Incomprehensible likeness.

There! – At last! Charousek was coming.

Or not?

Joyous surprise: it was Mirjam.

– – –

"Do you know, Mirjam, just now I was about to go down
and ask you to go on a carriage outing with me?" It was not
the strict truth, but I did not worry about that. – "You won't
refuse, will you? Today I'm so infinitely glad at heart that
you, no one but you, Mirjam, must put the crowning touch
to my joy."

" – go on an outing?" she repeated, so bewildered that I
had to laugh out loud.

"Is it such a preposterous suggestion?"

"No, no, but – – " she searched for words, "strange, unheard of. Go on an outing!"

"Not at all unheard of, considering that hundreds of
thousands of other people do it – really spend their lives doing nothing else."

"Yes, *other* people!" she admitted, still completely taken
aback.

I seized both her hands:

"I wish you, Mirjam, to enjoy the joy which *other* people experience, but to an infinitely greater degree."

Suddenly she went pale as death, and the rigid vacancy
of her gaze told me what she was thinking of.

I felt a pang.

"You mustn't carry it around with you always, Mirjam",
I cajoled her, "the – the miracle. Won't you promise me that
– out of – out of friendship?"

She heard the fear in my words and looked at me in astonishment.

"If it didn't take such a toll on you, I could rejoice too,
but as it is? Do you know, I'm deeply concerned for you,
Mirjam? – For – for – how should I say it? – for your psychic health! Don't take it literally, but – I wish the miracle
had never happened."

I expected her to contradict me, but she only nodded, lost
in thought.

"It consumes you. Aren't I right, Mirjam?" She pulled
herself together:

"Sometimes I almost wish it hadn't happened too."

It sounded like a ray of hope for me. – "When I think",
she spoke very slowly, lost in dreams, "that times could
come when I must live without such miracles – – –"

"But you could become rich overnight, and then you
wouldn't need –" I interrupted her thoughtlessly, but quickly broke off as I saw the horror in her face. "I mean: you
might suddenly be relieved of your cares in a natural manner, and the miracles you experienced then would be of a
spiritual nature: inner experiences."

She shook her head and said harshly: "Inner experiences
are no miracles. It is surprising enough that there seem to be
people who have none whatsoever. – Since my childhood,
day after day, night after night, I have experienced –" (she
broke off abruptly, and I guessed that there was something
more within her she had never told me of, perhaps a web of
invisible happenings like mine) – "but now is not the time to
speak of that. Even if someone went and healed the sick by
laying on hands, I could not call it a miracle. Only when
spirit animates lifeless matter – the earth – and the laws of

nature are broken, that alone is what I have longed for as long as I could think. – My father once told me that there are two sides to the Cabala: a magical one and an abstract, which can never be made to coincide completely. The magical can attract the abstract, but never the other way around. The magical is a gift, the other *can* be mastered, though only with the help of a guide." – She picked up the first thread again: "The *gift* is what I thirst for; what I can master is indifferent to me and worthless as dust. When I think that times could come, as I said before, when I will have to live without these miracles again", – I saw her fingers clench, and remorse and sorrow rent me – "I believe I could die this very minute at the mere possibility."

"Is that why you wished the miracle had never happened?" I probed.

"Only in part. There is something else. I – I –" she thought for a moment, "was not yet mature enough to experience a miracle in this form. That's it. How can I explain it to you? Assume, just for example, that for years I had one and the same dream every night, weaving its way on and on, in which someone – let us say: an inhabitant of another world – instructs me, not only showing me, in a mirror image of myself and its gradual changes, how far I am from the magical maturity of being able to experience a 'miracle', but also enlightening me in the kind of rational questions that occasionally occupy me by day, enabling me to verify it at any time. I know you will understand me: such a being is one's substitute for all the happiness conceivable on earth; for me it is the bridge which links me to 'beyond', the Jacob's ladder on which I can climb above the darkness of daily life and into the light – is my guide and friend, and I place in 'him', who has never lied to me, all my faith that on the dark paths my soul takes I cannot stray into insanity and darkness. – And then, all at once, contrary to all he has told

me, a 'miracle' crosses my life! Whom should I now believe? Was it an illusion that filled me all those many years
unceasing? If I doubted that, I would plunge headfirst into a
bottomless abyss. – And yet the miracle happened! I would
shout with joy if –"

"If – – –?" I interrupted her breathlessly. Perhaps now
she herself would say the words of deliverance, and I would
be able to confess everything to her.

"– if I learned that I had been wrong – that it was not a
miracle at all! But I know as surely as I am sitting here that
I would perish of it." – My heart stopped. "To be torn back,
forced to return from heaven to earth – do you believe a person could bear that?"

"Ask your father for help", I said, at my wits' end with
fear.

"My father? For help?" – She looked at me uncomprehending. – "When there are only two ways for me, can he
find a third one? – – Do you know what my only salvation
would be? If what happened to you would happen to *me*. If,
this very minute, I could forget all that lies behind me: my
whole life up to the present day. – Isn't it strange: what you
experience as a misfortune would be the pinnacle of happiness for me!"

For a long time we both were silent. Then she seized my
hand and smiled. Almost brightly.

"I don't want you to worry for my sake" – she comfort-
ed me – me! – "just now you were so filled with joy and
gladness at the spring outside, and now you're gloom itself.
I shouldn't have told you anything at all. Tear it out of your
memory and go on thinking the same cheerful thoughts as
before! – I'm so glad –"

"You? Glad? Mirjam?" I interrupted her bitterly.

She put on a look of conviction: "Yes! Really! Glad!
When I came upstairs to you, I was so indescribably fearful

– I don't know why: I couldn't escape the feeling that you are in great danger" – I pricked up my ears –, "but instead of being glad to find you healthy and well, I doomed and gloomed you and – –"

I put on a show of joviality: "And now the only way you can make up for it is by going on an outing with me." (I made an effort to fill my voice with as much gaity as possible:) "Mirjam, I'd like to see if I can't manage to chase away your gloomy thoughts. Tell me what you want: you're no Egyptian sorcerer by a long shot, for now you're just a young girl the wind of thaw can still play many a wicked trick on."

Suddenly she was in high spirits:

"Now, what's the matter with you today, Herr Pernath? I've never seen you like this before. By the way, 'wind of thaw', with us Jewish girls, you know, the parents send the wind of thaw, and we can only obey. And of course we do. It's in our blood. – Not mine", she added more seriously, "my mother went on quite a strike when she was supposed to marry that horrible Aaron Wassertrum."

"What? Your mother? The junk dealer down there?"

Mirjam nodded. "Thank God it didn't come off. – Of course, it was a devastating blow for the poor man."

"Poor man, you say?" I burst out. "The fellow is a criminal."

She rocked her head thoughtfully from side to side: "Certainly, he's a criminal. To live in such a skin and not become a criminal one would have to be a prophet."

I moved closer, curious:

"Do you know any more about him? It interests me. For very particular – –"

"If you had ever seen his shop from the inside, Herr Pernath, you would know how it looks in his soul. I say that because I was there quite often as a child. – Why do you look so surprised? Is that so strange? – He was always kind and friendly to me. Once, I remember, he even gave me a big, glittering stone which, out of all his things, had struck my fancy. My mother said it was a diamond, and of course I had to bring it back immediately.

For a long time he refused to take it back, and then he snatched it from my hand and hurled it far away from him in a fury. All the same I saw the tears gush from his eyes; and even then I knew enough Hebrew to understand what he murmured: 'Everything my hand touches is cursed.' – –It was the last time I was allowed to visit him. Never again did he ask me to come to him. And I know why: if I hadn't tried to comfort him, everything would have remained as before, but as it was, because I felt no end of pity for him and told him so, he never wanted to see me again. – – – You don't understand that, Herr Pernath? But it's so simple: he's a man obsessed, a man who immediately turns suspicious, incurably suspicious, when someone touches his heart. He thinks himself much uglier than he is in reality – if that's at all possible – and that is the root of all his thoughts and actions. They say his wife was fond of him, it may have been more pity than love, but in any case many people believe it. The only one profoundly convinced of the opposite was he. He smelled betrayal and hatred everywhere.

The sole exception he made was with his son. Whether it was because he had watched him grow up from infancy, so to speak experiencing the germination of the child's every trait from its very beginnings, and never reaching a point at which his suspicions could stir, or whether it was in his Jewish blood: to smother his progeny with all the capacity to love which dwelt within him – in the instinctive fear of our race: that we might die out without having fulfilled a mission which we have forgotten, but which lives on darkly within us – who can say!

He arranged his son's education with a prudence bordering on wisdom, miraculous in an unlearned person such as him. With the acumen of a psychologist he sheltered the child from every experience which could have contributed to the development of the conscience, in order to spare him future emotional torments.

As his teacher he hired an outstanding scholar who held that animals are without sensation, their cries of pain a mechanical reflex.

To wring from every creature as much selfish delight and pleasure as possible, and then throw away the useless husk: that, more or less, was the ABC of his far-sighted system of upbringing.

You can well imagine, Herr Pernath, that money played a crucial role as power's emblem and key. And just as he painstakingly conceals his own wealth, veiling the boundaries of his influence in obscurity, he devised a means for his son to do the same, at the same time sparing him the torment of a seemingly impoverished existence: he imbued him with the infernal lie of 'beauty', taught him the outward and inward show of aesthetics, taught him: to play the lily of the field *outwardly* while being a vulture *within*.

Of course, the notion of 'beauty' was anything but his own invention – no doubt an 'improvement' on a suggestion given him by some person of cultivation.

He never resented the fact that his son later disavowed him wherever and whenever possible. On the contrary: he made it his *duty*: for his love was selfless and, as I once said of my father, of the kind which reaches beyond the grave."

Mirjam fell silent for a moment, and I saw that she was mutely pursuing her thoughts, heard it in the changed sound of her voice when she said:

"The tree of Judaism bears strange fruits."

"Tell me, Mirjam", I asked, "have you ever heard that Wassertrum keeps a wax figure in his shop? I can't remember who told me that – maybe it was just a dream – –"

"No, no, that's quite right, Herr Pernath: there's a life-sized wax figure standing in the corner where he sleeps on his straw-mattress in the midst of the craziest collection of junk. They say he haggled it off a show-man years ago, just because it resembled a girl – a Christian – who had once been his lover."

"Charousek's mother!" it dawned on me.

"You don't know her name, Mirjam?"

Mirjam shook her head. "If it's important to you – should I find out?"

"Oh goodness, no, Mirjam; it doesn't matter to me at all." (I saw from her shining eyes that she had talked herself into a fervor. She could not be allowed to come to herself again, I decided.) "But I'd be far more interested in the subject you touched on before. I mean the 'wind of thaw'. – Your father surely wouldn't dictate whom you must marry?"

She laughed merrily:

"My father? The very idea!"

"Well, that's very fortunate for me."

"Why?" she asked innocently.

"Then I still have a chance."

It was only a joke, and she took it as such, but all the same she jumped up quickly and went to the window so that I should not see her blush.

To help her out of her perplexity I added:

"I ask one thing as an old friend: you must let me in on the secret when the time comes. – Or do you plan to remain unwed?"

"No, no, no!" – She protested so energetically that I could not help but smile. – "I'll have to marry some day."

"Naturally! It goes without saying!"

She grew as nervous as a half-grown girl.

"Can't you be serious for a minute at a time, Herr Pernath?" – I obediently made a schoolmaster face, and she sat down again. – "You see: when I say I'll have to marry some day, I mean that I haven't worried about the details yet, but surely I would have failed to understand the purpose of life if I were to suppose I had come into this world as a woman only to remain childless."

For the first time since I had known her I saw the womanliness in her features.

"It is a dream of mine", she went on softly, "to imagine that it is an ultimate goal for two beings fuse into one – into – – have you ever heard of the ancient Egyptian cult of Osirus? – into that which the 'hermaphrodite' may symbolize."

I listened intently: "The hermaphrodite –?"

"I mean: the magical union of the male and female aspects of humanity as a demigod. As an ultimate goal! – No, not as an ultimate goal, as the beginning of a new path which is eternal – has *no* end."

"And do you hope", I asked, shaken, "to find the man you seek one day? – Isn't it possible that he lives in a distant land, might not even be on this earth?"

"I don't know about that", she said simply; "I can only wait. If we are separated by space and time – which I do not believe, or why would I have been born here in the ghetto? – or by the chasm of a mutual failure of recognition – and I cannot find him, then my life has had no purpose and was the thoughtless game of an idiotic demon. – But please, please, let us speak no more of it", she begged; "the moment the thought is expressed it acquires an ugly, earthly flavor, and I don't want –"

She broke off abruptly.

"What don't you want, Mirjam?"

She raised her hand, stood up quickly and said:

"You have a visitor, Herr Pernath!"

Silken skirts rustled in the corridor.

Furious knocking. Then: Angelina!

Mirjam was about to go; I held her back:

"May I present: the daughter of a dear friend – Countess –"

"One can't even drive up to your house anymore. The pavement's torn up everywhere. Will you never move to a decent neighborhood, Master Pernath? The snow is melting outside, and the sky rejoices to make your heart break, and you hunch here in your stalactite cave like an old frog. – By the way: do you know, I was at my jeweler's yesterday, and he said: you're the greatest artist, the finest lapidary around today, if not one of the greatest who has ever lived?!" – Angelina chattered away like a waterfall, and I was enchanted. Saw nothing but her radiant blue eyes, her little feet in the tiny patent-leather boots, saw the capricious face shining out from the riot of furs, and the rosy earlobes.

She hardly allowed herself time to let out a breath.

"My carriage is waiting at the corner. I was afraid I wouldn't find you at home. You haven't eaten lunch yet, I hope? First – yes, where shall we go first? First we'll drive – wait – – yes, maybe to the Orchard, or simply: somewhere out in the country, where you truly sense the budding and secret germination in the air. Come, come, take your hat; and then eat with me – and then we'll chat on into the evening. So take your hat! What are you waiting for? – There's a warm, soft blanket down in the carriage: we'll wrap ourselves up to the ears and cuddle together until we're seething hot."

What could I say?! – – "I was just about to go on a drive with the daughter of my friend here – –"

Even before I could finish, Mirjam had hastily taken her leave of Angelina.

I accompanied her out into the hall, despite her friendly protests.

"Listen to me, Mirjam, here on the stairs I can't possibly tell you how fond I am of you – – and that I'd a thousand times rather – – "

"You mustn't keep the lady waiting, Herr Pernath", she urged, "adieu and have a wonderful time!"

She said it warmly, genuine and undisguised, but I saw that the light had died away in her eyes.

She hurried down the stairs, and I choked with pain.

I felt as if I had lost a world.

– – –

I sat at Angelina's side in a transport. We drove at a quick trot through the crowded streets.

Such surges of life all around me that, half-dazed, I could make out only the little gleams of light in the picture which rushed past me: flashing jewels in earrings and muff chains; glossy top hats; ladies' white gloves; a poodle with a pink bow around its neck, yapping and trying to bite at our wheels; black horses in a lather hurtling toward us, silver-harnessed; a shop window filled with shimmering bowls holding strings of pearls and glittering trinkets – the sheen of silk about slender girlish hips.

The raw wind which cut into our faces made the warmth of Angelina's body all the more perturbing to my senses.

The policemen at the intersections jumped aside respectfully as we raced past.

Then we passed at a walking pace along the quay – one solid line of carriages – past the caved-in stone bridge, thronged by gaping faces.

I barely looked – the least word from Angelina's mouth, her lashes, the rapid play of her lips – all that, all that was infinitely more important than the sight of the stone rubble below bracing its shoulders against the on-reeling ice floes. –

Park paths. Then – stamped-down, springy soil. Then the rustle of leaves beneath the horses' hooves, damp air, towering leafless trees filled with crows' nests, the dead green of meadows with whitish islands of vanishing snow, all that passed me by as if in a dream.

Only in a few brief words, almost indifferently, did Angelina mention Dr. Savioli.

"Now that the danger is past", she said with enchanting childish frankness, "and I know he's better again, all I went through seems so awfully tedious. – I want to be happy again at last, to close my eyes and plunge into life's glittering spray. I think all women are like that. They just don't admit it. Or are they too stupid to realize it themselves? Don't you think so?" She paid no attention to my reply. "Anyway, women don't interest me in the slightest. Of course, you mustn't take it as flattery: but – truly, down to my little finger I prefer the mere proximity of a congenial man to the most stimulating conversation with a woman, however clever she may be. It's all foolishness anyway, the things one ends up chattering. – At most: the latest finery – what of it! The fashions don't change all that often. – – I'm frivolous, aren't I?" she suddenly asked coquettishly, and, enthralled by her charm, I had to force myself not to take her little head between my hands and kiss the nape of her neck. – "Say that I'm frivolous!"

She nestled still closer and slipped her arm through mine.

We left behind the tree-lined avenue and drove past bosquets which looked, in their wrappings of straw, like the trunks of monsters with lopped-off limbs and heads.

People sat on benches in the sun and gazed after us, putting their heads together.

We were silent for a while, both lost in thought. How utterly different was Angelina than she had lived in my memory! – As if she had not entered the present for me until this day!

Was this really the same woman I had consoled in the cathedral church back then?

I could not tear my eyes from her parted lips.

Still she did not speak a word. Seemed to glimpse an image in her mind's eye.

The carriage turned to cross a damp meadow.

There was a scent of awaking earth.

"Do you know – – Frau – –?"

"Please call me Angelina", she interrupted me softly.

"Do you know, Angelina, that – that I dreamed of you all last night?" I choked out.

She made a quick little movement, as if to withdraw her arm from mine, and looked at me wide-eyed. "Strange! And I of you! – And just this moment I thought the same."

Again our conversation flagged, and we both guessed that we had also dreamed the same.

I felt it in the quaking of her blood. Her arm trembled almost imperceptibly against my chest. She looked away from me spasmodically, out of the carriage. – – – –

Slowly I drew her hand to my lips, peeled back the perfumed white glove, heard her breath come faster, and, mad with love, sank my teeth into the ball of her thumb. – – –

– – – – Hours later I walked down to the city through the fog like a drunken man. I chose streets at random and walked in a circle for a long time without realizing it.

Then I stood by the river, leaning over an iron railing, and stared down into the raging waves.

I still felt Angelina's arms around my neck, saw before me the stone basin of the fountain where we had parted once before many years ago, filled with decaying elm leaves, and once again, as she had done just now, she wandered silently with me through the chilly, twilit park of her manor.

I sat on a bench and pulled my hat down over my face to daydream.

The water surged over the weir, and its roar drowned out the last murmurs of the drowsing city.

From time to time I drew my coat more tightly about me and looked up to see how the river lay deeper and deeper in shadow, until at last, crushed by the heavy night, it poured past black-grey, and the foam of the weir slanted across to the other bank in a blinding white line.

I shuddered at the thought of returning to my dismal house.

The splendor of one brief afternoon had forever made me a stranger in my home.

A few weeks, perhaps only days, then the brief happiness would be over – leaving nothing but a lovely, agonizing memory.

And then?

Then I would be homeless here and yonder, on this side of the river and that.

I stood up! Before going to the dark ghetto I wanted to glance through the park fence at the manor behind whose windows she slept. – – – I went back the way I had come, groped along the rows of houses and across slumbering squares in the dense fog, saw black monuments rear up threateningly, lonely sentry-boxes and the flourishes of baroque facades. The dull glimmer of a lantern bloomed out of the mist in enormous, fantastic rings of faded rainbow colors, became a piercing, sallow yellow eye, and dissolved into the air behind me.

Underfoot I felt broad stone stairs, strewn with gravel. Where was I? A sunken path leading steeply upward?

Smooth garden walls right and left? The bare branches of a tree hang over. They reach down from the sky: the trunk is hidden behind the wall of fog. –

174

A few thin, brittle twigs snap off as my hat brushes them and fall down my coat into the misty grey abyss that hides my feet from me.

Then a shining point: a solitary light in the distance – somewhere – enigmatic – between heaven and earth. – – –

I must have lost my way. These can only be the "Old Castle Steps" along the slopes of the Fürstenberg Gardens. –

– – – – –

Then long stretches of clayey earth. – A paved path.

A massive shadow looms up high, a stiff black peaked cap on its head: "the Daliborka" – the hunger tower where people once languished while kings hunted game down in the "Stag Moat".

A narrow, winding alleyway with arrow slits, a tortuous passage, barely wide enough to admit the shoulders – and I stood before a row of houses, none of them taller than I.

I could touch the roofs by reaching out my arm.

I had blundered into the "Alchemists' Lane", where in medieval times the alchemist adepts forged the philosophers' stone and poisoned the moonbeams.

There was no way out but the way I had come.

But I could no longer find the gap in the wall which had admitted me – ran up against a wooden gate.

It's no use, I'll have to wake someone to show me the way, I said to myself. How strange, a house at the end of the street – larger than the others and with an inviting look to it! I can't remember noticing it before.

I go through the gate and across the narrow strip of garden, press my face against the panes – all is dark. I knock at the window. – Inside an ancient man holding a burning candle comes through a door with senile tottering steps, stops in the middle of the room, slowly turns his head toward the dusty alchemical retorts and alembics on the wall, stares thoughtfully at the enormous cobwebs in the corner and then fixes his gaze upon me.

The shadows of his cheekbones fill his eye sockets, making them seem empty as a mummy's. He does not appear to see me.

I knock on the glass.

He does not hear me. Leaves the room again, silent as a sleepwalker.

I wait in vain.

Knock at the front door: no one opens. – – –

I had no choice but to search until at last I found the way out of the alley.

– – –

Wouldn't it be best to seek company now, I thought. – To the "altes Ungelt", where my friends: Zwakh, Prokop and Vrieslander were sure to be – to drown out my consuming desire for Angelina's kisses for a few hours at least? I set off quickly in that direction.

– – –

Like a triad of the dead they hunched at the worm-eaten old table – all three with white, thin-stemmed clay pipes between their teeth, filling the room with smoke.

One could hardly make out their features, the way the dark brown walls swallowed up the meager light of the old-fashioned hanging lamp.

In the corner the spindly, taciturn, weathered waitress perpetually knitting a stocking, with her colorless gaze and her yellow duck-bill of a nose!

Dull-red cloths curtained the closed doors, making the voices of the guests in the next room reach us like the faint humming of a swarm of bees.

Vrieslander, with the conical, straight-brimmed hat on his head, his Vandyke beard, blue-grey complexion and the scar under his eye, looked like a drowned Dutchman from a forgotten century.

Josua Prokop had stuck a fork through his mane of curls, pattered ceaselessly with his preternaturally long bony fingers and watched admiringly as Zwakh attempted to dress the pot-bellied arrack bottle in a marionette's purple coat.

"That'll be Babinski", Vrieslander explained to me, dead earnest. "You don't know who Babinski was? Zwakh, hurry and tell Pernath who Babinski was!"

"Babinski", Zwakh began immediately, without looking up from his work for a second, "was once a famous cutthroat in Prague. – He went about his infamous work for years, and no one was the wiser. Little by little, however, it began to strike the better families that one or the other member of the clan would fail to come to dinner and was never seen again. At first nothing was said, as the matter had its good sides too, so to speak, allowing one to cook less, but on the other hand one could not ignore the fact that one's reputation in society might well suffer and gossip could spread.

Especially when it was a matter of marriageable daughters vanishing without a trace.

Besides, self-respect demanded that one display a proper regard for bourgeois family values.

The newspaper advertisements: 'Come back, all is forgiven!' multiplied and multiplied – a circumstance which Babinski, careless like most professional murderers, had not included in his calculations – and finally attracted broader attention.

In the lovely little village of Krtsch by Prague, Babinski, privately of quite an idyllic character, had established a small but cozy home over time with his tireless activity. A cottage, spic and span, and a little garden in front of it with blossoming geraniums.

As his income did not permit expansion, to dispose of his victims' corpses discreetly he was forced to lay out – instead of the flowerbed he would have liked – a grass-grown, simple, yet – in keeping with the circumstances – practical grave mound which could be extended effortlessly as the business or the season demanded.

On this holy mound Babinski would sit in the rays of the setting sun every evening after the day's toils and play all sorts of melancholy tunes on his flute." – –

"Stop!" Josua Prokop interrupted gruffly, took a house-key from his pocket, held it up to his mouth like a clarinet and sang:

"Tsimtserlim tsambuzla – deh."

"Were you there, that you know the melody so well?" Vrieslander asked in astonishment.

Prokop gave him a scathing look: "No. Babinski lived too long ago for that. But as a composer I ought to know best what he might have played. You have no right to judge: you are not musical. – – Tsimtserlim – tsambuzla – buzla – deh."

Zwakh listened, moved, until Prokop put his house-key away again, and then went on:

"The continuous growth of the mound eventually aroused the suspicions of the neighbors, and a policeman from the suburb of Zizkov, who occasionally watched from afar as Babinski strangled an old woman of good family, deserves the credit for putting an end to the monster's egotistical activities once and for all:

Babinski was arrested in his tusculum.

Conceding the extenuating circumstances of an otherwise excellent reputation, the court sentenced him to death by hanging and immediately charged the firm of the Leipen Bros. – cordage en gros and en detail – to deliver the necessary execution utensils, within their field of expertise, to a high State Exchequer for civil prices against receipt.

Now it happened, however, that the rope snapped and Babinski's sentence was commuted to life in prison.

The cutthroat has served twenty years behind the walls of Saint Pankraz without letting a single reproach escape his lips – to this day the official staff of the institution is full of praise for his exemplary conduct; indeed, he was even permitted to play his flute now and then on the birthday of our supreme lord and ruler –"

Prokop immediately groped for his house-key again, but Zwakh restrained him.

"– in a general amnesty the rest of Babinski's sentence was lifted, and he was given a job as porter in the convent of the 'Sisters of Mercy'.

Due to the great skill with the spade which he had acquired in his former sphere of activity, the simple garden work went quickly, leaving him sufficient leisure hours to ennoble heart and soul with good, carefully selected reading material.

The results thereof were highly gratifying.

Whenever the Lady Superior sent him to the tavern on Saturday evening to gladden his soul a bit, he would return home punctually before nightfall, remarking that the decay of public morals depressed him and that shady characters of the worst sort made the road so unsafe that all peace-loving people were well-advised to wend their way homeward before it was too late.

In the Prague of those days the wax-chandlers had inaugurated the deplorable custom of selling figurines wearing a red coat and depicting the cutthroat Babinski.

None of the bereaved families were without one.

Usually, though, they were displayed in the shops under bell jars, and nothing provoked Babinski's ire more than the sight of these wax figurines.

'It's unseemly to the extreme, testimony to a callousness without compare, to constantly confront a person with the lapses of his youth,' Babinski would say at such moments, 'and it is deeply regrettable that the authorities do nothing to prevent such out and out roguery.'

Even on his deathbed he expressed sentiments of the kind.

Not in vain, either, for soon the authorities forbade the sale of the scandalous Babinski statuettes." – – –

Zwakh took a mighty swallow from his grog glass, and all three of them grinned like devils; then he surreptitiously turned his head toward the colorless waitress, and I saw her wink away a tear.

– – –

– "Well, have you nothing to share with us, aside – of course – from footing the bill in gratitude for the artistic pleasure just endured, esteemed colleague and lapidary?" Vrieslander asked me after a long pause of general profundity.

I told them of my wanderings through the fog.

When I came to the point at which I saw the white house, all three of them took the pipes from their teeth in excitement, and when I finished Prokop pounded his fist on the table and cried:

"That's sheer – –! All the legends there are, Pernath lives them in the flesh. – Apropos, the Golem of the other day – you know: the matter's been cleared up."

"Cleared up how?" I asked, flummoxed.

"You know the crazy Jewish beggar 'Haschile'? No? Well then: this Haschile was the Golem."

"A beggar was the Golem?"

"Yes indeed, Haschile was the Golem. This afternoon in broad daylight, wearing his infamous old-fashioned clothes from the seventeenth century, the phantom coolly went on a stroll down Salnitergasse, and there the knacker managed to catch it in a dog snare."

"What's that supposed to mean? I don't understand a word", I flared up.

"I'm telling you: it was Haschile! I hear he found the clothes some time ago inside the front door of a house. – Anyway, to come back to the white house on the Lesser Side: it's a terribly interesting affair. According to an old legend, there's a house up there on the Alchemists' Lane which can only be seen in the fog, and then only by Sunday-children. It is called the 'Wall at the Last Lantern'. If you go up by day you see nothing but a big grey stone – behind that the ground drops off, into the Stag Moat. You can thank your lucky stars that you didn't take another step, Pernath: no doubt about it, you would have fallen and broken every bone in your body.

Under the stone they say an immense treasure is hidden; it's said to have been laid by the 'Asiatic Brothers', who are supposed to have founded Prague, as the corner-stone for a house which a person will occupy at the end of all days – a hermaphrodite, rather – a creature made of man and woman.

And it will bear the image of a rabbit on its coat of arms – incidentally: the rabbit was the symbol of Osiris, and no doubt *that* is where the custom of the Easter Bunny comes from.

Until that time has come, it is said, Methuselah himself keeps watch over the place so that Satan doesn't beflutter the stone and beget a son with it: the so-called Armilos. – Have you never heard tell of this Armilos? – They even know what he would look like – that is, the old rabbis know it – if he came into the world: he'd have hair of gold, bound back in a pig-tail, then: two partings, sickle-shaped eyes and arms down to his feet."

"Someone ought to draw a picture of this swell", Vrieslander muttered, looking for a pencil.

"So Pernath: if you should ever have the good fortune to become a hermaphrodite and find the buried treasure en passant", Prokop concluded, "please don't forget that I've always been your best friend!"

– I was in no mood for joking, and I felt a faint ache in my heart.

Zwakh must have noticed, even if he did not know the reason, for he quickly came to my assistance.

"At any rate, it's most odd, almost sinister, that Pernath had a vision in a place so closely tied to an ancient legend. – It seems impossible for a person to free himself from the embrace of these contingencies, if his soul has the ability to see forms which are concealed from the sense of touch. – I can't help it: the *metaphysical* is the most delightful! What do you think?"

Vrieslander and Prokop had grown earnest, and none of us found it necessary to reply.

"What do you think, Eulalia", repeated Zwakh, turning back, "isn't the metaphysical the most delightful?"

The old waitress scratched her head with a knitting needle, sighed, blushed and said:

"Go on with you! You're a bad one, you are."

– – –

"There was a hell of a tension in the air all day", Vrieslander began once our outburst of merriment had settled down; "I couldn't get a stroke of work done. I kept thinking of Rosina dancing in the dress coat."

"Did they ever find her?" I asked.

"Find her is good. The vice squad has secured her a permanent engagement! – Maybe she caught the eye of the Herr Commissar – 'at Loisitschek' that time? At any rate now she's – feverishly at work and doing much to boost the tourist trade in the Jewish Town. She's become a damned strapping thing in that short time, incidentally."

"When you think what a woman can make out of a man just by having him be in love with her: it's amazing", Zwakh put in. "To raise the money to go to her, the poor boy Jaromir has become an artist overnight. He goes around in the taverns and cuts out silhouettes for guests who want to have their portraits made."

Prokop, overhearing the last remarks, smacked his lips:

"Really? Has she turned out so pretty, that Rosina? – Did you ever steal a kiss from her, Vrieslander?"

At once the waitress jumped up and left the room indignantly.

"The old biddy! She of all people – attacks of virtue! Pah!" Prokop muttered angrily after her.

"What do you want, she left at the wrong moment. Besides, the stocking was finished", Zwakh soothed him.

– – –

The tavern-keeper brought fresh grog, and the conversation began to take a sultry turn. So sultry that it could not but sink into my blood, what with my feverish mood.

I resisted, but the more I shut myself off inwardly and thought back on Angelina, the hotter was the roaring in my ears.

I took my leave rather abruptly.

The fog had thinned out, spraying me with fine needles of ice, but was still so dense that I was unable to read the street signs and strayed slightly from my path.

I had turned onto the wrong street, and was about to turn around, when I heard someone calling my name:

"Herr Pernath! Herr Pernath!"

I looked around me, up.

No one!

An open house door, over it a discreet little red lantern, gaped next to me, and a pale figure – it seemed to me – stood far down the hall.

Again: "Herr Pernath! Herr Pernath!" In a whisper.

Surprised, I entered the hall – a woman's warm arms twined themselves about my neck, and in the beam of light which fell through the slowly widening crack of a door I saw that it was Rosina pressing up to me hotly. – – –

RUSE

A grey, blind day.

I had slept until late in the morning, dreamless, senseless, like a dead man

My old servant-woman had not come, or had forgotten to heat the rooms.

Cold ash lay in the stove.

Dust on the furniture.

The floor unswept.

I paced up and down, shivering.

The revolting exhalations of cheap alcohol hung in the room. My coat, my clothes stank of stale tobacco smoke.

I flung open the window, shut it again – the cold, filthy draft from the street was unbearable.

Sparrows with soaked plumage huddled motionless on the gutter outside.

Dingy gloom wherever I looked. Everything in me was torn, tattered.

The cushion on the armchair – how threadbare it was! The horsehair spilled out the edges.

It ought to be taken to the upholsterer – – oh, what of it, let it stay that way – for one more barren human lifetime, until everything fell to pieces!

And what tasteless, pointless trumpery, those rags hanging at the windows!

Why didn't I twist them to a rope and hang myself from it?!

Then at least I'd never need to see these offensive things again, and the whole grey, grinding misery would be over – once and for all.

Yes! That was the most sensible thing to do! Put an end to it.

This very day.

Now – this morning. Without even going to eat first. A vile thought, to exit this world with a full stomach! To lie in the damp soil with undigested, rotting food inside.

If only the sun would never shine again, twinkling its impudent lie about the joy of existence into one's heart!

No! I would be played for the fool no longer, would no longer be the toy of a clumsy, pointless fate which lifted me up and then shoved me into puddles again, just to make me see the transience of all earthly things, something I knew long ago, something every child knows, every dog on the street knows.

Poor, poor Mirjam! If only I could help *her*.

It was time to make a decision, a serious and unalterable resolution, before the cursed urge toward existence could reawaken within me and conjure up new phantasms before my eyes.

What use had they been to me: all these messages from the realm of the incorruptible?

None, none at all.

At most to make me reel about in a circle and experience the earth now as an intolerable torment.

There was only one thing to do.

In my head I calculated how much money I had in the bank.

Yes, *that* was the only way. That was the only, trifling deed of mine which could have any value in life!

Bundle up all I possessed – including the few gems in the drawer – in a package and send it to Mirjam. For a few years, at least, it would relieve her of the cares of everyday life. And write a letter to Hillel telling him the truth about the "miracle".

He alone could help her.

I felt: yes, he would know what to do for her.

I gathered up the gems, put them in my pocket, looked at the clock: if I went to the bank now – in an hour everything would be taken care of.

And then buy a bunch of red roses for Angelina! – – – – Pain and wild longing cried out within me. – Let me live one day more, one single day!

Only to go through this same choking despair once again?

No, there was not a single minute to lose! Something like gratification overcame me: I had not given in to myself.

I looked around. Was there anything left for me to do?

Right: the file there. I slipped it into my pocket – I would throw it away somewhere on the street, as I had recently intended.

I hated the file! It had almost made me into a murderer.

– – –

Who was that coming to bother me again?

It was the junk dealer.

"Jessa moment, Herr von Pernath", he pleaded, nonplussed, when I told him I had no time. "Jes half a moment. Jessa few words."

The sweat poured down his face, and he trembled with agitation.

"Can we talk in private, Herr von Pernath? I don't want that – that Hillel to barge in again. Lock the door, or let's go into the next room" – he dragged me after him in his accustomed forcible fashion.

Then he looked about warily a few times and whispered hoarsely:

"You know, I thought it over – our talk the other day. It's better that way. There ain't no point in it. Fine. Over is over."

I tried to read his eyes.

He held my gaze, but dug his hands into the arms of the chair, so great an effort did it cost him.

"I'm glad to hear that, Herr Wassertrum", I said as amiably as I could, "life is gloomy enough without souring it for each other with hatred."

"Jes like hearing a printed book talk", he grunted in relief, dug in the pockets of his trousers and pulled out the golden watch with the dented case, "and so you know I mean it honest, lemme give you this trifle. As a present."

"What are you thinking of?" I protested. "You can't possibly think – –" – then I recalled what Mirjam had said about him, and I reached out my hand so as not to offend him.

He paid no attention, suddenly went white as the wall, listened, and gasped:

"There! There! I knew it. Hillel again! He's knocking."

I listened, went back into the other room and, to reassure him, half-closed the communicating door behind me.

This time it was not Hillel. *Charousek* came in, laid a finger to his lips as if in token that he knew *who* was in the next room, and without waiting to hear what I might say, drowned me in a flood of words:

"Oh, my dear, esteemed Master Pernath, how can I possibly find the words to express my joy at finding you at home alone and well." – – He spoke like an actor, and his pompous, unnatural manner of speaking was in such glaring contrast to his contorted face that I felt a profound dread of him.

"Never, Master, would I have dared to come to you in the ragged state in which, surely, you have often seen me on the street – but what am I saying: seen! You who have so often reached out your hand to me in benevolence.

Today I can appear before you with a white collar and in a clean suit – and do you know who is to thank for it? One of the noblest and – alas – most misunderstood people in our city. Emotion overcomes me when I think of him.

Despite his own humble circumstances, he has always been open-handed toward the poor and the needy. As long as I can remember, whenever I see him standing sadly outside his shop, I have always wished from the bottom of my heart to go up and mutely clasp his hand.

Several days ago he called out to me as I went past and gave me money, enabling me to buy a suit on installments.

And do you know, Master Pernath, who my benefactor was? –

I say it with pride, for I have long been the only one to suspect the golden heart which beats in his bosom: it was – Herr Aaron Wassertrum!" – –

– – Of course I understood that Charousek's act was for the benefit of the junk dealer listening in the next room, though it was still unclear to me what he hoped to gain by it; the crude flattery hardly seemed likely to take in the suspicious Wassertrum. My doubtful face must have betrayed my thoughts to Charousek; he shook his head with a grin, and his next words seemed calculated to tell me that he knew his man and was aware how thick he could lay it on.

"Yes indeed! Herr – Aaron – Wassertrum! It almost breaks my heart that I can't tell him myself how grateful I am to him. I entreat you, master, never divulge to him that I was here and told you everything. – I know, the selfishness of mankind has embittered him and planted deep, irremediable – alas, all too justified – mistrust in his breast.

I am a mind-healer, but my instinct, too, tells me that it is best if Herr Wassertrum never learns – not even from my lips – how highly I think of him. – For that: would sow doubts in his unhappy heart. Far be it from me to do such a thing. Better he should think me ungrateful.

189

Master Pernath! I myself am an unhappy man and have known from infancy what it means to be alone and forsaken in the world! I do not even know my father's name. And I never saw my dear mother face to face. She must have died young" – Charousek's voice grew strangely mysterious and penetrating – "and, as I firmly believe, she was one of those profoundly spiritual natures who can never say how deeply they love, a nature such as Herr Aaron Wassertrum's.

I possess a page torn from my mother's diary – I always carry the sheet upon my bosom – and there it is written that she loved my father, though he is said to have been ugly, as never a mortal woman on earth did love a man.

Yet it seems she never told him so. – Perhaps for the same reasons why, for example, I could never tell Herr Wassertrum – and though my heart might break – the gratitude I feel for him.

But the page of her diary points to one more thing, even if I can only guess at it, for the words are rendered almost illegible by tears: my father, whoever he may have been – may his memory vanish from heaven and earth! – must have acted atrociously by my mother."

Suddenly Charousek fell to his knees with a thud, and screamed in such blood-curdling tones that I was not sure whether he was still playacting or had really gone mad:

"Thou Almighty One whose name man must not speak, here on my knees I prostrate myself before Thee: cursed, cursed, cursed be my father in all eternity!"

He virtually bit the last word in two and listened for a second with staring eyes.

Then he grinned like Satan himself. It seemed to me that Wassertrum had let out a soft groan in the next room.

"Forgive me, master", Charousek went on after a pause in an exaggeratedly choked voice, "forgive me for letting it get the better of me, but morning and night I pray that the

Almighty may one day ordain my father, whoever he may be, the most dreadful end imaginable."

I was about to reply in spite of myself, but Charousek quickly interrupted me:

"But now, Master Pernath, I must make a request of you:

Herr Wassertrum had a protégé of whom he was fond beyond measure – it must have been a nephew of his. It is even said that it was his son, but I do not believe it, or he would have had the same name; in reality his name was: Wassory, Dr. Theodor Wassory.

Tears fill my eyes when I see him before me in spirit. I was devoted to him with all my soul, as if bound to him by the immediate bonds of love and kinship."

Charousek sobbed as if emotion barely allowed him to go on.

"Alas, that that noble man had to leave this world! – Alas! Alas!

Whatever the reason may have been – I never learned it – he put an end to his own life. And I was among those summoned to help – – alas, alas, too late – too late – too late! And when I stood alone at his deathbed and covered his cold, pale hand with kisses, well – why should I not admit it, Master Pernath? – after all, it was no theft – I took a rose from the corpse's breast and secured the little bottle with whose contents the unfortunate had put a rapid end to his flourishing existence."

Charousek produced a vial and went on in a quavering voice:

"Both these things – I – lay – here –on – your table, the withered rose and the phial; they were my mementos of the deceased friend.

How often in hours of inner desolation, when I wished for death in the solitude of my heart and my longing for my departed mother, did I toy with this little bottle, and it was a blessed comfort to know: *I needed only to pour the liquid onto a cloth and breathe it in*, and I would painlessly drift off to the realm where my dear, good Theodor rests from the toils of our vale of tears.

And now I beg you, esteemed master – and it is for this reason I have come – take them both and bring them to Herr Wassertrum.

Say that they were given you by someone who was close to Dr. Wassory, but whose name you had promised never to divulge –from a lady, perhaps.

He will believe it, and it will serve him as a memento, as it was a precious memento for me.

That shall be the secret thanks I give him. I am poor, and it is all that I have; but it makes me glad to know: both will now belong to *him*, and yet he does not suspect that *I* am the giver.

I find infinite sweetness in that.

And now farewell, dear Master, and thank you in advance a thousand times."

He gripped my hand, winked and, when I still failed to understand, whispered something barely audible to me.

"Wait, Herr Charousek, I'll come down with you a ways", I mechanically repeated the words I read from his lips, and went out with him.

We stopped on the dark landing of the second floor, and I made to take my leave from Charousek.

"I can imagine what you aimed to achieve with that farce. – – You – you want Wassertrum to poison himself with the vial!" I said it to his face.

"Quite so", Charousek admitted cheerfully.

"And you expect me to help you do *that*?"

"Quite unnecessary."

"But you said just now that I was to bring Wassertrum the vial!"

Charousek shook his head.

"When you return, you will see that he has already pocketed it."

"How can you possibly assume that?" I asked in astonishment. "A person like Wassertrum would never kill himself – he's much too cowardly – never acts on sudden impulses."

"Then you don't know the insidious poison of suggestion", Charousek interrupted me earnestly. "If I had spoken in everyday words, you might have been right, but I calculated every last intonation ahead of time. Only the most revolting pathos has an effect on filthy curs! Believe me! I could have drawn you the expression he wore at each phrase of mine. – No 'kitsch', as the painters call it, is too base to coax tears from the perfectly hypocritical masses – and pierce them to the heart! Don't you think all the theaters would long since have been obliterated with fire and sword if it were not so? Sentimentality betrays the scoundrel. Thousands of poor devils can starve, and no one cries, but when a greasepaint camel on the stage, disguised as a country wench, rolls her eyes, they squeal like stuck pigs. – – Even if Daddy Wassertrum has forgotten by tomorrow what just cost him – heart-swill: each word of mine will return to life in him, come the ripening of the hours in which he seems infinitely pitiable to himself. – In such moments of great misery it takes only a nudge – that I will provide – and even the most cowardly paw will reach for the poison. It need only be within reach! Teddy probably wouldn't have grabbed for it either if I hadn't made it so easy for him."

"Charousek, you're a monster", I cried out, appalled. "Don't you have any sense of – – –"

Swiftly he put his hand over my mouth and pushed me into a niche.

"Quiet! There he is!"

Tottering, leaning against the wall, Wassertrum came down the stairs and staggered past us.

Charousek shook my hand hastily and slunk after him.

– – –

When I returned to my room I saw that the rose and the vial were gone; in their place lay the junk dealer's golden, dented watch.

– – –

I had to wait eight days to withdraw my money; that was the usual notice period, I was told at the bank.

Then they should fetch the director – I pretended that I was in great haste and had to leave town in an hour.

He was unavailable and could not change the bank's policy either, I was told, and a fellow with a glass eye who had stepped up to the counter along with me laughed at that.

Thus I was compelled to wait eight grey, fearful days for death!

It seemed like an endless period of time. – – –

I was so dejected that I had lost track of how long I had been pacing back and forth outside the door of a coffee-house.

At last I went inside, merely to get rid of the loathsome fellow with the glass eye who had followed me here from the bank, sticking to my heels; whenever I looked at him, he immediately began to look around on the ground as if he had lost something.

He was wearing a pale, checked, much too tight jacket and black, greasy pants which hung like sacks around his legs. His left boot had been patched with a bulging egg-shaped piece of leather which made it look as if he were wearing a signet-ring on his toe.

As soon as I had taken a seat he came in too and sat at a neighboring table.

194

I thought he was going to beg money from me, and I was reaching for my wallet when I saw the glitter of a large diamond on his puffy butcher's fingers.

I sat in the coffeehouse for hours and hours and thought I would go mad with inward agitation– but where could I go? Home? Wandering about? One seemed more frightful than the other.

The stale air, the eternal, idiotic clacking of the billiard balls, the dry incessant rasping of a half-blind, fanatical newspaper-reader across from me, a stork-legged customs officer who alternately picked his nose and combed his moustache with yellow smoker's fingers in front of a pocket mirror, a brown velvet gaggle of revolting, sweaty, chattering Italians around the card table in the corner, now screeching and slamming their trumps down with their knuckles, now spitting into the room, retching. And to be forced to see all that doubled and trebled by the wall mirrors! It slowly sucked the blood from my veins. – – –

Slowly darkness fell, and a flat-footed waiter, soft in the knees, reached a pole up to the gas lamps, at last satisfying himself, with a shake of his head, that they refused to be lit.

Whenever I turned my head I met the squinting wolf's gaze of the glass-eyed man, who quickly hid behind the newspaper every time, or dipped his filthy moustache into the coffee cup he had long since drained.

He had pulled down his stiff, round hat until his ears virtually stood out at right angles, but made no move to go.

It had become unendurable.

I paid and left.

As I closed the glass door behind me, someone snatched the handle from my hand. – I turned around:

That man again!

195

Angry, I was about to turn to the left, toward the Jewish Town, when he pushed his way to my side and stood in my path.

"That's going a bit too far!" I yelled at him.

"Ve go to de right", he said curtly.

"What's that supposed to mean?"

He stared at me insolently:

"You're Pernath!"

"I'm sure you mean *Herr* Pernath?"

He only laughed mockingly:

"No foolery now! You're coming yerrself wid me!"

"Are you crazy? Who are you, anyway?" I snapped.

Without replying, he threw open his jacket and discreetly pointed to a scuffed tin eagle pinned to the lining.

I understood: the scoundrel was a secret policeman, and he was arresting me.

"Then for Heaven's sake, tell me what's going on!"

"You'll find yerrself out soon enough. At de Station", he replied roughly. "Now forrward marrch!"

I suggested that I would rather take a cab.

"Nothing doing!"

We went to the police.

– – –

A gendarme led me up to a door.

> ALOIS OTSCHIN
> Police Inspector

I read on the porcelain name-plate.

"You kin come yerrself in", said the gendarme.

Two grubby desks with yard-high hutches stood across from each other.

Between them a few dilapidated chairs.

A picture of the Emperor on the wall.

A bowl of goldfish on the windowsill.

Nothing else in the room.

A club-foot and next to it a fat felt slipper under frayed grey pant legs behind the left-hand desk.

I heard a rustle. Someone murmured a few words in Bohemian, and a moment later the Police Inspector emerged from behind the right-hand desk and came up to me.

He was a small man with a grey goatee and the peculiar habit of baring his teeth before he spoke, like someone peering into bright sunlight.

Then he screwed up his eyes behind his glasses, which gave him the appearance of alarming villainy.

"Your name is Athanasius Pernath and you are" – he glanced at a piece of paper on which nothing was written – "a lapidary."

At once the club foot under the other desk came to life: it whetted itself against the table leg, and I heard the scratching of a quill.

I affirmed: "Pernath, lapidary."

"Well, then we're in agrreement rright off, Herr – – – Pernath – yes indeed, Pernath. Yes indeed, yes." – All at once the Police Inspector was astonishingly amiable, as if he had just received the most delightful news in the world; he reached out both his hands to me and made a laughable effort to assume the expression of an honest man.

"So, Herr Pernath, tell me, what do you do all day?"

"I don't believe that concerns you, Herr Otschin", I replied coldly.

He screwed up his eyes, waited for a moment, and then shot out:

"Since when has the Countess been having her affair with Savioli?"

I had been prepared for something of the sort and did not even bat an eye.

With skillful cross-questioning he tried to snare me in contradictions, but though my heart beat in my throat with horror I did not betray myself, repeating over and over again that I had never heard the name Savioli, that I knew Angelina through my father and that she had often commissioned cameos from me.

All the same I felt distinctly that the Police Inspector saw through my lies and was seething with inward rage at his inability to get anything out of me.

He thought for a while, then drew me up close by the jacket, jerked his thumb warningly to the left-hand desk and whispered into my ear:

"Athanasius! Your departed father was my best friend. I want to save you, Athanasius! You must tell me everything about the Countess. – Do you hear: everything."

I had no idea what that was supposed to mean. "What do you mean: you want to save me?" I asked out loud.

The club-foot stamped angrily. The Police Inspector went ashen with hatred. Drew up his lip. Waited. – I knew he was about to jump at me again (his system of surprise reminded me of Wassertrum); and I waited too – saw a goat's face, the owner of the club-foot, loom up warily from behind the desk – –, then the Police Inspector suddenly shrieked at me:

"Murderer!"

Astonishment rendered me speechless.

The goat's face retreated sullenly behind the desk.

The Police Inspector also seemed disconcerted by my calm, but he concealed it skillfully by pulling up a chair and instructing me to take a seat.

"So you refuse to provide me the information I require about the Countess, Herr Pernath?"

"I cannot provide it, Herr Police Inspector, at least not in the sense you anticipate. First of all, I know no one by the name of Savioli, and then I am firmly convinced that it is sheer slander if the Countess is said to deceive her husband."

"Are you prepared to swear to that?"

My breath caught. "Yes! By all means!"

"Good. Hm."

There was a long pause as the Police Inspector seemed to make an effort to think.

When he looked at me again there was a farcical strain of distress on his ugly mug. I had to think of Charousek when he began in a tear-choked voice:

"You can tell me, Athanasius – me, your father's old friend– I who carried you in my arms" – I could hardly bite back my laughter: he was at most ten years older than I – "it was self-defense, wasn't it, Athanasius?"

The goat's face reappeared.

"What was self-defense?" I asked uncomprehending.

"The business with – – – *Zottmann*!" the Police Inspector shouted a name into my face.

The word caught me like a dagger thrust: Zottmann! Zottmann! The watch! The name Zottmann was engraved on the watch.

I felt all the blood rush to my heart: that monster Wassertrum had given me the watch to frame me for the murder!

At once the Police Inspector shed his mask, bared his teeth and screwed up his eyes.

"Then you confess to the murder, Pernath?"

"It's all a mistake, a terrible mistake. For God's sake listen to me. I can explain it to you, Herr Police Inspector – –!" I screamed.

"Are you ready to tell me everything concerning the Countess now?" he interrupted me quickly. "I advise you: it will improve your situation."

"I can say no more than I already have: the Countess is innocent."

He gritted his teeth and turned to the goat's face:

"Write! – So: Pernath confesses to the murder of the insurance clerk Karl Zottmann."

I was seized by insensate fury.

"You police rotter!" I bellowed. "How dare you?!"

I looked around me for a heavy object.

A moment later two policemen had grabbed and handcuffed me.

Now the Police Inspector puffed himself up like a cock on a dungheap:

"And the watch here?" – Suddenly he held up the dented watch. – "Was the unfortunate Zottmann still alive when you robbed him, or not?"

I was quite calm again, and stated in a clear voice:

"The junk dealer Aaron Wassertrum gave me the watch this morning – as a present."

A whinny of laughter burst out, and I saw the club foot and the felt slipper perform a dance of delight together under the desk.

– – –

RACK

Hands bound, a gendarme with fixed bayonet behind me, I was marched through the lamp-lit evening streets.

Catcalling throngs of street urchins trailed along to the left and right of us, women tore open the windows, threatened with ladles and cursed after me.

From afar I saw the massive stone cube of the courthouse drawing near, and the inscription on its pediment:

"The scourge of justice is
the shield of the law-abiding."

Then I was swallowed up by an enormous gate and a vestibule which stank of the kitchen.

A bearded man with a saber, uniform jacket and cap, barefoot, his legs clad in long johns tied together around the ankles, stood up, put away the coffee-grinder which he had been holding between his knees, and ordered me to undress.

Then he searched my pockets, removed everything he found there, and asked me whether I had – bedbugs.

When I replied in the negative, he took the rings from my fingers and said, good, I could put on my clothes again.

I was led up several stories and along corridors in which large, grey, locked chests stood here and there in the window recesses.

Iron doors with bolts and tiny barred openings, over each one a gas flame, stretched down along the wall in unbroken sequence. A colossal, soldierly-looking warder – the first honest face in hours – unlocked one of the doors, shoved me into a noisome, dark, closet-like opening and locked the door behind me.

Standing in utter darkness, I groped my way around.

My knee struck a tin pail.

At last – the space was so cramped that I could barely turn around – I hit upon a doorknob and stood in – a cell.

Two cots with straw mattresses against each wall.

The aisle between them only a step across.

A square meter of barred window high up in the far wall admitted the dull shimmer of the night sky.

Unbearable heat, air fouled by the smell of old clothes filled the room.

Once my eyes had adjusted to the darkness, I saw that people in grey convicts' garb sat on three of the cots – the fourth was empty – their elbows propped on their knees and their faces buried in their hands.

No one said a word.

I sat down on the empty bed and waited. Waited. Waited. One hour.

Two – three hours!

Every time I thought I heard a step outside, I gave a start:

Now, now they were coming to fetch me, to take me to the examining magistrate.

Every time it was an illusion. Again and again the steps faded away down the corridor.

I tore open my collar – thought I would suffocate.

I heard one prisoner after the other stretch out with a groan.

"Can't that window up there be opened?" I asked out loud, desperately, into the darkness. I almost took fright at the sound of my own voice.

"Can't", came the surly reply from one of the straw mattresses.

Nonetheless I groped my hand along the narrow wall: a board ran across at chest height – – – two pitchers of water – scraps of breadcrust.

I scrambled up with an effort, clung to the bars and pressed my face to the cracks in the window to catch at least a breath of fresh air.

– – –

I stood like that until my knees trembled. Monotonous, black-grey fog before my eyes.

The cold iron bars sweated.

It must be nearly midnight.

I heard snoring behind me. Only one seemed unable to sleep: he tossed and turned on the straw and groaned softly now and then.

Wouldn't the morning come at last?! There! The clock struck again.

I counted with trembling lips:

One, two, three! – Thank God, only a few more hours, and the dawn would come. It went on striking:

Four? Five? – The sweat broke out on my brow. – Six! – Seven – – – it was *eleven* o'clock.

– – –

Slowly I put my thoughts in order:

Wassertrum had pinned the watch of the missing Zottmann on me in order to frame me for a murder– thus he himself must be the murderer; how else could he have gotten hold of the watch? If he had found the corpse somewhere and then robbed it, surely he would have claimed the thousand gulden reward which had been offered for the discovery of the missing man. – But this could not be the case: the posters still hung on the street corners, as I had distinctly seen on my way to prison. – – –

It was obvious that the junk dealer must have turned me in.

Likewise: that he was working hand in glove with the Police Inspector, at least as far as Angelina was concerned. Why else interrogate me about Savioli?

203

On the other hand, this suggested that Wassertrum *hadn't
yet* gotten his hands on Angelina's letters.

I pondered. – – – –

All at once everything appeared before me with appalling clarity, as if I had seen it with my own eyes.

Yes, it had to be: Wassertrum, suspecting that my iron
casket contained evidence, had pocketed it as he was rummaging through my apartment with his police accomplices
– was unable to open it immediately, as I carried the key on
my person, and – – – might this very moment be attempting
to force it open in his lair.

In a frenzy of despair I shook at the bars, pictured
Wassertrum rummaging through Angelina's letters. – –

If only I could give word to Charousek so that he could
at least warn Savioli in time!

For a moment I clung to the hope that the news of my ar-
rest must already have spread through the Jewish Town like
wildfire, and I trusted in Charousek as in a guardian angel.
The junk dealer had no chance against his infernal cunning.
"I'll have him by the throat the very moment he goes for Dr.
Savioli's", Charousek had said once before.

The very next minute I lost faith in everything, and wild
fear seized me: what if Charousek came too late?

Then Angelina was lost.

– – –

I bit my lips until they bled, and clawed my breast in remorse at not having burned the letters at once – – – I swore
to myself that I would rid this world of Wassertrum the very
hour I was set free again.

Whether I died by my own hand or on the gallows –
what did it matter to me!

The magistrate would believe my words if I could convince him of the story with the watch, tell him of Wassertrum's threats – I did not doubt that for a moment.

Surely I would be free again by the morrow; at least the court would have to have Wassertrum arrested as well on suspicion of murder.

I counted the hours and prayed for them to pass more quickly; stared out into the blackish haze.

After an unspeakably long time it finally began to grow brighter, and like a dark fleck at first, then clearer and clearer, an enormous copper face emerged from the fog: the face of an old tower-clock. But the *hands were missing* – putting me to the rack again.

Then it struck five.

I heard the prisoners wake and chat, yawning, in Bohemian.

One voice seemed familiar to me; I turned around, climbed down from the shelf and – saw pock-marked Loisa sitting on the cot across from mine and staring at me in astonishment.

The other two, insolent-faced fellows, regarded me disparagingly.

"Embezzler, huh?" the one asked his comrade under his breath, nudging him with his elbow.

The other replied in a scornful mutter, rummaged in his straw mattress, took out a piece of black paper and laid it on the floor.

Then he poured a little water onto it from the pitcher, knelt down, mirrored his face in it and combed his hair over his forehead with his fingers.

Whereupon he dried the paper with tender care and hid it under the cot again.

"Pan Pernath, Pan Pernath", Loisa murmured to himself the whole time wide-eyed like someone seeing a ghost.

"The chentlemen arre acqvainted, I see", said the uncombed one, noticing this, in the stilted dialect of the Czech Viennese, half-bowing to me mockingly. "Perrmit me

to intrroduce myself: Vóssatka my name. Black Vóssatka. –
– –Arrson", he added proudly an octave deeper.

The coiffured one spat between his teeth, looked at me
for a while contemptuously, pointed at his own chest and
said laconically: "Burglary".

I was silent.

"Vell, Herr Count, vat zey got on you?" asked the Viennese after a pause.

I thought for a moment, then said calmly: "Robbery and
murder."

Both leapt up in astonishment, the scorn on their faces
gave way to boundless esteem, and they cried as one:

"Reshpect, reshpect."

When they saw that I took no notice of them they withdrew into the corner and spoke in whispers.

Only once did the coiffured one get up, come over to me,
silently scrutinize the muscles of my upper arms and return
to his friend, shaking his head.

"You must also be here on suspicion of murdering
Zottmann?" I asked Loisa quietly.

He nodded. "Yes, some time now."

A few more hours passed.

I closed my eyes and pretended to sleep.

"Herr Pernath. Herr Pernath!" I suddenly heard Loisa's
voice, very softly.

"Yes?" – – – I pretended to wake up.

"Herr Pernath? Please excuse me – please – please, do
you know what Rosina's doing? – Is she at home?" the poor
boy stammered. I felt no end of pity for him, the way his inflamed eyes clung to my lips and his hands clenched with
excitement.

"She's fine. She – she's a waitress now at – – the 'altes
Ungelt'", I lied.

– – –

Three prisoners silently carried in tin pots of hot sausage broth on a board and set down three of them in the cell; several hours later the bolt gave another clatter, and the warder took me to the examining magistrate.

My knees trembled in anticipation as we went up and down the stairs.

"Do you think it's possible I could be released today?" I asked the warder anxiously.

I saw him suppress a smile, pityingly. "Hm. Today? Hm – – my God – anything's possible." –

I went ice cold.

Once again I read a porcelain name-plate on a door and a name:

> KARL BARON VON LEISETRETER
> Examining Magistrate

Once again an unadorned room and two desks with yard-high hutches.

A tall old man with a white, parted beard, black frock-coat, thick red lips, creaking boots.

"You are Herr Pernath?"

"Yes."

"Lapidary?"

"Yes."

"Cell no. 70?"

"Yes."

"Suspected of the murder of Zottmann?"

"I beg of you, Herr Magistrate – –"

"Suspected of the murder of Zottmann?"

"Probably. At least I think so. But – –"

"Confessed?"

"What ought I to confess, Herr Magistrate, I'm innocent!"

207

"Confessed?"

"No."

"Then I order that you be confined pending trial. – Take the man out, warder."

"Please, hear me out, Herr Magistrate – I absolutely must be home today. I have important business to take care of – –"

Someone bleated behind the second desk.

The Herr Baron chuckled. –

"Take the man out, warden."

– – –

Day crept after day, week after week, and still I sat in the cell.

At twelve o'clock every day we were permitted to go down to the prison yard and walk in a circle on the wet ground for forty minutes with the other remand prisoners and convicts, two by two.

We were forbidden to speak to each other.

In the middle of the yard stood a bare, dying tree with an oval glass picture of the Virgin Mary half swallowed by its bark.

Scraggly privet shrubs grew against the walls, their leaves nearly black from falling soot.

On all sides the barred cell-windows of the cells, now and then a putty-grey face with bloodless lips staring down.

Then we went back up into the familiar crypt for bread, water and sausage broth and, on Sundays, to spoiled lentils.

I was interrogated only one more time:

Were any witnesses present when "Herr" Wassertrum supposedly gave me the watch?

"Yes: Herr Schemajah Hillel – – that is – no" (I remembered that he had not been there) – – "but Herr Charousek – no, he wasn't there either."

"In short then: no one was there?"

"No, no one was there, Herr Magistrate."

Once again the bleat from behind the desk and again the: "Take the man out, warder!"

My anxiety about Angelina had given way to a dull resignation: the time to tremble for her had passed. Either Wassertrum's vengeful scheme had long since succeeded, or Charousek had intervened, I told myself.

But fear for Mirjam almost drove me mad.

I pictured her waiting hour after hour for the miracle to be renewed – running out early in the morning when the baker came and searching the bread with trembling hands – perhaps swooning with fear for my sake.

Often it shook me out of my sleep at night, and I climbed onto the shelf and stared up at the copper face of the tower-clock, consumed by the desire that my thoughts might reach Hillel and cry into his ear: help Mirjam and release her from the racking torment of hoping for a miracle.

Then I threw myself back down onto the straw and held my breath until my chest nearly burst – to summon up the image of my double before me so that I could send him to comfort her.

And once he did appear next to my bed with the letters: "Chabrat Zereh Aur Bocher" in mirror writing on his breast, and I wanted to cry out with joy that everything would be set right again, but the ground swallowed him up before I could command him to appear before Mirjam. – – – –

To have no news whatsoever from my friends!

Was it forbidden to receive letters, I asked my cellmates. They did not know.

They had never gotten any – but then, there was no one to write them, they said.

The warder promised me to ask if the occasion arose. – –

My nails were bitten to the quick, and my hair was unkempt, for we had neither scissors, comb nor brush.

Nor water for bathing.

I fought down an almost perpetual nausea, for the sausage broth was seasoned with soda, not salt. A prison regulation to "curtail the sexual urge". – –

Time passed in frightful grey monotony.

Revolved in a circle like a wheel of racking pain.

Then there were those moments we all knew, when one or the other of us would suddenly jump up and pace back and forth for hours like a wild animal, only to collapse onto the cot again, broken, and again, in a stupor, wait – wait – wait.

When evening came, the bedbugs trooped along the walls like ants, and I asked myself in astonishment why the fellow with the saber and the long johns had so conscientiously searched me for insects.

Did the provincial court fear the emergence of a *hybrid* of alien insect species?

On Wednesday mornings, as a rule, came a pig's head with a slouchhat and twitching trouser legs, the prison doctor Dr. Rosenblatt, and satisfied himself that all were bursting with health.

And if anyone had complaints, no matter what they were, he prescribed – zinc-ointment to rub on the chest.

Once the president of the provincial court came – a tall, perfumed high-society scoundrel with the basest vices written all over his face, and looked to see whether – everything was as it should be: "dat no vone's hengt himself yet", as the coiffured one put it.

When I went up to him with a request, he leaped behind the warder and pointed a revolver at me. – What did I want, he screamed at me.

Were there letters for me? I asked politely. Instead of a reply I got a shove in the chest from Herr Dr. Rosenblatt, who took to his heels forthwith. The Herr President withdrew as well and sneered through the aperture in the door:

I'd do better to confess to the murder. Otherwise I'd get no more letters in this lifetime.

– – –

I had long since grown used to the bad air and the heat, and shivered constantly. Even when the sun shone.

Two of the prisoners had already changed several times, but I paid little notice to that. This week a pickpocket and a highwayman were brought in, the next week it was a counterfeiter or a fence.

What I had experienced one day was forgotten the next.

All external circumstances paled before the gnawing fear for Mirjam.

One incident alone made a deeper impression upon me – now and then it pursued me into my dreams in distorted form.

I was standing on the shelf to stare up at the sky when I suddenly felt a sharp object poke me in the hip. When I looked, I saw that it was the file, which had bored its way into my coat lining. It must have been there for some time, otherwise the man in the vestibule would surely have noticed it.

I pulled it out and tossed it carelessly onto my straw mattress.

When I climbed back down, it was gone, and I had no doubt that only Loisa could have taken it.

Several days later he was removed from the cell and taken to the floor below.

It would not do to have two remand prisoners accused of the same crime kept in a cell together, like him and me, the warden said.

With all my heart I hoped that the poor boy would manage to free himself with the help of the file.

May

When I asked the date – the sun shone as hotly as in mid-summer, and the weary tree in the yard had put out a few buds – the warder was silent at first, then whispered to me that it was the 15th of May. Really he was not allowed to tell me, for it was forbidden to speak with the prisoners – in particular, those who had not yet confessed had to be kept in the dark about the time.

I had been in prison for three whole months, then, still without news from the world outside.

– – –

When evening came, the faint sounds of a piano drifted through the barred window, which was now open on warm days.

The daughter of the caretaker was playing, a convict told me. – –

Day and night I dreamed of Mirjam.

How could she be faring?!

Now and then I had the comforting sensation that my thoughts had made their way to her to stand at her bedside as she slept and lay a soothing hand on her brow.

Then again, in moments of hopelessness, when one after the other my cellmates were taken to be interrogated – all but me – I was choked by the dull fear that she could be long dead.

Then I asked fate whether she was still alive or not, sick or well, and the number of a handful of straws I tore from the mattress was to give me the answer.

And almost every time "it turned out badly", and I delved within me for a glimpse of the future – attempted to outwit my soul, which concealed the secret from me, with the apparently unrelated question of whether a day would ever come when I could be happy and laugh again.

In these cases the oracle's reply was always affirmative, and then for an hour I would be glad and joyous.

As a plant secretly germinates and grows, a deep, profound love of Mirjam had gradually woken within me, and it baffled me that I could have sat with her and spoken to her so often without realizing it at the time.

In such moments the tremulous desire that she might think of me with the same feelings often grew to a presentiment of certainty, and then when I heard a footstep in the corridor outside I almost feared that I might be fetched and released and that my dream would fade away to nothingness in the crude reality of the outside world.

During my long imprisonment my ears had grown so sharp that I could hear the faintest sound.

Each nightfall I heard a carriage driving in the distance, and I racked my brains as to who might be sitting inside.

There was something strangely incongruous in the thought that there were people out there who could do as they pleased – who could move freely and go here and there and yet did not experience it as indescribable exhilaration.

That I too could ever be fortunate enough to wander along the streets in the sunlight – – I was no longer capable of imagining it.

The day I held Angelina in my arms seemed to belong to a long-fled existence – I thought back to it with the faint melancholy which steals over one upon opening a book and discovering dried flowers once held by the love of one's youth.

Did old Zwakh still sit with Vrieslander and Prokop in "Ungelt" evening after evening, addling the brain of dried-up Eulalia?

No, it was May – the time when he traveled the provincial towns with his marionette theater, playing Sir Bluebeard on green meadows outside the gates.

– – –

I sat alone in my cell. Vóssatka, the arsonist, for a week my only companion, had been taken to the magistrate a few hours before.

This interrogation lasted an unusually long time.

There. The iron bolt clattered at the door. And Vóssatka burst in with a radiant face, tossed a bundle of clothes on the cot and began to change at lightning speed.

Piece by piece he tossed the convict's uniform onto the floor with a curse.

"Dey couldn't prove a ting on me, de hallodri. – Arson! My eye!" he pulled down his bottom lid with one index finger. "Black Vóssatka vasn't born yesterday. – It was de vind, said I. And stuck by my story. Dey can lock up him if dey catch him – Herr von Vind. – Vell, servus till tonight, den. Dey'll paint de down red. At Loisitschek." – He spread out his arms and danced a "G'strampfter". – "But once in life de May-hay does bloom." With a whack he jammed a stiff hat with a little blue-speckled jay feather onto his skull. – "Yeah, right, you'll be inter'sted to hear, Count: wanna know somethin' new? A frienda yours, Loisa flew de coop. – I just heard from de hallodri up dere. Las' mont' already – around de las' of de mont' he made a break for it, an' by now – pbhuit" – he drummed his fingers on the back of his hand – "he's long gone." –

"Aha, the file", I thought to myself with a smile.

"Vell denn, dey'll be calling you soon enough, Count" the arsonist gave me his hand companionably, "and you'll get out one a dese days. – And if you ever don't have no money, just go to Loisitschek and ask for Black Vóssatka. – All de girls know me dere. So! Well den, servus, Count. My bleasure."

Just as he went out the door the warder pushed a new remand prisoner into the cell.

At the very first glance I recognized him as the bounder with the soldier's cap who had stood next to me in the archway on Hahnpassgasse during the downpour. A pleasant surprise! Perhaps he might know something about Hillel and Zwakh and the others?

I wanted to start questioning him at once, but to my great surprise he laid a finger to his mouth with a mysterious mien and motioned me to be quiet.

He did not come to life until the door was locked from the outside and the warder's steps had faded away down the hall.

My heart pounded with excitement.

What could that mean?

Did he know me, and what did he want?

The first thing the bounder did was sit down and take off his left boot.

Then he pulled a plug from the heel with his teeth, took a small bent iron plate from the resulting cavity, tore off the sole of the shoe, which apparently was only loosely secured, and handed both to me with a look of pride. –

All that at lightning speed and without paying the slightest attention to my excited questions.

"So! Greetings from Herr Charousek."

I was too staggered to say a word.

"Ya jes' needa take a bitta iron and break up de sole at night. Or whenever no one's lookin'. – I's hollow inside, see", – explained the bounder with a look of superiority, "and dere you'll find yerself a letter from Herr Charousek."

In the excess of my delight I fell on the bounder's neck, and tears poured from my eyes.

He fended me off gently and said with reproach:

"You'll hafta pull yerself together, Herr von Pernath! I don't got myself time to lose a minute. Dey can figure out any time dat I'm in de wrong cell. Franzl an' I switched numbers on each other down at de porder."

I must have made a very stupid face, for the bounder went on:

"Don't matter if you don't understand. I'm here, and dat's dat!".

"Tell me", I interrupted him, "tell me, Herr – – Herr – – –"

"Wenzel", the bounder assisted me, "dey call myself de Han'some Wenzel".

"Tell me, Wenzel, what news is there of the archivist Hillel, and how is his daughter?"

"Dere ain't no time for dat", Handsome Wenzel interrupted me impatiently. "I can get myself thrown outta here any minute. – So: I'm here 'cause I confessed to a robbery 'specially – –"

"What, Wenzel, you committed a robbery just for my sake, just to reach me?" I asked, shocked.

The bounder shook his head contemptuously: "If I'da *committed* a robbery for real, I ain't *gonna* confess it. Whaddaya take me for!?"

I was beginning to understand – the fine fellow had used a ruse to smuggle Charousek's letter to me in prison.

"So! Firstavall" – he made an extremely important face –" I hafta give you a lesson in ebilebsy".

"In what?"

"In ebilebsy! – So look sharp and dontcha missa thing – Look here: firsht you puts some spit in yer choppers " – he puffed up his cheeks and moved them back and forth as if rinsing out his mouth – "den ya froth at de mouth, like dis"– and that he did. With revolting realism. "And den ya clench yer fists. – Den ya pop yer eyes out" – he squinted appallingly – "and den – dis is de hard part – you let outta kinda scream halfway. See, like dis: buh-buh-buh – and at de same time ya keel yerself over." – He fell to the floor full length, rocking the building, and said, getting to his feet:

"Dat's de nacherl ebilebsy de way de late Dr. Hulbert learned us in de 'Badalyon'."

"Yes, yes, it's a perfect imitation", I admitted, "but what is the point of it all?"

"To throw yerself outta de cell, first off!" explained Handsome Wenzel. "Dat Dr. Rosenblatt's an ox! You could come to him wid no head on yer shoulders, he'd still say: de man's fit as a fiddle! But he's got a beastly reshpect of ebilebsy. If ya can pull it off, you're in de sick ward like dat. – – And breaking outta dere is child's play" – he assumed an air of profound mystery – "Ya see, da bars of da window are sawed open and jest stuck together with dirt. – It's isself a Batalyon secret! – Den you jes needa look sharp a few nights, and when ya see a noose lowering down to de window from de roof, you take out de bars quiet like, so no one hears, stick yer shoulders through the noose, and we pull you up on de roof and let you down in de street on de oder side – an dat's dat."

"Why should I break out of prison?" I protested shyly. "After all, I'm innocent."

"Dat ain't no reason not to break out!" Handsome Wenzel objected, goggling in astonishment.

It took all my eloquence to talk him out of the daring plan which, he said, was the result of a "Battalion" decision.

It was inconceivable to him that I could turn down the "gift of God" and preferred to wait until I was freed on my own.

"At any rate, I thank you and your fine comrades most heartily", I said, touched, and shook his hand. "When these hard times of mine are over the first thing I do will be to show you my appreciation."

"Ain't no need", Wenzel demurred amiably. "If ya buy a few glasses a 'pils', we'll be glad to take you up on it, but dat's about it. Pan Charousek, who's now de dreasurer of de Batayon, he already told us about yer being a secret bene-factor. Anything I should tell him when I get out in a few days?"

"Yes, please", I said quickly, "tell him to go to Hillel and let him know how greatly I fear for the health of his daughter Mirjam. Herr Hillel must not let her out of his sight. – Will you remember the name? *Hillel*!"

"Hirrel?"

"No: Hillel."

"Hiller?"

"No: Hill-el."

Wenzel nearly twisted his tongue on the name, impossible for a Czech, but at last he mastered it with savage grimaces.

"And then one more thing: Herr Charousek should also – I entreat him so – do all that is in his power to look after the 'genteel lady' – he'll know who is meant."

"You probl'y mean de fine floozy what had de fling wit de Neemetz – Dr. Sapoli? – Well, she got herself a divorce and up an' left with her kid and de Sapoli."

"Are you sure of that?"

I felt my voice tremble. As much as I rejoiced for Angelina's sake – still my heart contracted.

How many cares I had borne for her sake, and now – – – I was forgotten.

Perhaps she thought I really was a murderer.

A bitter taste rose in my gorge.

With the delicacy strangely characteristic of hard-bitten people in all things having to do with love, the bounder seemed to sense how I felt, for he looked away shyly and did not reply.

"And do you know how Herr Hillel's daughter, Fräulein Mirjam, is faring? Do you know her?" I choked out.

"Mirjam? Mirjam?" – Wenzel wrinkled his brow though-fully. – "Mirjam? – Is she at Loisitschek's nights?"

I smiled in spite of myself. "No. Certainly not."

"Then I don't know her", Wenzel said dryly.

We were silent for a while.

Maybe there is something about her in the letter, I hoped.

"Dat de debbil came for Wassertrum", Wenzel began again suddenly, "you musta heard about dat, right?"

I jumped up, horrified.

"Yessir." – Wenzel pointed to his throat. – "Murxi, mur-xi! I'm telling you, dat was a grisly sight fer ya. When dey broke into his store, 'cause he hadn't showed his face a few days, I was de first one in, natcherly – what else! – And dere he sat, dat Wassertrum, in a grotty armchair, his chest fulla blood and his eyes like glass. – – – Ya know, I'm as hard as dey come, but my head took a turn, I tell you, and I thought I'd go out like a li-ight. Over an' over I hadda tell myself: Wenzel, I said to myself, Wenzel, don't work yerself up, it's jest a dead Yid.' He had a file sticking in his throat, and de shop was all dopsy-durvey. – Burglary, 'course."

"The file! The file!" I felt my breath go cold with horror. – The file! So it had found its way after all!

"And I know who it was", Wenzel went on under his breath after a pause. "None odder dan pocky Loiso, I tell ya. – See, I found his pocket knife on de floor of de shop, and I put it away quick so de police don't find it. – He got into de shop through an unnerground passage – –"

All at once he broke off, listened intently for a few seconds, then threw himself down on the cot and began to snore appallingly.

A moment later the padlock clattered, and the warder came in and looked at me suspiciously.

I made a poker face, and Wenzel was barely to be woken.

After many more snorts he straightened up with a yawn and staggered out drunk with sleep, followed by the warder.

– – –

Feverish with anticipation, I unfolded Charousek's letter and read:

"May 12.

My poor, dear friend and benefactor!

Week after week I have waited for you to be freed – in vain – have tried all possible means to gather material to exonerate you, but found none.

I asked the examining magistrate to expedite the proceedings, but was told every time that he could do nothing – it was the public prosecutor's affair, not his. Red tape!

But, just an hour ago, I managed a coup from which I expect *great results*: I learned that Jaromir sold Wassertrum a golden pocket watch he found in his brother Loisa's bed after his arrest.

At 'Loisitschek', which, as you know, is frequented by the police, rumor has it that the watch of the supposedly murdered Zottmann – whose corpse still has not turned up, incidentally – was found in *your* apartment as a corpus delicti. I figured out the rest myself: Wassertrum et cetera!

I spoke to Jaromir at once, gave him 1000 florins – – –"
I lowered the letter, and tears of joy filled my eyes: only Angelina could have given Charousek that sum. Neither Zwakh nor Prokop nor Vrieslander had that much money. – So she had not forgotten me after all! – I read on:

"– gave him 1000 florins and promised him 2000 florins more if he goes to the police with me immediately and admits that he stole this watch from his brother at home and sold it.

But by the time this can be done, this letter will already be on its way to you, in Wenzel's hands. There is not enough time.

But rest assured: it *will* be done. *Today.* I swear it to you.

I do not doubt for a moment that Loisa committed the murder and that the watch is Zottmann's.

If, against all expectations, that should not be the case – well, then Jaromir knows what he must do: *at any rate he will identify it as the one found in your apartment.*

So: persevere, and do not despair! The day of your liberation may be at hand.

Yet will a day come when we see each other again?

I do not know.

I am almost inclined to say: I believe not, for my end is rapidly approaching, and I must be on my guard lest my last hour take me by surprise.

But rest assured: we *will* see each other again.

If not in *this* life and not, like the dead, in *that* life, but on the day when time is sundered – when, as it is written in the Bible, the LORD will spit out *those* from his mouth who were neither hot nor cold, but lukewarm. – – –

Do not be surprised at my words! I have never spoken to you of these things, and once when you mentioned the word 'Cabala' I evaded your questions, but – I know what I know.

Perhaps you understand what I mean, and if not, I beg of you, strike what I have said from your memory. – – Once, in my delirium, I thought – I saw a sign on your breast. – It may be that I was dreaming with open eyes.

If you really do not understand me, take it that I have had certain experiences – inwardly! – virtually from my childhood on, which have taken me on a strange path – realizations which cannot be reconciled with the teachings of medicine and which, thank God, medicine will never know – and hopefully will never learn.

But I have never let myself be hoodwinked by science, whose loftiest goal is to furnish a – 'waiting room' it would be better to demolish.

But enough of that.

Instead I will tell you what has happened in the meantime:

By the end of April Wassertrum had reached the point when my suggestion began to take effect.

I could tell by the way he constantly gesticulated and talked loudly to himself on the street.

That sort of thing is an unmistakable sign that a person's thoughts are banding together to take their master by storm.

Then he bought a notebook and made notes.

He wrote!

He wrote! I could laugh! He *wrote*.

And then he went to a solicitor. Below, outside the house, I knew what he was doing up there: he was drawing up his will.

It never crossed my mind that he would make me his heir. I probably would have gotten the St. Vitus dance out of sheer delight if it had occurred to me.

He made me his heir because I was the only person in the world he could make amends to, as he thought. Conscience outwitted him.

Or perhaps it was the hope that I would bless him once his death suddenly rendered me a millionaire by his grace, thus making up for the curse he was compelled to hear from my lips in your room.

Thus my suggestion worked threefold.

Hilarious, that in secret he did believe in retribution beyond the grave, after making such efforts to talk himself out of it all his life.

But all the oh-so-clever are like that; you can tell from the frenzy they fly into when you say it to their faces. They feel caught out.

From the instant Wassertrum left the solicitor, I never let him out of my sight.

At night I listened at the shutters of his shop, for the decision could come at any minute. –

I believe I would have heard it through the walls, that yearned-for smack when he pulled the cork from the vial of poison.

Another hour, perhaps, and my life's work would have been complete.

Then an interloper stepped in and murdered him. With a file.

Let Wenzel tell you the details, it is too bitter for me to write all that down.

Call it superstition – but when I saw that blood had been *spilled* – the things in the shop were stained with it – it seemed to me that his soul had escaped.

Something within me – a keen, infallible instinct – told me that it is not the same whether a person dies by a stranger's hand or by his own: that Wassertrum should have taken his blood with him into the ground, and only then would my mission have been fulfilled. – Now that it has turned out differently, I feel like an outcast, a tool found wanting in the hand of the Angel of Death.

But I shall not rebel. *My hatred is of the kind which reaches beyond the grave,* and I have my own blood yet, which I can spill as I wish, that it may follow on the heels of his into the realm of shadows. – – –

Since they buried Wassertrum I sit out in the cemetery with him every day, listening to my heart for counsel.

I believe I know already, but I will wait until the inner word which speaks to me grows clear as a spring. – We human beings are impure, and often it takes long fasting and vigils before we understand the whispers of our soul. – – –

Last week the court informed me officially that Wassertrum had made me his universal heir.

I need hardly assure you, Herr Pernath, that I will not touch a kreuzer of it for myself. – I will see to it that I give 'him' no bargaining point for 'over there'.

I will auction off the houses he owned, the objects which he touched will be burned, and of the resulting money and money value, one third will pass to you after my death. –

In my mind's eye I see you jump up and protest, but I can reassure you. What you will receive belongs to you by right with interest and compound interest. I have long known that Wassertrum, years ago, robbed your father and his family of everything – only now do I have the documents to prove it.

The second third will be distributed among the twelve members of the 'Battalion' who knew Dr. Hulbert personally. I want each one of them to become rich and gain an entrée to Prague's 'high society'.

The last third belongs in equal part to the next seven cutthroats in the country who are released for lack of evidence.

I am duty bound to that scandalization of public morals."

So. That would seem to be all.

And now, my dear, dear friend, farewell, and think now and then of

Your

sincerely grateful
Innocenz Charousek."

Shaken to the core, I put down the letter.

I could not rejoice in the news of my impending release.

Charousek! Poor man! He took an interest in my fate like a brother. Simply because I had once given him a hundred guldens. If only I could shake his hand again!

I felt: yes, he was right: the day would never come.

I saw him before me: his flickering eyes, the consumptive shoulders, the high, noble brow.

Perhaps everything would have turned out quite differently if a helping hand had reached out sooner toward this withered life.

I read the letter one more time.

How much method there was in Charousek's madness! Was he even mad at all?

I was almost ashamed to have harbored the thought for a single moment.

Did not his allusions say enough? He was a person like Hillel, like Mirjam, like myself; a person swayed by his own soul – led through the wild gorges and ravines of life up into the snowy summits of an undiscovered land.

He, who had schemed murder all his life, was he not purer than any of those who wrinkle their noses and pretend to follow the rote-learned commandments of an unknown, mythical prophet?

He kept the commandment dictated to him by an overpowering urge, with no thought of a "reward" here or in the beyond.

What he had done, was it anything but the most pious fulfillment of duty in the deepest sense of the word?

"Cowardly, devious, murderous, sick, a problematic – a criminal nature" – I all but heard the rabble's inevitable judgment of him, if they came to shine their blind stable-lanterns into his soul – this slavering mob, which will never, ever understand that the poisonous autumn crocus is a thousand times more beautiful and noble than the practical chives. – – –

Again the bolt slid back outside, and I heard a person being thrust in.

I did not even turn around, so full was I with the impression the letter had made.

There was not a word about Angelina, nothing of Hillel.

Of course: Charousek must have written in great haste, as I could tell from his handwriting.

Would I be passed another secret letter from him?

I set my hopes on the morrow, on the prisoners' walk in the yard. – That would be the easiest opportunity for someone from the "Battalion" to slip me something.

A soft voice startled me out of my meditations.

"Sir, would you permit me to introduce myself? My name is Laponder. Amadeus Laponder."

I turned around.

A short, slight, still quite young man in elegant clothing, but, like all remand prisoners, without a hat, bowed to me quite correctly.

He was smooth-shaven like an actor, and his large, pale-green gleaming, almond-shaped eyes had the peculiar quality of seeming not to see me, however directly they were focused upon me. – There was something like – abstraction in them.

I murmured my name, bowed too, and was about to turn away again, but for a long time I was unable to take my eyes from the man, so exotic did he seem with the perpetual idol-like smile which the upturned corners of his finely-curved lips constantly imprinted upon his face.

He resembled a Chinese Buddha figurine of rose quartz, with his unwrinkled, transparent skin, the girlishly slender nose and the delicate nostrils.

"Amadeus Laponder, Amadeus Laponder", I repeated to myself.

"What could his crime have been?"

MOON

"Have you been interrogated yet?" I asked after a while.

"I was just now. – Hopefully I won't have to inconvenience you here much longer", Herr Laponder replied pleasantly.

"Poor devil!" I thought to myself. "He has no idea what is in store for a remand prisoner."

I decided to break it to him gradually:

"The first few days are the worst; after a while you get used to sitting still." – – –

He adopted an attentive expression.

Pause.

"Did your interrogation last very long, Herr Laponder?"

He smiled distractedly:

"No. I was only asked whether I confessed to the crime, and had to sign the statement."

"You signed a confession?" I blurted out.

"Precisely."

He said it as if it were self-evident.

It can't be anything serious, I surmised, if he shows no sign of agitation. Probably a challenge to a duel or something of the sort.

"Alas, I've been here for so long that it seems a whole lifetime to me" – I sighed in spite of myself, and at once he made a sympathetic face. "I wish for your sake that you won't need to go through the same thing, Herr Laponder. As far as I can see, you'll soon be free again."

"It all depends how you look at it", he replied tranquilly, but it sounded like a veiled double entendre.

"You don't think so?" I asked with a smile. He shook his head.

"How do you mean that? What have you done that was so very terrible? Forgive me, Herr Laponder, I ask not from curiosity – only out of sympathy."

He hesitated a moment, then said without batting an eye: "Sex murder."

I felt as if he had clubbed me over the head.

Filled with revulsion and horror, I could not utter a sound.

He seemed to notice this and looked away discreetly, but not the slightest shift of expression on his smiling automaton face revealed injury at the sudden change in my manner.

Without exchanging another word, we gazed past each other mutely. – – –

When I went to bed at nightfall, he followed my example at once, undressed, fastidiously hung his clothes on a nail in the wall, stretched out and, to judge from his calm, deep breaths, fell fast asleep immediately.

I was unable to rest all night.

The constant awareness of having such a monster in my immediate vicinity and having to breathe the same air as he was so awful and agitating that the impressions of the day, Charousek's letter and all the new things I had experienced receded far into the background.

I lay so as to keep an eye on the murderer at all times; I could not have stood to know that he was behind my back.

The shimmer of the moon dully suffused the cell, and I could see that Laponder lay there motionless, almost rigid.

His features had taken on a corpse-like appearance, and the parted lips heightened this impression.

For hours on end he did not even change position.

Only long after midnight, when a thin moonbeam fell onto his face, did a slight unrest seize him, and he moved his lips soundlessly as if talking in his sleep. It seemed to be the same word over and over again – perhaps a sentence of two syllables, something like:

"Spare me. Spare me. Spare me."

– – –

The next few days passed without my taking notice of him, and he never broke the silence either.

His manner remained as considerate as before. Whenever I was seized by the urge to pace up and down, he saw it at once, and when he was sitting on his cot he would tuck in his feet politely so as not to obstruct my path.

I began to reproach myself, but with the best will in the world I could not get over my revulsion toward him.

However I had hoped to accustom myself to his presence – it was impossible.

Even at night it kept me awake. I would sleep barely a quarter of an hour.

Evening after evening exactly the same procedure was repeated: he waited respectfully for me to stretch out, then took off his clothes, folded them methodically, hung them up, and so on and so forth.

One night – it must have been around two – I stood on the shelf again, drunk with exhaustion, staring into the full moon, whose beams were reflected on the copper face of the tower clock like glistening oil, and thought sorrowfully of Mirjam.

When suddenly I heard her soft voice behind me.

At once I was awake, beyond awake – I spun around and listened.

A minute passed.

I was beginning to think I had been mistaken, when it came again. I could not understand the exact words, but it sounded like:

"Ask me. Ask me."

Quaking with excitement I climbed down as quietly as I could and crept to Laponder's bed.

The moonlight shone him full in the face, and I could clearly distinguish his open lids, but only the whites of his eyes were visible.

The rigidity of his cheek muscles showed me that he was sound asleep.

Only his lips moved, as they had recently.

And gradually I understood the words which emerged between his teeth:

"Ask me. Ask me."

The voice was deceptively like Mirjam's.

"Mirjam? Mirjam?" I cried out involuntarily, but lowered my voice at once for fear of waking the sleeper.

I waited for his face to grow rigid again, then repeated softly:

"Mirjam? Mirjam?"

His mouth formed a barely audible yet distinct:

"Yes."

I put my ear close to his lips.

After a while I heard *Mirjam's voice* whispering – so unmistakably her voice that my blood ran cold.

I drank in the words so greedily that I grasped only the gist of them. She spoke of her love for me and of the unutterable good fortune that we had found each other again at last – and would never be parted again – hastily – without a pause, like someone who fears she will be interrupted and wants to take advantage of every second.

Then the voice faltered – now and then fading away entirely.

"Mirjam?" I asked, trembling with fear and sucking in my breath. "Mirjam, are you dead?"

For a long time no answer came.

Then, almost unintelligible:

"No. – I'm alive. – Asleep." – –

Nothing more.

I listened and listened.

In vain. Nothing more.

Trembling with emotion, I had to support myself on the edge of the bed so as not to collapse onto Laponder.

The illusion had been so perfect that for a moment I actually thought I saw Mirjam lying before me, and had to muster all my strength not to plant a kiss on the murderer's lips.

"Henoch! Henoch!" I heard him stammer, then clearer and more articulate: "Henoch! Henoch!"

I recognized Hillel at once.

"Is that you, Hillel?"

No reply.

I remembered having read that to make sleepers talk one must direct one's questions not into their ear but at the plexus in the pit of the stomach.

I did so:

"Hillel?"

"Yes, I hear you!"

"Is Mirjam well? Do you know everything?" I asked quickly.

"Yes. I know everything. Long known it. – Be untroubled, Henoch, and fear not!"

"Can you forgive me, Hillel?"

"I say to you: be untroubled."

"Will we meet again soon?" – I feared I would not be able to understand the answer; the last words had only been breathed out.

"I hope so. I will wait – for you – if I can – then I must – land –"

"Where? To what land?" I nearly fell over onto Laponder. – "To what land? To what land?"

"– Land – Gad – south – Palestine –"

The voice died away.

In my confusion a hundred questions flashed through my mind: why did he call me Henoch? Zwakh, Jaromir, the watch, Vrieslander, Angelina, *Charousek*.

"Farewell, and think of me now and then", came, suddenly clear once more, from the murderer's lips. This time with Charousek's inflections, but as if I had said it myself.

I remembered: it was word for word the last sentence of Charousek's letter. –

Laponder's face now lay in darkness. The moonlight fell onto the head of the straw mattress. In a quarter of an hour it would have vanished from the cell.

I asked question after question, but received no more answers:

The murderer lay immobile as a corpse, and his lids were closed.

– – –

I reproached myself bitterly for having seen only the criminal in Laponder all these days, never the human being. –

From what I had just seen, he was clearly a somnambulist – a creature influenced by the full moon.

Perhaps he had committed the sex murder in a kind of trance. In fact, there was no doubt about it. –

Now that dawn was breaking, the rigidity had left his features, giving way to an expression of blissful peace.

A man with a murder on his conscience couldn't possibly sleep that peacefully, I said to myself.

I could hardly wait for him to wake up.

Did he know what had happened?

At last he opened his eyes, met my gaze and looked away.

I went up to him at once and seized his hand: "Forgive me, Herr Laponder, for being so rude to you. It was the shock of the unaccustomed, the –"

"Rest assured, my dear man, I understand perfectly", he interrupted me warmly, "that it must be a dreadful feeling to be cooped up with a sex murderer."

"Speak no more of it", I begged. "I was mulling things over last night, and I can't escape the thought that you might –" I groped for words.

"You think I'm sick", he helped me out.

I assented: "Certain signs lead me to that conclusion. I – I – may I ask you a blunt question, Herr Laponder?"

"Please."

"It sounds a bit strange – but – would you tell me what you dreamed last night?"

He shook his head with a smile: "I never dream."

"But you talked in your sleep."

He looked up, surprised. Thought for a bit. Then he said firmly:

"That can only have happened if you asked me something." – That I admitted. – "For as I said, I never dream. I – I wander", he added in a low voice after a pause.

"You wander? How do you mean that?"

He seemed reluctant to come out with it; considering it prudent to tell him my reasons for questioning him, I told him roughly what had happened that night.

"You can depend upon it", he said gravely once I had finished, "that there is truth to everything I said in my sleep. If I said just now that I 'wander' rather than dream, I meant that my dream life is of a different nature than that of – let us say: *normal* people. Let us call it, if you like, a departure from the body. – – Last night, for example, I was in a most peculiar room which could only be entered from below, through a trapdoor."

233

"What did it look like?" I asked quickly. "Was it unlived-in? Empty?"

"No; there was furniture in it, but not much. And a bed where a young girl slept – or lay as if in a trance – and a man sat next to her and held his hand on her forehead." Laponder described the faces of the two. No doubt about it, they were Hillel and Mirjam.

I hardly dared breathe with excitement.

"Please go on. Was anyone else in the room?"

"Anyone else? Wait – – – no: there was no one else in the room. A candelabra with seven candles burned on the table. – Then I went down a spiral staircase."

"And it was in ruins?" I interrupted.

"In ruins? No, no; it was perfectly intact. A chamber branched off to the side, and there sat a man with silver buckles on his shoes, of a foreign type such as I have never seen before: with a yellow complexion and slanting eyes – he was leaning forward and seemed to be waiting for something. For a command, perhaps."

"A book – didn't you see an old, big book anywhere?" I probed.

He rubbed his forehead.

"A book, you say? – Yes. Quite right: a book lay on the floor. It was all made of parchment, opened, and the page began with a big, golden 'A'."

"You must mean with an 'I'?"

"No, with an 'A'."

"Are you sure of that? Wasn't it an 'I'?"

"No, it was definitely an 'A'."

I shook my head and began to have my doubts. It seemed that Laponder, half-asleep, had browsed in the contents of my imagination and jumbled everything together: Hillel, Mirjam, the Golem, the Book of Ibbur and the underground passageway.

"Have you had this gift of 'wandering', as you call it, for a long time?" I asked.

"Since I was twenty-one – – –" he faltered, seemed loath to speak of it; then his face suddenly took on an expression of boundless astonishment, and he stared at my chest as if he saw something there.

Heedless of my astonishment, he sized my hand and pled – almost desperately:

"For heaven's sake, tell me *everything*. Today is the last day I may spend with you. Another hour, perhaps, and I will be taken away to hear my death sentence – –."

I interrupted him, shocked:

"Then you must take me with you as your witness! I'll swear that you're sick. – You're moonstruck. They can't possibly execute you without looking into the state of your psyche. Please listen to reason!"

He protested nervously: "That's so unimportant – please, tell me everything!"

"But what can I tell you? Let's speak of *you* and – –"

"Now I am sure of it: You must have experienced certain things which concern me closely – more closely than you can imagine – – I implore you, tell me everything!"

It was inconceivable to me that my life was of more interest to him more than his own affairs, which were certainly urgent enough; but to pacify him I told him all the enigmatic things that had happened to me.

After each main episode he nodded in satisfaction like someone seeing to the bottom of a matter.

When I came to the point when the apparition without a head stood before me and held out the black-red seeds, he could hardly wait to hear the end.

"So, you struck them out of his hand", he murmured pensively. "I hadn't thought that there could be a *third* 'way'."

235

"It wasn't a third way", I said, "it was the same as if I had refused the seeds."

He smiled.

"Don't you think so, Herr Laponder?"

"If you had refused them, you would have gone the 'Way of Life' as well, but the seeds, which represent magic powers, would not have remained behind. – This way, as you say, they rolled onto the ground. That means: they remained here and will be tended by your ancestors until the time of germination has come. Then the powers which still slumber within you will come to life."

I did not understand: "The seeds are tended by my ancestors?"

"You must understand what you experienced partly in symbolic terms", Laponder explained. "The circle of people with the blue radiance which surrounded you was the chain of inherited 'I's' which all born of woman carry about with them. The soul is nothing 'individual' – it is only meant to become so, and that is called: 'immortality'; your soul is still made up of many 'I's' – as an ant colony is made of many ants; you bear the psychic remains of many thousands of ancestors within you: the heads of your family. So it is with all beings. How could a chicken artificially hatched from an egg immediately seek the right nourishment if it were not filled with the experience of millions of years? – The existence of instinct betrays the presence of the ancestors in body and soul. – But forgive me, I did not mean to interrupt you."

I told the story to the end. Everything. Including what Mirjam had said about the "hermaphrodite".

When I paused and looked up I saw that Laponder had gone white as the lime on the wall, and tears were running down his cheeks.

I got up hastily, pretending not to notice, and paced up and down the cell to wait until he had calmed himself again.

Then I sat down across from him and mustered all my eloquence to convince him how urgently necessary it was to inform the judges of his mental state.

"If only you hadn't confessed to the murder!" I finished.

"But I had to! They appealed to my conscience", he said naively.

"Do you think a lie is worse than – than a sex murder?" I asked, baffled.

"Perhaps not in general, but in my case certainly. – You see: when the examining magistrate asked me whether I confessed, I had the strength to tell the truth. Thus I had the choice to lie or not to lie. – When I committed the sex murder – – please, spare me the details: it was so hideous that I would rather not revive the memory – – when I committed the sex murder, I had *no* choice. Even though I acted with perfectly lucid consciousness, I *still had no choice*: something whose existence within me I had never suspected woke and was stronger than I. Do you believe that I would have murdered if I had had the choice? – I have never killed – not even the tiniest animal – and now I would be absolutely incapable of it.

Supposing the law of man were: to murder, and failure to do so were punishable by death – as is the case in war – I would be condemned at once. – Because I would have no choice. I quite simply could not murder. When I committed the sex murder, it was the other way around."

"Now that you feel like a different person, so to speak, you should try all the harder to escape the sentence!" I objected.

Laponder waved his hand in protest: "You're mistaken! From their point of view the judges are quite right. Should they let a person like me run around on the streets? And have catastrophe strike tomorrow or the day after?"

"No; but they should commit you to a sanatorium for the mentally ill. That's what I'm saying!"

237

"If I were mad, you would be right", Laponder replied calmly. "But I am not mad. I am something quite different – something which closely resembles madness, but is its exact opposite. Please listen. You will understand me shortly. – – – What you told me just now of the phantom without a head – a symbol, of course, this phantom, you can find the key easily enough if you think about it – happened to me once just like that. Only I *accepted* the seeds. So I am going the 'Way of Death'! – For me the holiest thing I can imagine is: to let my steps be guided by the spiritual part of me. Blindly, trustingly, wherever the way may lead: to the gallows or the throne, to poverty or wealth. Never have I hesitated when the choice was placed in my hands.

And that is why I did not lie when the choice was in my hands.

Do you know the words of the Prophet Micha:

'You are told, Man, what is good for you,
and what the Lord demands of you'?

If I had lied, I would have created a cause, because I had the choice – when I committed the murder, I did not create a cause; the effect of a *cause* long since planted and slumbering within me, over which I no longer had control, was merely set free.

So my hands are clean.

By making me into a murderer, my spiritual part executed me; when the people string me up on the gallows, my fate will be severed from theirs – I will be set free."

He is a saint, I felt, and my hair stood on end in horror at my own smallness.

"You told me that a doctor's hypnotic intervention in your consciousness long made you lose the memory of your youth", he went on. "That is the mark – the stigma – of all those who have been bitten by the 'serpent of the spiritual realm'. It almost seems that two lives must be grafted together within us like a scion onto the wild tree before the *miracle of awakening* can occur – what is otherwise sundered by death is done here by the extinguishing of memory – sometimes only by a sudden inner conversion.

In my case, I woke up altered one morning in my twenty-first year, apparently without external cause. All that had previously been dear to me all suddenly seemed of no consequence: life seemed as foolish as a tale of cowboys and Indians, and lost its reality; my dreams became certainty – adoptive, conclusive certainty, mark my words: *conclusive, real certainty*, and the daytime life became a dream.

This all could do, if they had the key. And the key lies simply and solely in becoming conscious, in sleep, of one's 'I-form', one's skin, so to speak – finding the narrow chink through which consciousness squeezes itself from waking to profound sleep.

That is why I said before: I 'wander', and not: I 'dream'.

The struggle for immortality is a battle for the scepter against our indwelling sounds and phantoms; and to wait for the kingship of our own 'I' is to wait for the Messiah.

The spectral Habal Garnim you saw, the 'Breath of Bones' of the Cabala, that was the king. When he is crowned – snap goes the rope which, through the external senses and the chimney of reason, ties you to the external world.

How could it happen, you ask, that despite my detachment from life I could become a sex murderer overnight? People are like glass tubes through which colored balls roll: only one in a lifetime for most people. If the ball is red, the person is called: 'bad'. If it is yellow, then the person is: 'good'. If two pass in succession – a red and a yellow one, then 'one' has an 'unbalanced' character. In one lifetime we 'serpent-bitten' ones go through what the whole race undergoes in an age: the colored balls race through the glass tube one after the other, and when they have passed – – then we are prophets – have become the mirror of God."

Laponder fell silent.

For a long time I was unable to say a word. His words had dazed me.

"Why were you so anxious to learn what *I* have experienced, when you are so very far above me?" I began again at last.

"You are wrong", said Laponder, "I am far *below* you. – I asked you because I felt that you possess the key I still lacked."

"I? A key? O God!"

"Yes, *you*! And you gave it to me. – I don't believe there is a happier person on earth than I am today."

There was a noise outside; the bolt slid back – Laponder barely heeded it:

"The hermaphrodite was the key. Now I possess the certainty. For that reason alone I am glad that they are coming to take me away, for I will soon be at my goal."

For tears I could no longer make out Laponder's face, I only *heard* the smile in his voice.

"And now: farewell, Herr Pernath, and remember: tomorrow only my clothes will be hanged; you have revealed the most beautiful thing to me – the last thing I did not know. Now off to the wedding – – – –." He stood up and followed the warder. – "It is closely tied to the sex murder", were the last words which I heard and only dimly understood.

– – –

After that night, whenever the full moon shone in the sky, I thought I saw Laponder's sleeping face against the grey linen of the bed.

For several days after he was taken away, I heard a hammering and sawing resound up from the execution yard, sometimes lasting until dawn.

I guessed its meaning, and for hours I held my ears shut in despair.

Month after month went by. I saw the summer's decline in the ailing of the meager foliage in the yard; smelled it in the fuzzy exhalations of the walls.

Every time my eyes fell upon the dying tree on my walks, and the glass picture of the Virgin swallowed by its bark, I drew an involuntary parallel to the way in which Laponder's face had embedded itself into me. I carried it about within me constantly, this Buddha face with the un-wrinkled skin and the strange, unceasing smile.

Once more – in September – the magistrate fetched me and asked me skeptically to account for the fact that at the bank window I had said I was about to leave town, and why I had been so agitated in the hours after my arrest and had carried all my gems on my person.

When I replied that I had intended to put an end to my life, another mocking bleat came from behind the desk. –

Until then I had been alone in my cell and could give free play to my thoughts, my grief for Charousek, who, I felt, must long since have died, and Laponder, and my long-ing for Mirjam.

Then new prisoners came again: thievish clerks with used-up faces, paunchy bank clerks – "orphans", as Black Vóssatka would have called them, fouling my air and my mood.

One day one of them indignantly announced that a sex murder had been committed in the city some time ago. Fortunately the perpetrator had been caught at once, and short shrift had been made with him.

"Laponder dey called him, de miserble wretch", shrieked a fellow with a feral cat's mug, a child abuser who had been sentenced to – fourteen days in prison. "Caught him red-handed, dey did. De lamp fell over in de scuffle and de room burned out. De gal's corpse got fried to a crisp, and to dis very day dey can't figure out who she was. Black hair she had, an' a narrow face, dat's all we know. And Laponder wouldn't let onta her name for de life a him. – If I'da hadda say in de matter, I'da skinned him and peppered him alive. – Dat's de fine chentlemen for ya. Cutthroats alla dem. – – – – As if dere weren't enough odder ways ta get rid of a gal", he added with a cynical smile.

I seethed with rage, and longed to strike the scoundrel to the ground.

Night after night he snored in the bed where Laponder had lain. I breathed a sigh of relief when he was finally released.

But even then I was not free of him. His words had bored their way into me like a barbed arrow.

Almost constantly, especially in the dark, I was consumed by the awful suspicion that Mirjam could have fallen victim to Laponder. The more I struggled against it, the deeper I entangled myself in the notion, until it almost became an obsession.

Sometimes, especially when the moon shone brightly through the bars, it was better: I could summon up the hours I had spent with Laponder, and my deep feeling for him banished the torment – but only too often did the awful moment return when I saw Mirjam murdered and charred in my mind's eye, and fear nearly made me lose my reason.

At such moments the flimsy evidence I had for my conjecture joined to a complete whole – a scene filled with indescribably appalling details.

At the beginning of November, around ten in the evening – it was already pitch-black, and the desperation within me had reached such a height that I sank my teeth into my straw mattress like a thirsting animal so as not to scream out loud, the warder suddenly opened the cell and ordered me to follow him to the magistrate. I felt so weak that I staggered rather than walked.

The hope of ever leaving this terrible place had long since died within me.

I resigned myself to be asked another cold question, hear the standard bleat from behind the desk and then be forced to return into the darkness.

Herr Baron Leisetreter had gone home, and only an old, hunchbacked clerk with spider fingers stood in the room.

I waited dully to see what would happen to me.

It struck me that the warder had come in with me and twinkled at me kindly, but I was much too dejected to grasp the meaning of all that.

"The investigation concludes", the clerk began, bleated, climbed onto a chair and first rummaged about on the bookshelf for documents before continuing: "concludes that before his death the Karl Zottmann in question, on the occasion of a clandestine assignation with the unmarried former prostitute Rosina Metzeles, known at that time by the nickname 'red Rosina' and later bought off from the 'Kautsky' wine salon by a silhouette cutter by the name of Jaromir Kwássnitschka, now under police surveillance, who has for several months been cohabiting with His Highness Prince Ferri Athenstädt in disorderly concubinage as his mistress, was treacherously enticed into an open subterranean cellar vault in the house number conscriptionis 21 873 slash Roman numeral III on Hahnpassgasse, locked into the same and left to his own devices, that is to say, left to die by starvation or exposure. – – The above-mentioned Zottmann, that is –" the clerk explained, glancing over his glasses, and turned a few pages.

"Furthermore the investigation concludes that to all appearances the above-mentioned Karl Zottmann – after the onset of demise – was robbed of all the possessions on his person, in particular the enclosed sub fascicle Roman P slash 'Bee' double-cased pocket watch" – the clerk held up the watch on its chain. "No importance could be attached to the statutory declaration on the part of the silhouette cutter Jaromir Kwássnitschka, orphaned son of the host baker of the same name, seventeen years deceased: that he had found the watch in the bed of his now-fugitive brother Loisa and alienated it to the second-hand storekeeper and multiple, now deceased, property owner Aaron Wassertrum in exchange for money value, due to lack of credibility.

Furthermore, the investigation concludes that at the time of its discovery the corpse of the above-mentioned Karl Zottmann carried in its back trousers pocket a notebook in which, presumably several days before ensuing decease, it had made several notes illuminating the facts of the case and facilitating the apprehension of the perpetrator by the Royal and Imperial authorities.

Accordingly the attention of a senior Royal and Imperial public prosecutor has been called to the presently fugitive Loisa Kwássnitschka, overwhelmingly implicated by Zottmann's testamentary notes, and at the same time decreed that the remand of Athanasius Pernath, lapidary, never previously convicted, be overturned and the proceedings against him be closed.

Prague, July

signed

Dr. Baron von Leisetreter"

– – –

The ground swayed beneath my feet, and for a minute I lost consciousness.

When I woke, I was sitting in a chair, and the warder clapped me amiably on the shoulder.

The clerk had remained perfectly calm; he sniffed, blew his nose, and said to me:

244

"The decree was not read until today because your name begins with a 'Pee' and naturally does not occur until the end of the alphabet." – Then he read on:

"Moreover, Athanasius Pernath, lapidary, is to be informed that according to the last will and testament of the stud. med. Innocenz Charousek, deceased in May, one third of the latter's entire estate has devolved upon him in inheritance, and he is herewith requested to sign the protocol."

At the last word the clerk dipped his quill and began to scribble.

Out of habit I expected him to bleat, but he did not bleat.

"Innocenz Charousek", I repeated absently under my breath.

The warder leaned over me and whispered into my ear:

"He visited me shortly before his death, Herr Dr. Charousek, and asked about you. He sends you many greetings, he said. Of course, at the time I couldn't pass them on. It's strictly prohibited. Incidentally, he came to a terrible end, that Herr Dr. Charousek. He made away with himself. He was found dead on Aaron Wassertrum's grave mound, lying face-down. – He dug two deep holes in the ground, slashed his wrists, and then buried his arms in the holes. He bled to death like that. He must have been mad, that Herr Dr. Char – – –"

The clerk pushed back his chair loudly and handed me the quill to sign my name.

Then he straightened up proudly and said in the exact same inflections as his baronial superior:

"Warder, take the man out."

– – –

– – –

As he had a long, long time ago, the man with the saber and the long johns in the gate room took the coffee mill from his lap; only this time he did not search me, and he gave me back my gems, the wallet with ten guldens in it, my coat and all the rest. – – –

Then I stood on the street.

"Mirjam! Mirjam! We'll see each other again at last!" – I suppressed a cry of wild delight.

It must have been midnight. The full moon floated lusterless behind veils of mist like a wan brass plate.

The pavement was covered with a stubborn layer of filth.

I staggered toward a coach which looked in the fog like a prostrated antediluvian monster. My legs almost failed me; having forgotten how to walk, I reeled – on insensate soles like a spinal patient. – –

"Coachman, take me to Hahnpassgasse 7 as fast as you can! – Do you understand me? – Hahnpassgasse 7."

FREE

After a few yards the coach stopped.

"Hahnpassgasseh, Sir?"

"Yes, yes, hurry, won't you."

Again the coach drove on a ways. Again it stopped.

"For heaven's sake, what's the matter?"

"Hahnpassgasseh, Sir?"

"Yes, yes. Exactly."

"But we can't drive to Hahnpassgasseh!"

"Why on earth not?"

"De streets are torn emselves up all over, de Jewish Town's a-razin' isself."

"Well, then drive as far as you can, but quickly, if you please."

The coach made one single galloping lurch and then stumbled on at a leisurely pace.

I lowered the rickety window and inhaled the night air with greedy lungs.

Everything had become so strange to me, so unfathomably new: the houses, the streets, the closed shops.

A white dog trotted past on the wet sidewalk, lonely and ill-tempered. I gazed after it. – How strange!! A dog! I had completely forgotten that such animals existed. – Childish with joy, I called after him: "Now, now! How can anyone be so surly." – –

Whatever would Hillel say!? – And Mirjam?

Only a few minutes more, and we would be together. I wouldn't stop knocking at the door until I had roused them from their beds.

Now all was well – all this year's misery was past! –

Would that be a Christmas!

This time I could not let myself sleep through it like the last one.

For a moment the old horror paralyzed me again: I remembered the words of the convict with the mug of a feral cat – the sex murder – but no, no! – I shook it off forcibly: no, no, it could not, it could not be. – Mirjam was alive! I had heard her voice from Laponder's lips.

One more minute – half a minute – – and then –

The coach stopped in front of a heap of rubble. Barricades of cobblestones everywhere!

Red lanterns burned on top of them.

An army of workmen dug and shoveled by torchlight.

Piles of debris and chunks of masonry blocked my way. I clambered around them, sinking down to the knee.

Surely this had to be Hahnpassgasse?!

I took my bearings with difficulty. Nothing but ruins all around. Wasn't that the house I had lived in?

The front was sheared away.

I climbed onto a pile of dirt; far below me a black, stone passageway ran the length of what had once been the street. I looked up: like the cells of an enormous beehive the exposed rooms hung in the air, lit half by torchlight, half by the dim light of the moon.

That up there had to be my room – I recognized it by the painted decoration on the walls.

Only a strip of it was left.

And next to it the studio – Savioli's. Suddenly my heart went vacant. How strange! The studio! – Angelina! – – All that was so distant, so immeasurably far behind me!

I turned around: of the house where Wassertrum had lived, not a stone was in place. Everything had been leveled: the junk shop, Charousek's basement dwelling – – – everything, everything.

"Man passes like a shadow" – I recalled words I had once read.

I asked a workman whether he knew where the people who had moved away now lived; whether he knew the archivist Schemajah Hillel.

"Nix daitsch", was the reply.

I gave the man a gulden: he understood German at once, but could give me no answer.

Neither could any of his comrades.

Perhaps I could learn something at "Loisitschek"?

"Loisitschek" was shut down, I was told, the house was being renovated.

Then wake someone in the neighborhood! – Was that impossible?

"Dere ain't a cat lives far and wide", said the workman, "it's prohibbeded by dauthorities. 'Cause of typhus."

"'Ungelt'? That must be open."

"Ungelt's shut isself."

"For certain?"

"For certain."

At random I mentioned a few names of peddlers and to-bacconists who had lived nearby; then the names Zwakh, Vrieslander, Prokop –

The man shook his head every time.

"Perhaps you know Jaromir Kwássnitschka?"

The workman pricked up his ears.

"Jaromir? Isself deaf an dumb?"

I rejoiced. Thank God. An acquaintance, at least.

"Yes, he's deaf and dumb. Where does he live?"

"Does he cut isself pictures? Outta black payper?"

"Yes. That's the one. Where can I find him?"

As circuitously as possible the man directed me to a night cafe in the inner city and immediately started shovel-ing again.

I spent more than an hour wading through fields of debris, balancing across wobbling boards and crawling under cross-beams which blocked the street. The Jewish Quarter was one great stony waste, as if an earthquake had destroyed the city.

Breathless with agitation, with torn shoes and covered with filth, I found my way out of the labyrinth at last.

A few more blocks, and I stood outside the dive I sought. "Café Chaos" said the sign.

A deserted hole-in-the-wall with barely enough room for the few tables which stood against the walls. In the middle, on a three-legged billiard table, a waiter slept, snoring.

A market-woman with a basket of vegetables in front of her sat in the corner and nodded over a glass of *čaj*.

At last the waiter saw fit to rise and ask me what I wanted. The insolent way he looked me over brought home to me for the first time how ragged I must look.

I glanced in the mirror and took fright: an unfamiliar, bloodless face stared out at me, wrinkled, grey as putty, with a bristly beard and long, wild hair.

Had the silhouette cutter Jaromir been there, I asked, and ordered a black coffee.

"Dunno what's keeping him", was the yawned reply.

Then the waiter lay back down on the billiard table and slept on.

I took the "Prager Tagblatt" from the wall and – waited.

The letters crawled across the pages like ants, and I did not take in a word I read.

Hours passed, and behind the panes there were already signs of the suspicious deep dark blue which presages the dawn in a tavern with gas lighting.

Now and then a few policemen with green-glinting plumes peered in and moved on with a slow, heavy tread.

Three soldiers came in, looking as if they had made a night of it.

A street sweeper took a schnapps.

At last, at last: Jaromir.

He had changed so greatly that I did not recognize him at first: his eyes extinct, his hair sparser, deep hollows behind his ears. I was so glad to see a familiar face after such a long time that I jumped up, went to meet him and seized his hand.

He seemed extraordinarily skittish and kept glancing at the door. With all kinds of gestures I tried to convey to him that I was glad to have run into him. – It was a long time before he seemed to believe me.

Whatever questions I asked, his hands made the same helpless gesture of incomprehension.

How could I possibly make myself understood?

Wait! An idea!

I asked for a pencil and drew the faces of Zwakh, Vrieslander and Prokop.

"What? None of them are in Prague anymore?"

His hands flew nimbly in the air, he made the gesture of counting money, marched his fingers across the table, struck the backs of his hands. I guessed: all three of them had probably gotten money from Charousek and were now wandering the world as a professional troupe with the expanded marionette theater.

"And Hillel? Where does he live now?" – I drew his face, a house next to it, and a question mark.

Jaromir did not understand the question mark – he could not read – but he understood what I wanted, took a match, seemed to toss it into the air and skillfully made it vanish like a conjurer.

What did that mean? That Hillel was away on a journey too?

I drew the Jewish Town Hall.

The deaf-mute shook his head vigorously.

"So Hillel is no longer there?"

"No!" (A shake of the head.)

"Where is he?"

The match trick again.

"He means, the chennleman up and left, and no one knows where to", was the instructive interjection of the street sweeper, who had been watching us the whole time with great interest.

My heart contracted with fear: Hillel gone! – Now I was all alone in the world. – – The things in the room began to flicker before my eyes.

"And Mirjam?"

My hand trembled so violently that I could produce nothing resembling a likeness of her face.

"Has Mirjam vanished too?"

"Yes. Also vanished. Without a trace."

I groaned loudly, paced up and down the room until the three soldiers looked at each other questioningly.

Jaromir attempted to soothe me, and made an effort to tell me something else he seemed to have found out: he laid his head on his arm like someone sleeping.

I clung to the tabletop: "For the love of God, Christ – is Mirjam dead?"

A shake of the head. Jaromir repeated the gesture of sleeping.

"Was Mirjam sick?" I drew a medicine bottle.

A shake of the head. Again Jaromir laid his forehead on his arm. – – – – – –

Dawn broke, the gas flames went out one after another, and still I was could not fathom what the gesture was supposed to mean. I gave up. Pondered.

All I could do was go to the Jewish Town Hall first thing in the morning to inquire where Hillel could have gone with Mirjam.

I had to follow him. – – –

I sat next to Jaromir without a word. Deaf and mute as he.

When I looked up, much later, I saw that he was cutting out a silhouette with a pair of scissors.

I recognized Rosina's profile. He handed me the sheet across the table, put his hand to his eyes and – – wept silently.

Then he jumped up and staggered out the door without a parting gesture.

– – –

The archivist Schemajah Hillel had failed to come to work one day for no reason and had never returned; he had taken his daughter with him, at any rate, for no one had seen her since, I was told at the Jewish Town Hall. That was all I could find out.

No clue as where they could have headed.

At the bank I was told that my money was still confiscated by the court, but that they expected permission to pay it out to me any day.

The inheritance from Charousek had to go through the official channels as well, though I waited for the money with burning impatience, ready to stake everything to seek Hillel's and Mirjam's trail.

– – –

I sold the gems I still had in my pocket and rented two small, furnished, adjacent garret rooms on Altschulgasse – the only street which had been spared in the clearing of the Jewish Town.

Strange coincidence: it was the same famous house into which, according to the legend, the Golem had once vanished.

I asked the occupants – mostly store clerks and craftsmen – whether there was any truth to the rumor of the "room without a door", and was laughed at. – How could anyone believe such nonsense!

In prison my own experiences in this connection had taken on the pallor of a long-fled dream, and I saw them as mere symbols without blood or life – struck them from the book of my memories.

Laponder's words, which I sometimes heard within as clearly as if he were sitting across from me and speaking to me as he had in the cell, confirmed me in the belief that what had once seemed tangible reality had been a purely inward vision.

Was not all that I had possessed now fled and vanished? The Book of Ibbur, the fantastic tarok deck, Angelina, and even my old friends Zwakh, Vrieslander and Prokop! – – –

It was Christmas Eve, and I had brought home a little tree with red candles. I wanted to be young once more, surrounded by the glow of candles and the scent of pine needles and burning wax.

Before the year was over I might already be on the road, searching cities and villages, or wherever my inner urge took me, for Hillel and Mirjam.

All impatience, all anticipation had gradually left me, all the fear that Mirjam could have been murdered, and in my heart I knew that I would find them both.

There was a constant joyful smile within me, and whenever I touched something with my hand I felt it radiated healing. In the strangest way I was filled with the contentment of a person who turns homeward after a long walk to see the towers of his home city glittering from afar.

Once I went back to the little coffeehouse to ask Jaromir to join me for Christmas Eve. – He had not been seen again, I learned, and I was about to go again, saddened, when an old peddler came in to hawk worthless little antiques.

I rummaged among all the watch fobs, little crucifixes, comb pins and brooches in his box when a heart of red stone on a faded silk band slipped into my hand. In astonishment

I recognized it as the token Angelina had once given me by the fountain of her manor, when she was still a little girl.

And all at once my youth rose before me as if I were looking deep into a peep show, to see a picture painted by a child. –

For a long, long time I stood there, shaken, and stared at the little red heart in my hand. – – –

I sat in the garret and listened to the pine needles crackle every now and then when a twig began to glow over the wax candles.

"Perhaps at this very moment old Zwakh is performing his 'Marionette Christmas Eve", I pictured to myself, "declaiming in a mysterious voice the strophes of his favorite poet Oskar Wiener:

> 'Where is the heart of red, red stone?
> It hangs upon a silken band.
> I loved it warm and loved it true,
> And served it seven toilsome years,
> That heart of stone, and loved it true.' "

All at once I felt a strange solemnity.

The candles had burned down. Only one still flickered. Smoke gathered in the room.

As if a hand had tugged me, I suddenly turned around and:

My likeness stood there at the threshold. My double. In a white mantle. A crown on his head.

Only for a moment.

Then flames broke through the wood of the door, and a cloud of hot, choking smoke burst in:

A blaze in the house! Fire! Fire! – – –

I tear open the window. Climb out onto the roof.

Already the shrill bell of the fire department races up from afar.

Glittering helmets and terse commands.

Then the sinister, rhythmic, sucking breath of the pumps, as the demons of the water crouch to spring upon their mortal enemy: the fire.

Glass shatters, and a red inferno shoots from all the windows.

Mattresses are thrown down, the whole street is covered with them, people leap after them, are carried away wounded.

Within me something cries out in wild, jubilant ecstasy; I know not why. My hair stands on end.

I walk toward the chimney to avoid being singed; the flames are reaching for me.

A chimney-sweep's rope is wrapped around it.

I unroll it, wind it around my wrist and leg, the way I learned in gymnastics as a boy, and calmly let myself down the facade of the house. –

Pass a window. Look in:

Inside everything is blindingly lit.

And there I see – – – there I see – – – my whole body becomes one single resounding cry of joy:

"Hillel! Mirjam! Hillel!"

I leap at the bars.

Miss. Lose my grip on the rope.

For a moment *I hang head down, legs crossed, between heaven and earth.*

The rope sings with the jolt. The fibers stretch, creaking.

I fall.

My consciousness is snuffed.

As I fall I reach for the windowsill, but I slide off. No hold:

The stone is smooth.

Smooth as a piece of
fat. – – –

END

"– – – as a piece of fat!"

That is the stone which resembles a piece of fat.

The words ring in my ears. Then I sit up, wondering where I am.

I am lying in bed, living in a hotel.

My name isn't Pernath at all.

Was all that just a dream?

No! No one dreams like that.

I look at the clock: I slept barely an hour. It is two-thirty.

And there hangs the strange hat I took by mistake in the cathedral on the Hradschin when I sat in the pew for High Mass.

Is there a name inside?

I take it and read, in golden letters on the white silk lining, that strange and yet so very familiar name:

ATHANASIUS PERNATH

Now it refuses to leave me in peace; I dress hastily and go down the stairs.

"Porter! Open up! I'm going to take an hour's walk."

"Where to, pliz?"

"To the Jewish Town. To Hahnpassgasse. Is there even a street of that name anymore?"

"Oh yes, oh yes", – the porter smiles maliciously – "but in the Jewish Town – may I point out: there's not much action now. All newly built, pliz."

"No matter. Where is Hahnpassgasse?"

The porter's fat finger points at the map: "Here, pliz."

"And the tavern 'Loisitschek'?"

"Here, pliz."

"Do you have a big piece of paper?"

"Here, pliz."

I wrap Pernath's hat in it. Strange: it is almost new, impeccably clean, and yet as fragile as an antique. –

On the way there I reflect:

All that this Athanasius Pernath experienced, I experienced with him in a dream, saw, heard, felt in *one* night as if I had been *he*. Then why don't I know what he saw through the barred window at the moment the rope snapped and he cried "Hillel, Hillel!"?

That was the moment he parted from me, I realized.

I *must* find this Athanasius Pernath, I decide, even if I have to roam three days and three nights.

– – –

So that is Hahnpassgasse?

Nothing like how I saw it in my dream! –

All the new houses.

– – –

A minute later I am sitting in Café Loisitschek. A tasteless, relatively clean cafe.

In the back, however, is a platform with a wooden balustrade; a certain resemblance to the old, dreamed "Loisitschek" cannot be denied.

"Yes, please?" asks the waitress, a buxom girl virtually stuffed in to a red velvet dress coat.

"Cognac, Miss. – Ah, thank you." – – – – –

"Hm. Miss!"

"Yes, please?"

"Who does the coffeehouse belong to?"

"Herr Councilor of Commerce Loisitschek. – The whole house belongs to him. A very fine rich gentleman."

– Aha, the fellow with the pig's teeth on his watch chain, I remember! –

I have a good idea to help me get my bearings:

"Miss!"

"Yes, please?"

"When did the Stone Bridge cave in?"

"Thirty-three years ago."

"Hm. Thirty-three years ago!" – I think it over: then the lapidary Pernath must be nearly ninety by now.

"Miss!"

"Yes, please?"

"Are there any guests here who might remember what the old Jewish Town was like back then? I'm a writer, and the subject interests me."

The waitress ponders: "The guests? No. – But wait: the billiard marker playing carom over there with the student – see him? The fellow with the hooked nose, the old one – he's always lived here, he can tell you everything. Should I call him over when he's finished?"

I followed the girl's gaze:

A slender, white-haired old man leans against the mirror over there, chalking his queue. A ravaged yet strangely noble face. What does he remind me of?

"Miss, what is the marker's name?"

The waitress props her elbows on the table, writing, licks a pencil, writes her first name quick as lightning on the marble tabletop countless times, quickly erasing it again each time with a wet finger. All the while she shoots me more or less smoldering looks –with variable success. Essential, of course, is the simultaneous raising of the eyebrows, which heightens the enchantment of the gaze.

"Miss, what's the marker's name?" I repeat my question. I can tell by looking at her that she would rather have heard: Miss, why aren't you wearing a dress coat with nothing underneath? Or something of the sort, but I do not ask it; my head is too full of the dream for that.

"What should his name be", she sulks, "Ferri's his name. Ferri Athenstädt."

"Indeed? Ferri Athenstädt! – Hm – another old acquaintance, then.

"Tell me ever so much about him, Miss", I coo, and must fortify myself with a cognac immediately. "What a charming little chat we're having!" (I revolt myself.)

She leans down mysteriously close to me, so that her hair tickles my face, and whispers:

"That Ferri, that used to be a crafty one for you. – He's supposed to come from an ancient noble family – of course it's just talk, 'cause he doesn't wear a beard – and had an awful lot of money. Then a red-haired Jewess who was a 'character' from childhood on" – again she quickly wrote down her name a few times –, "stripped him bare. I mean in terms of money, of course. Well, and then when he didn't have no more money she went off and got herself married by a distinguished gentleman – von dem..." She whispers a name in my ear which I don't understand. "Then of course the distinguished gentleman was stripped of all his honors and could only call himself Sir von Dämmerich from then on. Oh well. But she used to be a 'character', and he couldn't wash that off her. I always say –"

"Fritzi! The check, please!" someone calls down from the platform. –

I let my eyes wander about the cafe, when suddenly I hear a faint, metallic chirping, like that of a cricket, behind me.

I turn around, curious. Can hardly believe my eyes:

Face turned to the wall, old as Methuselah, a music box the size of a pack of cigarettes in his trembling skeletal hands, all huddled together – the *ancient blind Nephtali Schaffranek* sits in the corner cranking the little handle.

I go up to him.

In a whisper he sings to himself confusedly:

"Frau Pick,
Frau Hock.
Und rote, blaue Stern',
Die schmusen allerhand.
Von Mesinnung, an Räucherl und Rohn."

"Do you know the old man's name?" I ask a waiter as he hurries past.

"No, Sir, no one knows him or his name. He's forgotten it himself. He's all alone in the world. He's a hundred and ten years old, if you please! He gets a so-called charity coffee from us every night."

I lean over the old man – shout a word into his ear: *"Schaffranek!"*

It jolts through him like lightning. He murmurs something, rubs his forehead pensively.

"Do you understand me, Herr Schaffranek?"

He nods.

"Listen well! I want to ask you something, about the old days. If you answer all my questions well, you'll get a gulden, I'll put it here on the table."

"Gulden", repeats the old man, and begins to crank away maniacally at his twittering music box.

I hold onto his hand: "Think carefully
– *Did you know a lapidary by the name of Pernath about thirty-three years ago?"*

"Hadrbolletz! Hosenschneider!" – he babbles asthmatically and laughs from ear to ear, in the belief that I just told him a splendid joke.

"No, not Hadrbolletz – – *Pernath!*"

"Pereles?!" – He virtually exults.

"No, not Pereles either. – Per – *nath!*"

"Pascheles?!" – He crows with delight. – –

I give up the attempt, disappointed. – – –

"You wish to speak to me, Sir?" – The marker Ferri Athenstädt stands before me and bows coolly.

"Yes. Quite right. – We could play a game of billiards while we're at it."

"Do you play for money, Sir? I'll give you odds of ninety to a hundred."

"Fine then: for a gulden. Why don't you begin, marker."

His Highness takes the cue, aims, mis-cues, makes an exasperated face. I know the game: he'll let me get up to ninety-nine, and then he'll "clean up" in *one* break.

I have an increasingly peculiar feeling. I come directly to the point:

"Do you recall, Herr Marker: a long time ago, about the time when the Stone Bridge collapsed, did you know *a certain – Athanasius Pernath* in what was then the Jewish Town?"

A man in a red and white striped linen jacket, with squinting eyes and little gold earrings, sitting on a bench against the wall reading a newspaper, gives a start, stares at me and crosses himself.

"Pernath? Pernath?" repeats the marker, straining to remember. – "Pernath? – Wasn't he tall, slender? Brown hair, flecked with grey, a close-cut goatee?"

"Yes. Exactly."

"About forty years old at the time? He looked like – – " His Highness suddenly stares at me in surprise. – "You're a relative of his, Sir?!"

The squint-eyed man crosses himself.

"I? A relative? Funny idea. – No. I'm just interested in him. Do you know anything more?" I say calmly, but feel my heart turn ice-cold.

Ferri Athenstädt thinks again.

"If I'm not mistaken, in his day he was thought to be mad. – Once he insisted his name was – – wait a moment –

262

yes: Laponder! And then again he claimed to be a certain –
Charousek."

"Not a word of truth to it!" the squint-eyed man put in.
"*Charousek* really existed. My father inherited several thousand florins from him."

"Who is this man?" I ask the marker under my breath.

"He's a ferryman by the name of Tschamrda. – As far as
Pernath is concerned, all I remember, or I think I do – is that
in later years he married a lovely dark-skinned Jewess."

"Mirjam!" I say to myself, growing so agitated that my
hands tremble and I am unable to go on playing.

The ferryman crosses himself.

"What on earth is wrong with you today, Herr Tschamrda?" the marker asks in astonishment.

"Pernath didn't never live", the squint-eyed man
screams. "I don't believe it."

Immediately I pour the man a cognac to make him more
communicative.

"There are people say Pernath is still alive", the ferryman discloses at last, "I hear he's a comb-cutter and lives on
the Hradschin."

"Where on the Hradschin?"

The ferryman crosses himself.

"That's just it! He lives where no living man can live: *at
the Wall of the Last Lantern.*"

"Do you know his house, Herr – Herr – Tschamrda?"

"I wouldn't go up there for the world!" protests the
squint-eyed man. "What do you take me for? Jesus, Mary
and Joseph!"

"But you could show me the way up from far off, couldn't
you, Herr Tschamrda?"

"That I could", grumbles the ferryman. "If you can
wait until six in the morning; then I'll go down to the
Vltava. But I warn you against it! You'll fall into the Stag

Moat and break every bone in your body! Holy Mother of God!"

We walk together through the morning; a fresh breeze blows from the river. Full of expectation, I hardly feel the ground below me.

Suddenly the house on Altschulgasse appears before me.

I recognize every window: the bent gutter, the greasily gleaming stone sills – everything, everything!

"When did this house burn down?" I ask the squint-eyed man. My ears ring with tension.

"Burn down? Didn't never."

"Yes it did! I'm sure of it."

"No."

"But I know it did! Do you want to bet?"

"How much?"

"One gulden."

"Done!" – And Tschamrda summons the house-steward. "Did this house ever burn down?"

"The idea!" The man laughs. –

I simply cannot believe it.

"I've been living here for seventy years", affirms the house-steward, "I should know."

– – – Strange, strange! – – –

With odd, crooked, jerking movements the ferryman rows me across the Vltava in his boat made of eight un-planed boards. The yellow water foams against the wood. The roofs of the Hradschin gleam red in the morning sun. An indescribable awe comes over me. The faint dawn of a feeling as if from a previous existence, as if the world around me were enchanted – a dreamlike epiphany as if I were living in several places at the same time.

I disembark.

"What do I owe you, Herr Tschamrda?"

"A kreuzer. If youda helped row – it woulda cost you two kreuzers." – – –

I pass back up the same path I took last night in my sleep: the narrow, lonely Castle Steps. My heart pounds, and I know beforehand: now comes the bare tree whose branches reach over the wall.

No: it's covered with white blossoms.

The air is filled with the sweet scent of lilac.

The city lies at my feet in the first light like a vision of promise.

Not a sound. Only fragrance and light.

Every step is suddenly so familiar to me that I could find my way up to the curious little Alchemists' Lane with my eyes closed.

But where the wooden fence stood in front of the white, shimmering house last night, the street now ends at a splendid, bellied, gilded grille.

Two yew-trees tower amidst blossoming bushes, flanking the gate in the wall which runs along behind the grille.

I stretch to see over the bushes, and new splendor blinds me:

The garden wall is completely covered with mosaics. Turquoise with golden, strangely shelled frescoes depicting the cult of the Egyptian god Osiris.

The double-winged gate is the god himself: a hermaphrodite in two halves, forming the door – the right half feminine, the life masculine. – He sits on a magnificent, flat mother-of-pearl throne – in bas-relief – and his golden head is that of a rabbit. The ears stand up, side by side, so that they look like the two pages of an open book. –

There is a smell of dew, and the scent of hyacinths wafts over the wall. – – –

For a long time I stand there as if petrified, marveling. I feel as if a strange world is opening up before me; an old gardener or servant with silver-buckled shoes, a lace ruff and a strangely-cut coat comes up to me from the left behind the grille and asks me through the bars what I want.

Mutely I hand him the wrapped hat of Athanasius Pernath.

He takes it and goes through the gate.

When it opens I see a temple-like marble house behind it, and on its steps:

ATHANASIUS PERNATH

and leaning against him:

MIRJAM,

both gazing down at the city.

For a moment Mirjam turns around, sees me, smiles and whispers something to Athanasius Pernath.

I am enthralled by her beauty.

She is as young as I saw her in my dream last night.

Athanasius Pernath turns toward me slowly, and my heart stops:

I seem to see my mirror image, so closely does his face resemble mine. – – –

Then the wings of the gate fall to, and I see nothing but the gleaming hermaphrodite.

The old servant gives me my hat and says – I hear his voice as if from the depths of the earth –:

"Herr Athanasius Pernath thanks you most sincerely and begs you not to consider him inhospitable if he does not invite you into the garden, but such is the strict and ancient law of the house.

I am to tell you that he did not put on your hat, as the mistake struck him immediately.

He hopes only that his did not give you a headache."

Dear Herr Meyrink,

it is more than thirty years now since we perched on the crumbling wall of the Invaliden Cemetery one dark summer night up on the Hradschin, in old Prague, in the twilight-brown shadow of the Church of St. Loretto. We had climbed up there on one of our many expeditions through the nocturnal city which time and again bestowed new and strange miracles upon us in such hours. Everything was as it had to be and as we wished it back then. Darting moonlight on crumbling gravestones, the wind singing uncannily in the ghoulishly gnarled tree branches and owl cries in the black-blue depths where we sought presentiments of the unearthly. Each sought and found his adventure, you yours and I mine, and later, when we sat in the little Café Radetzki on the Lesser Side over a cup of "melange", amidst old-fashioned philistines and newfangled "Zwockeln"[4], as you ironically called the officers of the old Royal and Imperial army, our conversation touched discreetly upon all the uncanny and grotesque things in life we both observed around us every day. Those were strange years we lived back then, we, a small circle of close friends, young writers and artists into whose close-knit community you unexpectedly stepped one day. We marveled at you, you, the much older man who, in appearance alone, was so ill-suited to our rather formless and ebullient bohemianism, and at first we had no idea what brought you, the socially prominent banker *Meyer*, the elegant sportsman, into our circle. Like the entire city, we knew quite a bit about you. The press was full of your sensational

[4] Probably from Czech "zvok", "fool".

267

affairs of honor aimed at a Prague regiment's entire officer corps, of even more sensational trials in which you hauled this whole officer corps into court, and of all the gossip about you which was maliciously presented to the eager public with their morning coffee.

We knew that you had to defend yourself against a whole murky world of the very worst underground denunciations and knew that a power-bloated and extremely irate Royal and Imperial military and official caste was bent on destroying you. You defended yourself bravely against these attacks, and whoever was left on the battlefield in the end, it was not you. Did you ever hear the stories that circulated about you back then? The *Fama* of our old city, in those days no doubt more loquacious than elsewhere, was happily and exhaustively devoted to you and your life.

You were held to be a goldmaker and alchemist and versed in esoteric doctrines; it was said you were no longer a Christian, but a Brahman and a member of several Asiatic orders visited in Prague by Indian monks traveling through Europe; it was maintained that you were of royal descent, and fantastic evidence was produced. The wildest tales were told of your strangely decorated apartment, open only to the initiated, in which inexplicable, mystical things were supposed to have taken place. For the good Praguers you were quite simply a thoroughly peculiar person, and I believe in the end they began to fear you, for you did not fit at all into the closely circumscribed world and rigid views of the society of the "Deutsches Kasino"[5].

---

[5] Deutsches Kasino: another name for the "Deutsches Haus" (German House) at Na příkopě 22, which served as a cultural center for the Prague German community starting in 1873. Many German associations had their headquarters there, and prominent German writers such as Rainer Maria Rilke, Detlev von Lilienkron and Gerhard Hauptman gave readings of their works there. Since 1945 it has been known as the "Slavic House".

But we young artists flocked to you; for us you were adventure and inspiration, with you we wandered through the Old Town and sat with you in smoky taverns of ill repute. At night in the "Three Acorns", on one of the steep, abandoned streets of the Lesser Side, the blind harpist sang old Czech folksongs for us at night; dawning, frosty winter mornings found us among market-women and carters' men in the "White Wreath" on the fruit market, and the more than dubious crowd which gathered every night at "Serrabona" on Peter's Square gradually came to appreciate our interest in their activities. Often, in the low back room of the ancient tavern "Zum alten Ungelt", we inflamed our young minds in passionate discussions, until your razor-sharp logic and sarcastic wit put an end to the dispute.

And then you would often begin to speak in a soft, controlled voice of yourself and all sorts of experiences, tales in which one was soon unable to tell truth from invention; with your slender hands, one of which was adorned with a large, strange ring, you summoned your stories' characters out of the air with expansive, commanding gestures and set them before us compellingly, and the old city, this unique and matchless Prague, which you saw so differently than the others, became the fantastical background for these characters. But one day you read us one of these stories which you had written down; it was the story "The Hot Soldier", which was to become so famous.

Many years have passed since then. These first tales were followed by many more, some of which finished off your open and covert enemies of the time with elegant dagger thrusts or resounding boxes to the ear. You fell to decisively and without sentimentality, and Royal and Imperial officers, Royal Imperial officials, righteous police inspectors and infallible magistrates, lieutenants and captains, even staff-officers and generals with red stripes on their trousers and bobbing green feathers on gold-trimmed two-cornered hats – all flailed in your hands. And when you left Prague (we younger ones had scattered throughout the world ahead of you), you bade us farewell with the tale of that certain George Mackintosh who had hoodwinked Praguers into razing the initials of his name, G. M. (so very much like your own!) into the city blocks en masse in their greedy search for the supposed vein of gold under their houses.

All these events of thirty years ago are now dead and buried, and perhaps, my dear Herr Meyrink, you will be moved to sentimentality at the memory of those years, those people, and magical Prague.

The noisy metropolis of today has little place for the baroque, sinister romanticism of yore. It has intelligently conserved the beauties of the past, insofar as they contribute to its own standing and profitable tourism, but has made this city more or less a museum of "sights" which have long since lost the vital connection with the peculiar life which once linked them. Only here and there, hidden away, does an ancient nook, an old alley haunt the present like a ghost.

You will agree with me that in those days Prague was indeed something quite remarkable and very strange, a city obsessively mired in the past – not only its streets and houses, but its people as well. Thus grass grew between the bumpy cobblestones of many streets and squares on the Lesser Side; haughty, gold- and silver-laced doormen stood in the proud, emblazoned archways of the old palaces of the nobility; on the quieter streets one met strange human originals whose peculiarities all knew smilingly and who fit so perfectly into the ambience of the time: poor, genial madmen whom birth or fate had made into tragic or comic figures; puppeteers, balladeers and fortune-tellers at markets and festivals; pious beggars by chapels and statues, and

270

strange saints in the singing processions. On the left bank of the Vltava the districts of the nobility, palace after palace; on the right the old burghers' town; and crouching in the shadow of mighty churches the former ghetto, the old Jewish Town, which over the decades had changed from a rigorously isolated involuntary sanctuary into the haunt of criminals. Here the ancient somber temples of the Jews stood in the strangest contrast to notorious underworld taverns and countless bordellos; here the pious murmur of ecstatic prayers was often punctuated by the repulsive yowling of people drunk on bad schnapps. The ghostly graveyard of the Jews opened up like an uncannily improbable, tempestuous sea of stones among the dying houses of this quarter, canopied by fantastically branching elder trees which, in spring, covered this submerged world of thousands and thousands of gravestones with blossoms, including the sarcophagus of that High Rabbi Löw who is supposed to have created the "Golem" with his secret powers.

In a wild, stormy night in the winter of 1916, on a lonely North Sea island, I read for the first time the book to which you gave the name of this enigmatic creature. I read it from cover to cover, breathless and without stopping. The longer I read, the more vividly all these submerged years of my youth rose before me, the figures that peopled them and their whole remarkable world mingling with the events in your story. At one time I sat with many of these people in dark rooms, waited out the nights with many of them, and I often met them on the crooked streets of the Old Town. I recognized everything. In the gloom of the old archways they had waited for something or other, from half-blind windows they had gazed out at me until I was seized by fear of them, and this fear followed me into my dreams. And at last everything, the people, the houses, the churches and palaces, the noble gardens with their marble fountains and

271

the slums with their cares and torments, became one whole, tragic experience which took shape anew in the events of your Golem book.

Your book was old Prague, its characters created in the image of the people of our times.

In that year 1916, my 25 lithographs for your "Golem" appeared, several of which, in reduced form, are included in this new edition.[6]

Very truly yours

Hugo Steiner-Prag

Wendorf (Baltic), September 1931

---

[6] Hugo Steiner-Prag wrote this letter for the edition of *The Golem* published by Carl Schünemann Verlag, Bremen.